"Where

"She is giving a[...] our food baske[...] [women with those h...] children," Mrs. Kinnard said. "As she should. Now, about—"

"Excuse me," he said, pushing his way through the crowd again to get closer to the train.

He stood waiting on the platform, watching Kate progress all the way until she finally appeared. She was so…beautiful to him and had been since the first time he saw her in the downstairs hallway of his fath[...]

Maria was ri[...] preacher's wife—*his* wife—and he didn't see how their situation could be any more impossible.

I love her, Lord.

He didn't know when it had happened, or how. All he knew was that it was so, that she was in his mind night and day—and now he was only moments away from breaking her heart….

Books by Cheryl Reavis

Love Inspired Historical

The Soldier's Wife
An Unexpected Wife

CHERYL REAVIS

The RITA® Award-winning author and romance novelist describes herself as a "late bloomer" who played in her first piano recital at the tender age of thirty. "We had to line up by height—I was the third smallest kid," she says. "After that, there was no stopping me. I immediately gave myself permission to attempt my *other* heart's desire—to write." Her books *A Crime of the Heart* and *Patrick Gallagher's Widow* won a Romance Writers of America coveted RITA® Award for Best Contemporary Series Romance the year each was published. *One of Our Own* received a Career Achievement Award for Best Innovative Series Romance from *RT Book Reviews*. A former public health nurse, Cheryl makes her home in North Carolina with her husband.

An Unexpected Wife

CHERYL REAVIS

HARLEQUIN® LOVE INSPIRED® HISTORICAL

Recycling programs
for this product may
not exist in your area.

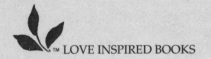

™ LOVE INSPIRED BOOKS

ISBN-13: 978-0-373-82972-9

AN UNEXPECTED WIFE

www.LoveInspiredBooks.com

Printed in U.S.A.

Be of good courage, and He shall strengthen your heart, all ye that hope in the Lord.
—*Psalms* 31:24

For my mother, in honor of her birthday—
92 years and counting. Thank you, Mommy,
for always being my biggest fan.

Chapter One

Kate Woodard stood looking out the parlor window, more than content to be in her brother's finally empty house and do nothing but watch the falling snow. It was deep enough to drift across the veranda now, a barricade—she hoped—from any outside intrusion.

The house was cold; a strong draft at the window made the lace curtains billow out from time to time. She could light a fire in the fireplace—if only one had been laid on the hearth and she knew how. When she made her impulsive decision to deliberately miss her train, she hadn't for one moment taken into consideration that it was the dead of winter and she knew next to nothing about managing parlor fires, much less the one in the kitchen. Tomorrow she would do something about all that—hire someone or…something. Now she would savor the peace and silence of the house, and it would be enough.

She had come to Salisbury, North Carolina, to visit her brother and his family in the hope that a change of scenery and the rowdy company of his adorable young sons—two adopted, one his by blood—would redirect her mind. She was so weary of living the false life that had been foisted upon her when she was hardly more than a child herself. She needed…respite. She needed the privacy to *feel* all the emotions she had to keep bottled up for the sake of propriety. She wanted to weep—or not to weep. She wanted to pace and fret, if that seemed more applicable to her state of mind. She wanted the freedom to think about her own son. Her lost son. He was thirteen now, and the web of lies surrounding his birth had held fast. No outsiders knew young Harrison Howe was *her* child and not the child of her parents' closest friends, nor did they know his brother was not his brother at all.

John.

He had made a much better brother than father—at least before the war had changed him so.

All these years Kate had lived on the fringes of Harrison's life, watching him grow, being his friend but always carefully exercising the restraint it took not to make Mr. and Mrs. Howe or her own family think that she might be trying to get close to him. She was so good at it that she sometimes thought the people who knew the truth forgot that she was Harrison's real mother.

Her latest news of him was that he had been sent to a prestigious boarding school deep in the Pennsylvania countryside, the alma mater of many—if not all—the males in the Howe family and the one place Kate believed he would not thrive. He wasn't like the Howe men— John—or the senior Mr. Howe. He was more like *her* father—and her—thoughtful and observant and studious, and the fact that he required spectacles would make him even more of a target for boarding school jibes and pranks.

But there was nothing she could do beyond sending him small gifts of books and candy. He had sent her a *carte de visite* in return. She cherished it, but seeing his wistful young face staring back at her from the photograph only underlined her growing fear that he was miserable.

So she had come to her brother's lively household in the hope of forgetting at least for a time the helplessness she was feeling—only now she had put herself squarely into a different kind of helplessness. If she'd taken the time to think about it, she might have been discouraged by her lack of housekeeping skills. The original plan— her brother Maxwell's plan—had been that she would return to her parents' home in Philadelphia while Max and Maria and the boys and their nanny were away. There were no other servants in the house; Max relied on his soldiers to accomplish what few of the heavy chores Maria would allow them to do. He had even assigned one of his nervous young officers and his wife, who were traveling to New York City, to see her safely to her destination. But she had forgotten the basket of food Maria had packed especially for her to take on her long train journey. When she hurried back inside to get it, she realized suddenly that she didn't have to go. She was the last person to leave. She could stay behind; no one would be the wiser. Without a second thought, she had feigned a sudden "sick headache," dismissing the fainthearted lieutenant despite his legitimate fear of what her brother might do to him for not carrying out his orders. She had felt sorry for him and for his young wife, but she had still embraced the opportunity to have the solitude she had craved for so long.

She gave a quiet sigh and pulled her cashmere shawl more closely around her, caressing the softness of the wool as she did so. The shawl was not quite rose and not quite lavender, and it suited her coloring perfectly. It had been a birthday gift from her father, and as such, it was very much a symbol of her social status, especially here. Ordinarily she was mindful of the fact that she was Kate Woodard, of the Philadelphia and Germantown Woodards, the seemingly respectable sister of Colonel Maxwell Woodard, commander of the occupation army garrisoned in this small Southern town—and she behaved accordingly.

She was also the Woodard family's twenty-nine-year-old bona fide spinster, and at this late date, there was little incentive for her to learn anything domestic. There had been a time when she had thought she could—would—marry. During the early months of the war she had become engaged to Lieutenant Grey Jamison, an amiable young cavalryman who, unlike so many of his peers, was more interested in doing his duty to save the Union than in becoming a great military legend. She'd found him brave and honorable and optimistic—so much so that he had made her brave, too. For the first time in her life she'd actually believed she could dare to be happy.

But Grey had been killed in the battle of Bentonville in what would turn out to be one of the last throes of the Confederacy. She had been devastated when the news of his death had come, and then all over again when his last letter had arrived. In it he had seemed so...troubled. He'd asked her to promise that if he came home changed, she wouldn't coddle him. She would treat him as she always had, and if she should feel sorry for him, she would never let him see it.

But he hadn't come home, and when she had lost him, she had lost all hope that she could be someone's wife. There were too many secrets, too many lies, and she hadn't known then how hard it would become to maintain them, even the one that defined her very existence. Had she married Grey, at some point, she would have had to tell him about her son—because she loved them both.

"At least I was brave once," she whispered, and perhaps she was being brave now. She suddenly smiled. Wandering around in a cold empty house wasn't brave; it was foolish. Even she could see that.

But she made a determined effort not to second-guess her decision to stay behind. There was no point in dwelling on it—or perhaps she *would* dwell on it—later—because she was free to do just that, if she wanted.

Free!

She had a meager basket of food and a cold hearth in the middle of a snowstorm—and she was happier than she'd been in a long while.

She began closing the heavy drapes in the parlor. She had no real plans beyond bundling up and going to bed. It occurred to her that it had been a long time since she'd eaten. She never ate much before a train trip. As a child she had learned the hard way that she was a far better traveler if she embarked with an empty stomach. But she was hungry now, and she picked up the oil lamp and stepped into the wide hallway that led to one of the two kitchens necessary for the running of her brother's household. The other one was outside, a summer kitchen with thick brick walls and a stone floor, and she hadn't the slightest idea how to manage either one of them.

It was so drafty in the hallway. And empty. Despite it being over five years since the war ended and the fact that Max could well afford whatever furniture Maria might want, the hallway was in serious need of some tables, a chair or two and perhaps a hall tree, the kind with marble shelves and a beveled mirror. According to her brother, many of those things had once been here—until General Stoneman and his men had raided the town. If Kate understood the situation correctly, the dearth of furniture and the mismatched sets of china, crystal and silverware still in use were somehow a badge of honor. Kate almost envied Maria the sense of pride she and the rest of the women here seemed to take in their years of deprivation.

In Philadelphia Kate had helped with the war effort, but she'd only done what was deemed proper for a young woman of Philadelphia's highest society. The truth of the matter was that the balls held to raise money for the Sanitary Commission and the gatherings where young ladies packed tins of cookies for homesick soldiers, or rolled bandages for the hospitals—none of which they actually believed would be needed—were as much an excuse for lively and supposedly patriotic socializing as anything. She hadn't gone into the hospitals to help with the wounded the way Maria and her friends here had. She certainly hadn't gone hungry or been deprived of new dresses or undergarments or anything else she might have wanted. *Wanted,* not needed. She sometimes wondered if she would have done anything at all if her brother and her fiancé hadn't been Union cavalrymen. And there was John, of course. He was the father of her child, and as such, he was on her very short list of males other than her son she cared enough to worry about. The war, the unbridled patriotism had been exciting—until Max and John had become prisoners of war and Grey had been killed.

She held the lamp higher as she made her way to the rear of the house, trying not to be disconcerted by the wavering shadows she cast as she moved along. This particular hallway always made her think of Max and John and their daredevil cavalryman tales of riding their mounts directly through the front doors of rebel houses like this one, just for a lark and with no thought that they could easily have been killed doing it. Back then, aside from the war, Max and John had been more than a little exasperating for the people who loved them. And who would have ever thought they would both end up completely domesticated, much less married to Southern women?

The door leading to the dining room was standing ajar and she moved to close it, hoping to interrupt the strong draft rushing through the house tonight. But then she stepped inside because she caught a glimpse of a toy lying on the floor—a small carved earless horse that belonged to Robbie, the youngest. The nanny, Mrs. Hansen, must have missed it when she packed up the boys' belongings for their trip.

Mrs. Hansen was yet another example of Kate's difficulty in understanding how the Southern mind worked. At first the woman's added presence in the household had led Kate to think that Maria was becoming more lax in her determination not to take advantage of Max's money. But then Kate realized that her wanting or needing help with the boys had very little to do with it. It was Mrs. Hansen who needed the help. She had been taking care of Suzanne Canfield, the adopted boys' sick mother, when Suzanne had been killed in a fire that also burned their house to the ground. The boys had barely escaped with their lives and then only because Max had braved the flames to go in and get them. Mrs. Hansen's grief and guilt at not having been there when the fire broke out had apparently been overwhelming, and Maria had deliberately given her perhaps the only thing that would ease her mind a little—the task of helping to take care of the little boys whom the fire had orphaned.

Kate picked up the wooden horse and put it into her pocket, smiling as she did so because Robbie's teething marks were all over it. He was such a dear little boy—indeed, they all were. Joe. Jake. Robbie.

Harrison.

"No," she said quietly. She wasn't ready to think about him just yet, not in the deep and intense way she wanted to.

She pulled the door firmly closed, and she saw the man immediately when she turned around. He wasn't wearing a hat, and his coat was still snowcovered, likely because it wasn't warm enough inside for it to have melted. Incredibly, he had taken the liberty of lighting not one but two of the kitchen lamps.

"Who are you?" he asked bluntly and with all the authority of someone whose business it was to know.

If her presence in the house had been authorized, she wouldn't have been so taken aback by the question, but as it was, she didn't reply. They stared at each other, Kate trying all the while to decide whether or not she was afraid.

"Why is the house so cold?" he asked next. He reached out as if to steady himself, but there was nothing in the hallway for him to grab onto. "There's plenty of wood… in the…box."

Kate eased backward, intending to make a run for the front door, snowstorm or no snowstorm. But she had the lamp. She couldn't run with it and she couldn't set it down without the man realizing her intent. The last thing she wanted was to light her unsuspecting brother's house ablaze.

"My apologies, miss," he said with some effort but in a slightly more genial tone. She tried to identify his accent. It was Southern, and yet it wasn't.

He took a few steps in her direction. "I didn't think… the questions were…that difficult."

"Who are *you?*" she asked finally, recovering at least a modicum of the snobbishness that was hers by birthright if not personality.

He took a few more steps, and she realized suddenly that something was indeed wrong. He was clearly unsteady on his feet now, and he seemed to want to say something but couldn't.

Drunk? Ill? She couldn't tell.

He suddenly pitched forward. She gave a small cry and jumped back in an effort to keep him from colliding with her and the lit oil lamp. He went sprawling face first on the parquet floor, his head hitting the bare wood hard.

"Sir," she said, keeping her distance. "Sir!"

He didn't move. She set the oil lamp on the floor and came as close to him as she dared. He was so still.

Someone rapped sharply on the front door, making her jump, and whoever it was didn't wait to be admitted. Sergeant Major Perkins, her brother's extremely competent orderly, came striding into the foyer and down the hallway, bringing much of the winter storm in with him.

"Miss Kate! I wondered why there were lamps burning— Who's that?"

"I don't know," Kate said, bending down to look at him again. He was still motionless.

"You didn't go and shoot him, did you?"

"No, I did not shoot him, Sergeant Major."

"What is he doing in here?"

"I don't know that, either."

"Then what are *you* doing in here? Colonel Woodard didn't say you were going to be on the premises."

"My brother doesn't know everything," she said obscurely.

"Well, you just go right on thinking that if you want to, Miss Kate, but if you want my advice, you'll revise that opinion, the sooner, the better. Don't much get by that brother of yours. Every soldier in this town can tell you that."

"Could we just address *this* first?" Kate said, waving her hand over the man still lying on the floor.

"That we can. Move the lamp so I can roll him over. I'm going to hang on to him. You see what's in his pockets."

Kate hesitated.

"We want to hurry this along, Miss Kate," he said pointedly. "While he's unaware."

"Yes," she decided, seeing the wisdom of that plan. She slid the lamp out of the way and knelt down by him again.

"He's not dead, is he?" it occurred to her to ask.

"If he was dead, we wouldn't need to be hurrying. Go ahead now. Look."

Far from reassured, she reached tentatively and not very deeply into a coat pocket.

"I don't reckon he's got anything in there that bites," Perkins said mildly.

She gave him a look and began to search in earnest. He didn't seem to be carrying anything at all.

"You let him in?" Perkins asked.

"No," Kate said pointedly, moving to another pocket. "He was just…here."

"Kind of like you are, I guess," he said. He was clearly suspicious about the situation, and he wasn't doing much to try to hide it. "You miss your train?"

"I didn't 'miss' it. I didn't get on."

"Colonel Woodard know about the…change in plans?"

"He does not."

"I was afraid of that."

"There is nothing for *you* to worry about, Sergeant."

"And yet here I am. Down on the floor with an unconscious and unknown man, helping you riffle through his pockets."

"The riffling was your idea," Kate reminded him.

"So it was," he agreed. "Anybody else here?"

"Just him—as far as I know."

"You're not sick or anything, are you?" he persisted, the question impertinent at best.

She didn't answer. Her fingers closed around a small book in the man's other coat pocket—a well-worn Bible, she saw as she pulled it free. She opened it. There was some kind of…card between the pages. The texture felt like a *carte de visite*. She moved closer to the lamp so she could see. It wasn't a photograph. It was a Confederate military card.

"Robert Brian Markham," she read. She looked at Perkins. "Max's wife was a Markham. She had a brother named Robert," she said, forgetting how long he had been Max's right hand and how likely it was that he knew more details about Maria Markham Woodard and her family than Kate did.

But that Robert Markham had been killed at Gettysburg, along with a younger brother, Samuel. Kate had understood for a long time why Max tried to be elsewhere during the first three days of July. His wife's heart had been broken by her brothers' deaths, and he was the last person who could comfort her. He had been at Gettysburg, too, fighting for the other side.

Kate picked up the lamp and held it near the man's face so she could see it better. It didn't help. She didn't recognize him at all and she couldn't see any family resemblance. She'd never actually met anyone with his kind of rugged features. She thought that he might have been handsome once, but then his face must have gotten… beaten and battered somewhere along the way.

She realized suddenly that Perkins was watching her. "He's not bleeding," she said, moving the lamp away.

Perkins reached out and briefly took the man's hand. "Prizefighter, would be my guess," he said. "Men fresh out of a war can have a lot of rage still. And they have to get rid of it."

"By beating another human being for sport?" Kate asked.

"There are worse ways to live—especially if you need to eat."

Kate looked at the man's face again. How much rage could be left after that kind of brutality? she wondered.

Perkins took the card from her, then stood. "I want you to go upstairs and lock yourself in, Miss Kate," Perkins said.

"Why?"

"I need to take care of all this and I'm going to have to leave to do it. I've only got the one horse and the snow's too bad to try it on foot. You'll be all right if you stay quiet and keep your door locked."

"I don't think he's in any shape to do me harm," Kate said, trying to sound calmer and more competent than she felt. "I'm not afraid. Just go."

Perkins hesitated, looking closely at the man again. "All right," he said after a moment. "I'll be back as quick as I can. Find something to cover him with. He needs to be kept warm until we find out what he's up to—just in case."

Kate was about to ask what "just in case" meant, but then she suddenly realized that Perkins was considering the possibility that this man might actually be Max's— and her—brother-in-law, or at least have some information about him.

"Light some more lamps so I can see the house easier from the outside. It's snowing so hard it's a wonder I noticed anything was going on in here at all. Wouldn't hurt to light a fire, too."

Kate nodded at his last suggestion. She wholeheartedly agreed, but she couldn't quite bring herself to admit that she didn't know how to do it.

He helped her get to her feet, then picked up the lamp and handed it to her. She kept staring at the man on the floor.

"Miss Kate," he said as he was about to go, and she looked at him.

"If he starts stirring, you get away from him."

"Yes, I will. Of course I will."

But Perkins still didn't go.

"What is it?" she asked. She knew him to be a straightforward and painfully blunt man—it was the main reason Max relied on him so. But he was having some difficulty saying whatever was on his mind now.

"You're…sure you don't know this man?"

She was so surprised by the question that she could only stare at him. Then she realized that he was considering every possible explanation for the man's being here and that he actually wanted to make certain she hadn't missed her train in order to keep some kind of secret assignation. If she hadn't been so cold and so upset, she might have been offended. Or she might have laughed.

"I don't know him, Sergeant Major Perkins," she said evenly.

"All right then," he said.

"I'd appreciate it if you hurried," she said in case he had any more questions he wanted answered.

"My plan exactly, Miss Kate."

"No, wait. I need a telegram sent to my parents. Say I've been delayed. Could you do that, please?"

"Yes, miss," he said.

She expected him to leave then, but he didn't. He was still looking at her in that sergeant major way he had. Not quite what her brother called a "sack and burn" face, but still…arresting.

"There is one other thing," he said. "My responsibility is to Colonel Woodard. I will do whatever is necessary to maintain his position and his authority in this town."

"Yes, all right," Kate said.

"Do you understand?"

"Yes," she said—which wasn't quite the truth. She understood that he made certain that her brother's life ran as smoothly as possible and that he wanted her to know something about that duty, which he felt was important. She just didn't know what that "something" was.

She had to turn away from the strong gust of wind that filled the hallway when he finally left by the front door. The man lying at her feet didn't react at all. She gave him a backward glance, then hurried upstairs to pull two of the quilts off her own bed because she didn't want to take the time to look through cedar chests for extra ones. He didn't seem to have stirred when she returned. She folded the quilts double, then knelt down to cover him, hesitating long enough to look at his face again before she went to light more lamps in the downstairs. One of his hands was outstretched, and she carefully lifted it. She could see the scarred knuckles, feel the calluses on his palm as she placed it under the quilt.

It was so cold on the floor. She couldn't keep from shivering, and she had to bite down on her lip to keep her teeth from chattering. For a brief moment she thought she saw a slight movement from him as well.

No, she decided. He wasn't waking. He was just cold. He had to be as cold as she was.

"I must learn how to build a fire. In a fireplace *and* in a cookstove," she said out loud as she got to her feet. "And that's all there is to it."

She went around lighting as many lamps as she could find—she did know how to do that, at least. She had no expectation that Perkins would return quickly, and after what already seemed a long time, she began to pace up and down the hallway in an effort to keep warm. She didn't know what time it was—only that it was nearly dark outside. She thought there had once been an heirloom grandfather clock in the foyer, but it, like the rest of the hall furniture, had become a casualty of the war, and Maria hadn't wanted another one. In this one instance, Kate thought she understood her sister-in-law's behavior. Some things were far too dear to be replaced, especially if all the replacement could ever be was a reminder of what had been lost.

Kate kept her eyes on the man as she walked the hallway, but she let her mind consider what she was going to tell Max about her being here instead of Philadelphia. After a time she decided that she wouldn't tell him anything. She would say the same thing to him she'd said to Perkins. She hadn't missed her train; she just didn't get on—and that was all these two representatives of the military occupation needed to know.

She suddenly stopped pacing. This time she had no doubt that the man had moved. She took a few steps closer because she couldn't tell for certain whether or not he was beginning to wake. If he tried to get up, if he seemed threatening in any way, she would do what Perkins said. She would run to her room and lock herself in.

She could tell that his eyes were still closed, and she took some comfort from that, but after a long, tense moment, he began stirring again. He gave a soft moan and turned his head in her direction.

"Eleanor," he said.

Am I wounded?

He tried to open his eyes and couldn't. He needed to get up, but he couldn't do that, either. He could hear the voices swirling around him. Women's voices.

"Move aside!" he heard one of them say. She must have been some distance away. There were sharp-sounding footsteps coming in his direction.

"You!" she suddenly barked. "Get the parlor and the kitchen fires lit! This house is freezing!"

"Yes, ma'am," a young-sounding male voice said.

"The kitchen first!" she said, still yelling. "We need hot water and heated blankets! Now!"

He could hear the scurrying of a heavier set of footsteps, and then a different woman's voice.

"That way," she said kindly, and the scurrying continued past him down the hall.

"Have you made no preparations whatsoever?" the first woman demanded.

"No, Mrs. Kinnard, I have not. I don't expect he'll be staying."

He struggled to make sense of what he was hearing. *Mrs. Kinnard? Acacia Kinnard?*

It couldn't be her. Acacia Kinnard was…was…

He couldn't complete the thought.

"Indeed, he will be staying," this Mrs. Kinnard said. "You cannot put Maria's brother out for all your thinking you've won the War. Shame on you, Robert Markham!" she suddenly barked. "Shame!"

"I don't think he can hear you," the younger woman ventured.

"Of course he can hear me! Robert Brian Markham! Where have you been!" Mrs. Kinnard demanded. "What would your dear sweet mother say! And poor Maria—if you'd bothered to come home, she might not be—"

Her voice suddenly drifted away, lost in the blackness that swept over him.

Chapter Two

Married to a Yankee, Kate thought. If Robert Markham had come home, as was his duty, then his sister might not have married a Yankee colonel. She was surprised that Mrs. Kinnard had stopped short of actually saying it.

Sergeant Major Perkins's plan to "take care of all this" left a great deal to be desired, in Kate's opinion. Her opportunity for solitude had completely disappeared when he'd returned with a number of soldiers, two hospital orderlies and Mrs. Kinnard, the indisputable Queen Bee of Salisbury Society. Mrs. Kinnard had an impeccable Southern pedigree, and she had used it to all but appoint herself head of just about everything, including the Confederate military wayside hospital down near the railroad tracks during the war. Mrs. Kinnard's word was still law in all matters not under the direct supervision of the United States Army, and, Kate suspected, in some of those, as well.

"Excuse me, Miss Kate," one of the hospital orderlies said.

She—and ultimately Mrs. Kinnard—moved out of the way so he could kneel down and assess the man's condition. It occurred to her that Robert Markham was going to have every bit as much trouble pacifying Mrs. Kinnard as her brother did.

"Is the doctor coming?" Kate asked the orderly.

"Just as soon as we can find him, Miss Kate," he said.

Kate stood watching as he uncovered the man and began to examine him, looking for a reason why he had fallen to the floor, she supposed.

"Well, can you do *anything* helpful?" Mrs. Kinnard said suddenly, and Kate realized she was once again in her sights.

"I…"

"*Exactly* as I thought. You do know where there is pen and paper, I hope."

Kate took a quiet breath before she answered. "Yes. I'll be happy to get it."

Kate escaped to Maria's writing desk in the parlor and returned with a sheet of paper and a short pencil. Mrs. Kinnard eyed the pencil, and Kate thought she was going to refuse to take it.

"The ink is frozen. I'm sorry," Kate added, because in a roundabout way, that could be considered her fault. "I assumed you were in a hurry," she said, still holding out the pencil.

Mrs. Kinnard gave an impatient sigh, then removed her gloves and bonnet and handed them to Kate in exchange for the pencil and paper. Kate had no idea what to do with them, given the dearth of furnishings in the hall. She held on to them in lieu of throwing them down on the parquet floor, then she opened the dining room door and went inside, ultimately placing the bonnet and gloves carefully on a chair next to the sideboard and nearly colliding with Mrs. Kinnard when she turned around to leave.

"They should be safe here," Kate said, because she

hadn't realized the woman had followed her and concern for her finery was the only conclusion Kate could come to as to why she did. She could hear the front door opening and a number of footsteps in the hall. Several more soldiers passed by the dining room door, two of them carrying a stretcher.

Mrs. Kinnard sat down at the dining table near the oil lamp Kate had lit earlier and began to write—a list, from the looks of it.

"Mr. Perkins!" she cried when she'd finished, clearly eschewing Perkins's military title, probably because he belonged to an army she considered of no consequence.

"Yes, ma'am, Mrs. Kinnard!" he called from somewhere at the back of the house.

"Take this," she said, when he finally appeared in the doorway. "I want this list filled as soon as possible."

He looked at the sheet of paper, then back at her. "Mrs. Russell isn't going to welcome a knock on the door this time of night from the likes of me, ma'am."

"Whether she welcomes it or not isn't important. Taking care of Robert Markham now that he has returned from the dead, is. I won't see him hauled off to your military infirmary, and this young woman is of no use whatsoever that I can see."

Kate opened her mouth to respond to the remark, but Perkins cleared his throat sharply and gave her a hard look. His sergeant major look. Again. She suddenly understood what he had been trying to tell her earlier. Neither she nor her tender feelings mattered in this situation. Maintaining her brother's authority and his rapport with the townspeople did.

Very well, then.

She stepped around him into the hallway. If she was

going to preserve Max's peace treaties, she'd have to get herself well away from this overbearing woman.

Honestly! she nearly said aloud. As she recalled, even Maria found the Kinnard woman hard going.

Robert Markham—if Mrs. Kinnard's identification could be trusted—still lay on the cold floor. The hospital orderly had lifted him slightly and was pouring brandy down his throat with all the skill of a man who had performed the treatment many times. Robert Markham eventually swallowed, coughed a time or two, but still did not wake.

"Miss Woodard!" Mrs. Kinnard said sharply behind her, making her jump. She closed her eyes for a moment before she turned around.

"Yes?" Kate said as politely as she could manage.

"We will put Robert in his old room," the woman said. "We have no idea what his mental state will be when he fully awakens. He needs to be in familiar surroundings. The bed must be stripped, new sheets put upon it—I'm sure Maria uses lavender sachet just as her dear mother did and he will no doubt recall that. And then the bed must be warmed and *kept* warm."

"The orderlies here will see to all that. Just tell them what you need, ma'am," Perkins said on his way out. "His old room is off the upstairs porch, Miss Kate. On the left."

And how in the world did Perkins know that? she wondered. It suddenly occurred to her that his room was also the one she was using—not that that would matter to Mrs. Kinnard. The woman had spoken, and Maria's brother was in need.

"Flannel," Mrs. Kinnard said, looking at Kate.

"I beg your pardon?"

"Flannel. We need flannel to wrap the heated bricks— you *are* heating bricks?" she said, looking at Kate hard.

"Yes, ma'am," one of the orderlies said for her. "The oven's full of them."

Undeterred, Mrs. Kinnard continued to look at Kate, now with raised eyebrows.

"I'll…see if I can find…some," Kate said, heading for the stairs.

Perkins hadn't left the house yet.

"Now try not to undo all your brother's hard work," he said quietly so Mrs. Kinnard wouldn't hear him. "He's finally got that old bat and her daughter where they don't set out to cripple everything he tries to do—and that's saying a lot. She's a mean old cuss and don't you go yanking her chain."

Kate sighed instead of answering.

"I'm telling you," Perkins said.

"I *don't* yank chains, Sergeant Major."

"Maybe not, but the Colonel says you are a strong woman, and it's my experience that strong women don't put up with much. This time it's important that you do, Miss Kate."

"Yes. All right. I'll…behave."

Easier said than done, she thought as he went out the door, but she was willing to try. She went upstairs and looked through the cedar chests, but there was no flannel in any of them. In an effort not to have to tell Mrs. Kinnard that, she went down the back stairs to the kitchen, hoping that flannel for hot bricks, if she just thought about it logically, might be found there.

Somewhere.

She found them at last in the pantry on a top shelf, a whole basketful of double-thickness, hand-sewn flannel bags she concluded were the right size to hold a brick, hot or otherwise. She gave them to the soldier manning the cookstove, then ended up holding the bags open so he could drop a hot brick inside—once he stopped protesting her offer of help.

"Mrs. Kinnard," she said simply, and he immediately acquiesced.

When the job was done, there was nothing else required of her beyond standing around and letting the Kinnard woman use her for target practice. She had intended to get the bed linens for what had only moments before been *her* bed, but apparently one of the hospital orderlies—Bruno—knew more about where the sheets and bedding were kept than she did.

She went upstairs again, intending to remove what few belongings she still had in the room—yet another consideration that had escaped her attention when she'd made her bold decision to miss the train and stay behind. Most of her clothes had been packed up in her travel trunk and were by now well on their way to Philadelphia.

But she couldn't get into the room. It was full of soldiers trying to stay ahead of Mrs. Kinnard.

"There's a fire in old Mr. Markham's sitting room, Miss Woodard," one of them said. "You might be more comfortable in there."

"Yes, thank you," she said, more than grateful for any suggestion that would keep her out of Mrs. Kinnard's way—for a while at least. But she could already hear the woman coming up the stairs, and she hurried away.

"The things I do for you, Max Woodard," she said under her breath. She was as intimidated as that young lieutenant who was supposed to see her safely to Philadelphia.

She slipped inside the sitting room and firmly closed the door, then thought better of it and left it slightly ajar. She didn't want Mrs. Kinnard sneaking up on her—not that the woman was given to anything resembling stealth. She was much more the charge-the-front-gates type.

A fire in the fireplace was indeed burning brightly. She savored the warmth for a moment, then moved to the nearest window and looked out. It was too dark to see anything but her reflection in the wavy glass.

Is that what a "strong woman" looks like?

She couldn't believe Max had described her in that way. She didn't feel strong. If anything, she felt...unfinished. What am I supposed to be doing? she wondered, the question stark and real in her mind and intended for no one. Clearly it wasn't going to be spending time alone thinking of her lost child.

Brooding.

Is that what she had actually planned to do? Perhaps, she thought, but she had never inflicted her unhappiness on anyone else, at least not consciously. To do so would have resulted in the decision to send her away—for her own good—and as a result, she would have had no contact with her son at all. She had worked hard to seem at least content with her life, so much so that she had nothing left over to nurture her better self. She always went to church, here and in Philadelphia, but the gesture was empty somehow. She felt so far away from anything spiritual and had for a long time. She still prayed for the people she loved, especially for Harrison. She had asked for God's blessing on him every night since he'd been born. But she never prayed for herself, and she had never asked for forgiveness. When she looked at Harrison, at what a fine young man he was becoming, she simply couldn't bring herself to do it. She might be a sinner, but *he* wasn't a sin.

Perhaps this was what living a lie did to a person— kept them feeling unworthy to speak to God. The best that could be said of her was that she had endured. Day after day. Year after year. In that context, she supposed Max was right. She was a strong woman.

She could hear the soft whisper of the snow against the windowpane. How much more pleasant the sound was when there was a warm fire crackling on the hearth behind her.

Is it snowing where you are, my dear Harrison? Are you warm and safe?

No, she thought again. She wasn't going to think about him now. She would wait until later. Until...

She couldn't say when. She gave a heavy sigh and looked around the room. It was no longer a combination sickroom, sitting room and library, but more a place to escape the domestic chaos of a household full of little boys. Even when Maria's ailing father had occupied it, it had been a pleasant place to be, with its floor-to-ceiling bookshelves, comfortable upholstered rocking chairs and windows that looked out over the flower and herb garden. She'd come in here often the first time she'd visited Max, shortly before he married Maria. Then the room had been a kind of *special sanctuary,* a place where old Mr. Markham had held court for the community and the conquering army alike, despite his doctor's orders. He'd been a witty and delightful man who'd enjoyed company—her company in particular, it had seemed—and she'd liked him very much. He'd been quite cunning, as well. He'd done his best to recruit her to bring him some forbidden cigars, and failing at that, it still hadn't taken him long to steer her into revealing all her misgivings about her brother's upcoming marriage to Mr. Markham's only daughter—some of which he harbored, as well.

She suddenly smiled to herself, thinking of Max and Maria and how suited they were to each other. "We were wrong to worry so, weren't we, Mr. Markham?" she whispered.

Or so she hoped. The chaos in Max's house tonight was of a completely different kind, the kind that had precipitated heavy footsteps and loud men's voices, Mrs. Kinnard barking orders like a sergeant major and some kind of commotion involving pots and pans in the kitchen. The house was annoyingly alive, and all because of the man who had collapsed in the downstairs hallway. If he was indeed Maria's brother, then it was no wonder he'd questioned Kate's presence here. He must have believed the house was still his home.

Where has he been? she wondered. *And why did he stay away?* She tried to imagine how she would have felt if Max had left her and their parents believing he was dead and grieving for him for years.

Kate suddenly realized that she wasn't alone. A woman carrying a heavy-laden tray stood tentatively at the doorway.

"I— Am I interrupting?" the woman asked.

"No, no, of course not. Do come in, Mrs.—"

"Justice," the woman said quickly, Kate thought in order to keep them both from being embarrassed if Kate happened not to remember her name—which she hadn't.

"Yes, of course."

The woman came into the room, a bit at a loss at first as to where to put the tray. After a moment she set it down on a small table next to one of the rocking chairs. There was a plain brown teapot on the tray, a sugar bowl, a cream pitcher, spoons and a cup and saucer—and a plate covered with a starched and finely embroidered— but slightly worn—tea towel.

"I thought you might like some tea and a little bread and butter to eat," Mrs. Justice said. "I brought the bread with me—events being what they are tonight. I baked it early this morning so it's fresh. And I took enough hot water to make a pot of tea when it started boiling—Mrs. Kinnard didn't see me," she added in a whisper, making Kate smile.

"You're very kind—will you join me? I'm sure we can find another cup."

"Oh, no," Mrs. Justice said quickly. "They'll be bringing Robbie upstairs shortly and I must be on hand for that—though I'm not quite sure why. Mrs. Kinnard always seems to require my presence, but she never really lets me *do* anything. I can't believe dear Robbie has come home. He's so like Bud, you know."

"Bud?" Kate asked as she poured tea into the cup.

"Mr. Markham Senior. We grew up together, he and I—well, all of us. Mrs. Russell, as well. You remember Mrs. Russell." It wasn't a question because Mrs. Russell was nothing if not memorable, especially if one happened to be associated with the occupation army in any way.

"I… Yes," Kate said. Maria had told her that the war was not over for Mrs. Russell—and never would be. She was as militant as Mrs. Kinnard was imperious, and she had single-handedly ended an alliance between her daughter and one of Max's officers. The disappointed young major had even reenlisted—much to Mrs. Russell's and his family's dismay—just to stay near her. So sad, Kate thought.

Together, Mrs. Russell and Mrs. Kinnard were a force majeure in this town, a walking, talking tribulation to all who had the misfortune to wander uninvited into their realms.

"Mr. Markham Senior was always 'Bud' to me," Mrs. Justice continued. "He was a bit of a rascal in his youth—and so was Robbie. You know, everyone says the love of a good woman is what turned Bud around, but that's not quite true. It's not enough that the good woman loves the rascal. The rascal has *got* to love the good woman, too. And if he loves her enough not to cause her worry or pain ever again, *that's* when it works out just fine. Or so *I* believe. And Robbie…well, before the war he was what you might call a regular brawler in the saloons and the…um…other places. Marriage to the right woman— somebody he loved—could have fixed him as well, I'm sure." She gave a quiet sigh. "Sometimes I think I can still feel Bud in this room. It's—" she looked around at everything "—nice. If only he'd lived to see this day and his older son come home again—or perhaps he does see it. His boys were everything to him. Everything."

"Mrs. Justice!"

"I do believe I hear my name," Mrs. Justice whispered with a slight giggle. "It's quite all right, though. I'd put my hand in the fire for Bud's son." She had such a wistful look on her face, and Kate suddenly realized that this woman had once loved Bud Markham beyond their having shared a childhood, perhaps loved him still, and Kate felt such a pang of loneliness and longing that she had to turn her face away.

"Oh, you should know our Mrs. Russell will be along shortly, too," Mrs. Justice said, turning to go. "Drink your tea, my dear," she said kindly. "You are likely to need it."

"Mrs. Justice!"

"Oh, dear," she whispered mischievously at Mrs. Kinnard's latest summons. She picked up her skirts and walked quickly toward the door.

"Mrs. Justice," Kate said just as she reached it. "Who is Eleanor?"

"Eleanor?" Mrs. Justice said, clearly puzzled.

"Robert Markham roused enough to say the name Eleanor. I think perhaps he thought I was she."

"Oh, that poor dear boy," Mrs. Justice said. "That *poor* boy. If *she's* the reason he's come home..."

"Mrs. Justice! We need you!"

Mrs. Justice held out both hands in a gesture that would indicate she couldn't linger because she was caught in circumstances far beyond her control. "Drink your tea!" she said again as she hurried away.

Chapter Three

"Miss Woodard! Where are you!" The fact that the question was whispered made it no less jarring.

Am I in a hospital? Robert thought. He tried to move, but he couldn't somehow. Blankets, he decided, tucked in tight. Perhaps he was in a hospital after all—except that it didn't smell like a hospital. It smelled like…

…coffee. Baked bread. Wood burning in a fireplace. Lavender sachet.

His head hurt—a lot, he soon realized. He managed to get one hand out from under the covers and reach up to touch his forehead.

Yes. Definitely a reason for the pain.

He finally opened his eyes. A fair-haired woman sat on a low stool in a patch of weak sunlight not far from his bed, her arms resting on her knees and her head down. He couldn't see her face at all, only the top of her golden hair and the side of her neck. Was she praying? Weeping? He couldn't decide.

"Miss Woodard!" the voice whispered fiercely right outside the door, making her jump.

She turned her head in his direction and was startled all over again to find him awake and looking at her.

She took a deep breath. "I'm hiding," she said simply, keeping her voice low so as not to be heard on the other side of the door.

He thought it must be the truth, given the circumstances.

"What…have you…done?" he managed to ask, but he didn't seem to be able to keep his eyes open long enough to hear the answer.

Kate took a hushed breath. He seemed to be sleeping again, and in that brief interlude of wakefulness, she didn't think he had mistaken her for the still-mysterious Eleanor, despite his grogginess. She knew that the army surgeon had given him strong doses of laudanum—to help his body rest and to make his return to the living less troubled, he said. The surgeon hadn't known that Robert Markham had already made his "return to the living," and thus missed the irony of his remark.

She hardly dared move in case Maria's brother was more awake than he seemed. She watched him closely instead. He was so thin—all muscle and sinew that stopped just short of gauntness. Both his eyes had blackened from the force of the fall in the hallway, and there was a swollen bruise on his forehead. He hadn't been shaved. She tried to think if she'd ever been in the actual company of a man so in need of a good barbering.

No, she decided. She had not. She had seen unkempt men out and about, of course—on the streets of Philadelphia and here in Salisbury—but generally speaking, all the men she encountered socially were…presentable. The stubble of growth on Robert Markham's face seemed so intimate somehow, as if he were in a state only his wife or his mother should see.

But still she didn't leave the room. She looked at his

hands instead, both of them resting on top of the latest warmed and double-folded army blanket the orderlies kept spread over him. The room was filled with the smell of slightly scorched wool.

His fingers moved randomly from time to time, trembling slightly whenever he lifted them up. She could see the heavy scarring on his knuckles, and she was sure Sergeant Major Perkins had been right. These were the kinds of scars that could have only come from fighting.

And rage.

I shouldn't be here, she thought, *Mrs. Kinnard or no Mrs. Kinnard.*

But it was too late for that realization. He was awake again.

Robert stared in the woman's direction and tried to get his vision to clear. When he finally focused, he could tell that she was the same woman he had seen earlier—in the same place—hiding, she'd said. Did he remember that right? Hiding?

She looked up at a small noise. She seemed only a little less startled to find him looking at her this time. "I didn't mean to disturb you," she said after a moment. "I'll go—"

"I wish you...wouldn't," Robert said, his voice hoarse and his throat dry. "I...don't seem to know...what has happened. Perhaps you could...help me with that."

"I don't think so," she said. "I'm somewhat bewildered myself."

"About what?"

"You, of course. You're supposed to be dead."

Robert looked away and swallowed heavily. He was so thirsty.

"Do you know where you are?" she asked, but he wasn't ready to consider that detail quite yet.

"Is there some…water?" he asked.

"Oh. Yes. Of course."

She rose from the footstool and moved to a small table near the bed. Someone had put a tray with a tin pitcher and a cup on it. She filled the cup with water, spilling a little as she did so. She hesitated a moment, before picking up one of several hollow quills used for drinking that had been left on the tray, then looked at it as if she wasn't quite sure how she was going to manage to give him the water.

Robert watched as she carefully brought the cup of water to him. He could see that it was too full and that her hands trembled, but he didn't say anything. As she came closer he could smell the scent of roses. How long had it been since he'd been this close to a woman who wore rosewater? He lifted his head to drink, his thirst making him forget the pain in his head. It intensified so, he couldn't keep still. Water spilled on the blanket, more of it than he could manage to swallow.

Appropriate or not, she put her hand behind his head to support him while he drank, but she took the cup away before he had drained it. "Not too much at first," she said. "As I understand it, when you're ill, what you want and what you can tolerate can sometimes be at odds."

"I'm not…ill."

"Not well, either," she said. She let his head down gently onto the pillow.

Robert looked at her, trying to decide if he felt up to arguing with her about it. No, he decided. He didn't. The persistent pounding in his head and the fact that he obviously couldn't manage something as simple as drinking from a tin cup on his own led him to conclude that, for the moment at least, he was some distance away from "well."

He watched as she returned the cup to the table and sat down again. He still couldn't decide who she was. *Not Eleanor* was the only thing he knew for certain—besides the fact that she was not a Southerner. Her diction was far too precise and sharp edged for her to have grown up below the Mason-Dixon Line. It was too painful to attempt any kind of conversation, so he kept looking at her. She seemed so sad.

Why are you sad, I wonder?

Since the war the whole world seemed to be full of women with sad eyes. She wasn't wearing a wedding ring; he thought she was far too pretty to be unmarried.

"My name is Robert Markham," he said after a moment because it seemed the next most socially appropriate thing to do.

"Yes," she said, watching him closely, apparently looking for some indication that she'd let him have too much to drink. "So I'm told. And you're sometimes called Robbie, I believe."

Robert frowned slightly. Incredibly, he thought she might be teasing him ever so slightly, and he found it… pleasant.

"Well, not…lately. How is it you know…who I am when I don't know you…at all?"

"I went through your pockets," she said matter-of-factly. "I found the Confederate military card inside your Bible. But three ladies who live here in the town actually identified you—Mrs. Kinnard, Mrs. Russell. And Mrs. Justice, of course. She's the one who calls you Robbie."

Robert drew a long breath in a feeble attempt to distance himself from the pain, but it only made his head hurt worse. Mrs. Kinnard. He certainly remembered that Mrs. Kinnard had identified him, and it was good that she had been correct in her identification. Mrs. Kinnard, as he recalled, was never wrong about anything. He nearly smiled at the thought that he might have had to assume whatever name she'd given him because no one had the audacity to contradict her. She would undoubtedly be the angry whisperer outside the door. It was no wonder this young woman had felt such a pressing need to stay out of sight.

He looked around the room, certain now of where he was at least, without having to be told.

Home.

In his own bed. It was so strange, and yet somehow not strange at all. It was the noise in the household that was so alien to him. Men's voices—accented voices and the heavy tread of their boots. Barked military orders and the quick, disciplined responses to them. What he didn't hear was his brother Samuel's constant racket; or his sister, Maria, playing "Aura Lee" on the pianoforte in the parlor; or his father and his friends laughing together in the dining room over brandy and cigars.

And he didn't hear his mother singing the second verse of her favorite hymn, "How Firm a Foundation," as she went about her daily chores. Always the second verse.

Fear not, I am with thee,
O be not dismayed;
For I am Thy God,
And will still give the aid...

He had never had her kind of faith, and for a long time he had lost all hope that the words of that particular hymn might be true.

I'll comfort thee, help thee,
And cause thee to stand...

And what about now? Did he believe them now?

He had thought he was prepared for the shame of returning, but he wasn't prepared at all for the overwhelming sense of loss. That was far beyond what he had expected, the direct result, he supposed, of having been so certain that he would never see his home again. And yet here he was, despite his vagueness as to precisely how he'd gotten here, and that was the most he could say for the situation.

Mrs. Russell suddenly came to mind—and her son, James Darson Russell. He tried to remember…something. Jimmy had died in the war; he was sure of that, and yet the memory seemed all wrong somehow. He frowned with the effort it took to try to sort out what was real and what was not.

Jimmy had been several years younger than he, but he had had the self-assurance not often seen in a boy his age. Most likely it had come from having had to become the head of the household after his father's death. His mother and his sister had needed him, and he'd accepted that responsibility like the man he was years from being.

Robert smiled slightly as another memory came into his mind. Jimmy had been confident and self-possessed—until he'd gotten anywhere near Maria. Then he couldn't seem to walk and talk at the same time. He'd turned into an awkward, inelegant boy who couldn't put two words together without sounding like a dunce. It was strange what a certain kind of woman could do to a man when he ardently believed her to be unattainable. He himself had suffered the same affliction when he'd been courting Eleanor and perhaps still would, had not a war intervened. But absence hadn't made her heart grow fonder; it had made it grow more discerning. So much so that shortly before the disaster at Gettysburg, she had written him a letter—her final letter to him—telling him plainly that she had decided that their reckless personalities, hers as much as his, would make for nothing but misery if they wed. He had been stunned at first, and then resigned— because he couldn't deny that their relationship was as volatile as she said it was. He'd lost the letter along with all the rest of his belongings somewhere on the Gettysburg battlefield, where it must have lain, who knew how long, soaked in blood and rain, and unreadable.

"He was killed at…" he said abruptly, aloud without meaning to.

"Who?" the woman sitting on the footstool asked. He had forgotten she was there. She was looking at him intently.

"Mrs. Russell's son. James Darson—Jimmy," he said with some effort, not remembering if she knew who Mrs. Russell was or not. "She was one of my mother's friends. Mrs. Russell and Mrs. Justice. And Mrs. Kinnard," he added as an afterthought. He deliberately called up the women's names because he'd lost his place in the conversation—if there had actually been a conversation— and he didn't want her to think he was any more addled than he was.

"Jimmy Russell had red hair—the good luck kind— a carrot top. I used to chase him down and rub his head before every card game and every horse race. He was always threatening to have his head shaved—just to break me of my gambling habit. Once, though, he hunted *me* down—because he heard I was going to play poker with Phelan and Billy Canfield's Up North cousins—do you know the Canfield brothers?"

"No—except by reputation," she added. He thought there was a slight change in her tone of voice, enough to signify something he didn't understand.

He looked at her for a moment. Yes. Her eyes were sad.

"Harvard men, these cousins were," he continued without really knowing why he should want to tell her—or anybody—about any of these things. Perhaps it was because he was starved for the company of another human being. Or perhaps it was the fact that she seemed to be listening that made his rambling recollections seem—necessary. "You could say they were arrogant."

"I can imagine," she said.

"Almost as arrogant as I was," he said. "It was important—a matter of honor—to win, you see."

"And did you?"

"I had to. Jimmy said he'd shave *my* head if I…didn't. Billy and Phelan would have helped him do it, too. I can't believe he's gone…so many of them…" His voice trailed away. He had to force himself to continue. "Jimmy's life was full of burdens, but he was always laughing…" He trailed away again, overwhelmed now by the rush of memories of the boy who had been his friend. He shook his head despite the pain. He had something important to do; he had to pull himself together. "I can't seem to recall where it happened—what battle. Early in the…war, I think. He was Mrs. Russell's life. It must have been… hard for her."

"It still is," she said quietly.

Footsteps sounded in the hallway again, but they continued past the door toward the back of the house. "I always…liked Mrs. Justice," he said when it seemed that they were safe from any outside intrusion.

"I believe the feeling is mutual."

"I liked all my mother's friends…but it was a little harder with…Mrs. Kinnard." He supposed that she must know about Mrs. Kinnard and her bossy nature—unless things had changed radically, everyone in this town longer than a day would know. But he only made the remark to see if she would smile. It pleased him that she did.

"All your mother's friends vouched for you. If they hadn't, I suspect you would have awakened in the stockade rather than in your own bed."

"I...don't look the same."

"Even so, they didn't hesitate."

"I'm most grateful, then."

They stared at each other until she became uncomfortable and looked away. It was time for her to identify herself, and he wasn't sure why she didn't. He supposed that hiding was one thing, and introductions were something else again.

"Miss Woodard," she said finally.

Robert frowned, trying to remember if he'd ever known a Woodard family. "Miss Woodard," he repeated. Half a name was not helpful. He still had no idea who she was. "And that would be the...Miss Woodard who... hides."

"The very one," she said agreeably. "I do apologize for intruding. I didn't intend to come in here at all, but I thought you were still unaware, and I was quite...trapped. My only excuse is that I've been charged not to upset the occupation by offending Mrs. Kinnard. I'm finding it...difficult."

"Yes, I can...see that. Tell me, do you often...go through men's pockets?"

"Thus far, only when Sergeant Major Perkins insists," she said.

"If he's like the...sergeants major I've known, he does that on a...regular basis. Insists."

"Well, he is formidable. They say my brother knows everything that goes on in this town and in the occupation army. If that is true, I believe the sergeant major is the reason." She stood and smoothed her skirts. "I must go now and tell him you're awake."

"Your brother is…?" he asked, trying to keep her with him longer, though why he wanted—needed—to do that, he couldn't have said, except that she was an anchor to the reality he suddenly found himself in.

She looked at him for a long moment before she answered. "Colonel Maxwell Woodard. Your brother-in-law. Which makes us relatives, I suppose, by marriage."

Robert heard her—quite clearly. He even recognized the implication of her brother's military title. He just didn't believe it. Maria married to a Yankee colonel was—impossible. It would have been no surprise to him at all to learn that she had wed during his long absence, but she would never have married one of them. Never.

And then he remembered. *Never* was for people who had viable options, not for the ones who found themselves conquered and destitute and occupied, especially the women. He should have been here. Who knew what circumstances had pushed Maria into such a union, and he had no doubt that she had been pushed.

A sudden downdraft in the chimney sent a brief billowing of smoke and ash into the room. He realized that his alleged sister-in-law was more concerned about him than about the possibility of a singed hearthrug. She was looking at him with a certain degree of alarm, but he made no attempt to try to reassure her. He stared at the far wall instead, watching the shifting patterns of sunlight caused by the bare tree limbs moving in the wind outside. It was his own fault that he was so ignorant. He supposed that some might find the situation ironic, his little brother dead at Gettysburg and his sister married to one of the men directly or indirectly responsible.

"I'm sorry to have put it so bluntly," she said after a

moment. "I should have realized that the news might be…difficult to hear."

He dismissed her bluntness with a wave of his hand. "Your brother and Maria…?" He couldn't quite formulate a question to ask; there were so many. Seven years' worth.

"They live here," she said, apparently making a guess as to what he might want to know despite her misgivings about him. She couldn't know if he had been so uninformed by choice or because of the circumstances he'd found himself in.

He had to struggle to keep control of his emotions. He hadn't expected to hear that the Markham household as he knew it was essentially gone. Finding out that Maria had married one of them was hard enough, but it was even more difficult to accept that this Yankee colonel had taken up residence in the house where his family—especially Samuel—had lived. Lying here now, he wanted to hear Samuel's boisterous presence in the house just one more time. Samuel, running down the hall, bounding up the stairs, whistling, dropping things, sneaking up on their mother and taking her by surprise with one of his exuberant hugs. Robert smiled slightly. It had cost the household a whole dozen eggs once when Samuel in his joyful enthusiasm had made her drop the egg basket she'd been carrying.

His smiled faded. There was nothing now but the tread of enemy soldiers.

No. The war is over. We aren't supposed to be enemies anymore.

"And you live here, as well?" it suddenly occurred to him to ask.

"No. I'm only visiting."

"Visiting," he said, because it all sounded so…normal. Only it wasn't normal at all. Nothing was normal anymore.

His head hurt.

"Are you—" she started to say, but he interrupted her.

"Is he good to her?" he asked with a bluntness of his own. "I want to know." He turned his head despite the pain so that he could see her face. The question was disrespectful at best, and far too personal under the circumstances. He knew perfectly well that she would likely be the last person to give him a truthful answer, especially when the question in and of itself suggested that he had no faith whatsoever that her brother could behave well toward a Southern woman.

But it couldn't be helped. She was his only opportunity, the only person who might actually know.

She didn't seem to take offense, however. "He is as good to her as she will let him be," she said. "He has to be careful of her Southern pride."

"And you see…that as a…problem?"

"No, I see it more as a token of his regard for her. He was quite smitten."

"Was. He isn't smitten now?"

"The word suggests to me a transient kind of emotion, Mr. Markham," she said, clearly trying to explain. "I believe what my brother feels for Maria is a good deal more than that. Maria has made him happy—when he thought he would never be happy again. The war…"

"Yes," he said when she didn't continue. "The war."

"He was a prisoner," she said after a moment. "Here."

"And now he's the…?"

"Occupation commander."

"That must be…satisfying, given his…history."

"If you're talking about an opportunity for revenge,

it might have been just that, but for Maria. He loves her dearly. And it isn't one-sided, Mr. Markham."

"What do the townspeople think of the marriage?"

"That would depend upon whom you ask, I believe."

"Has she suffered for it—for marrying a—the colonel?"

"The fact that Mrs. Justice and the others are here in the house ready to take care of her brother, and have been since you arrived, would suggest that she hasn't."

She was still looking at him steadily, trying to decide, it seemed to him, precisely how much he should be told of his sister's situation. At this point he was certain there was more. Perhaps Mrs. Justice would know. Asking Mrs. Russell and particularly Mrs. Kinnard was out of the question.

He loves her dearly.

And Maria apparently loved him in return. That was the most important thing, wasn't it? He couldn't want more for Maria than that. But, whether she was happy or not, he still had to face her—and his father. He closed his eyes. He dreaded it, almost as much as he dreaded facing Eleanor. He had never answered her letter, but even after all this time, there were things still to be said.

He took a wavering breath. The things he'd done— and not done—had become overwhelming and indefinable. His sins were so many he couldn't separate them out anymore. They had all melded into guilt, into sorrow, into a relentless sense of regret. There would be no fatted calf for his homecoming, nor should there be. He didn't deserve one, not when he'd abandoned what was left of his family the way he had, and the worst part was that, despite the progress he'd made, he was still lost in the relentless apathy that passed for his life.

I need Your help, Lord, he thought. *I have to make this*

right if I can. If I haven't waited too long. If the damage can be undone.

"Who is here in the house?" he asked abruptly.

"Right now? Mrs. Kinnard—she comes and goes. Mrs. Russell and Mrs. Justice are here on a more permanent basis for propriety's sake. And Sergeant Major Perkins. Several soldiers from the garrison who are usually assigned to the infirmary—they've been taking care of you. The army surgeon is in and out. And there are one or two other soldiers whose job it is to keep Mrs. Kinnard happy."

"And my father?" he asked. "Where is he?"

She looked surprised by the question. "I'm sorry, Mr. Markham. Your father died not long after Maria and Max were married," she said.

He took a deep breath, and then another, trying to distance himself this time from a different kind of pain. Coming home, getting this far, had been the hardest thing he'd ever done in his life. He had known that the old man might not still be alive, but he had hoped—prayed—that that would not be the case. Incredibly, he hadn't realized how much he was counting on his father being here.

Dead and gone. Like Samuel. Like Jimmy Russell. Like so much of his life. His faith was strong enough for him to believe that they would all meet again; in his heart he knew that. But surely he hadn't thought he could come home after all this time and find that the important things would have remained the same? The sorrow he felt at this moment told him that he had.

He knew she watched him as he tried to process the information she had given him so ineptly. He was grateful she hadn't just left him to try to understand all the things she'd told him on his own.

"My father— Do you know…what happened?" he asked after a moment.

"He was very ill. It was his heart," she said. "They had to hurry the wedding on account of it—at his request, because he wanted to see Maria as a bride. And his doctors advised that there could be no delay."

"My father approved of the marriage, then."

"Yes. He was quite fond of Max, and he…" She hesitated, apparently uncertain as to whether he was up to hearing the details of his sister's marriage to a Yankee colonel.

"Go on," he said. "I need to know."

"He made sure that Maria could live here as long as she wanted. It was in his will. He was worried that something might happen with the occupation and the house might be confiscated if Maria owned it. So he left it to Max. Your father trusted him to take care of her—they had long talks together about it. The ceremony was held here in the upstairs, the wide hallway right outside his room on the other end of the house. He could see and hear everything. Maria looked beautiful—she wore the earrings you and Samuel gave her before you left for the war—"

"We thought she would marry Billy Canfield. Where is he? Why didn't she?"

"You would have to ask her about that," Kate said.

"My father was pleased about her marrying your brother," he said. It wasn't a question, but the whole idea of such a thing was hard for him to believe.

"Yes. He was. I think it was a very enjoyable day for him. Lots of food and drink and good company, and I'm certain he sneaked at least one cigar."

Robert smiled briefly at hearing that his father's love of cigars had never waned. At least he had had something pleasant to focus on at the end of his life. "An enjoyable day. That's good. I'm…glad."

"I liked Mr. Markham very much," she said after a moment. "We would talk sometimes."

"Did he ever—" He suddenly stopped, unable to bring himself to ask the question.

"What were you going to ask?"

"I— Nothing."

"He spoke of you once," she said, and once again he thought she was trying to second-guess what he might want to know.

"He said you were his warrior son. And Samuel, his poet."

Robert looked away. He had thought he was ready to hear these things, but he wasn't. Had he not been such a hotheaded "warrior," Samuel might be alive today.

He forced himself to push the conversation in a different, but no less painful, direction.

"The colonel—isn't here?" he asked.

"He and Maria and the boys left for New Bern three days ago."

"Boys? There are…children?"

"Three. Two are adopted. One, the youngest, is their birth child. My brother had military business to attend to in New Bern and he wanted his family with him. And Mrs. Hansen."

He looked at her sharply. "Mrs. Hansen?"

"She helps Maria with the children. The boys are quite a handful."

"You're talking about Warrie Hansen?"

"Yes. You would know her, I think."

"I did," he said. "A very long time ago."

So, Robert thought. Now he knew where he could find Eleanor's mother at least.

"How…long have I been…?" He couldn't quite find a word to describe his current condition. He felt as if he had slept a long time, but he didn't know why or how. He reached up to touch his forehead again. It still hurt.

"You arrived the day they all left," she said.

"Poor…timing on my part. Or perhaps not," he added after a moment, primarily because of the look on her face.

"Given the circumstances," Kate said, "it would have been alarming for Maria to suddenly come upon you the way I did, but, given the state that you were in that day, I think it would have been even worse. When you fell in the hallway, you hit your head on the parquet floor. Hard. The army surgeon says your collapse was caused by hunger and exhaustion from trying to travel on foot through the deep snow. That, and the wound you received, I assume, at Gettysburg. He says it left you—"

"I know how it left me," Robert said. He lived with the pain every day and with being less than he'd once been both physically and mentally. He was thirty-three years old, and he felt like an old man.

But he suddenly remembered. "Mrs. Kinnard was there—when I was on the floor."

"Yes," she said.

"I remember…bits of it. She was upset with me. It was like…when the Canfield brothers and I tipped over…one of her outhouses."

She looked at him with raised eyebrows. "I can see why Maria thinks Robbie may demonstrate a mischievous streak when he's older."

"Robbie?"

"Max and Maria's little boy. He's named for you. The other two, Joe and Jake, are Suzanne and Phelan Canfield's sons. Max adopted them after she died."

Robert closed his eyes, his mind reeling. A nephew

named after him? Suzanne Canfield dead? And Eleanor. What had happened to Eleanor?

"I shouldn't be in here," she said suddenly. She moved quietly to the door, opening it slightly and peering into the hallway for some sign of Mrs. Kinnard.

"I think you should rest," she said over her shoulder. "The night you arrived, you were in no condition to either get or give explanations. You're better now, and you're going to need all the strength you can muster if you intend to try to make Maria understand why you did what you did. I don't think it will be easy. I know how I would feel if I were in her place and Max had suddenly come back from the dead. Truthfully, I don't envy you the attempt."

Robert didn't say anything. She was quite straightforward, this new sister-in-law of his.

"I have a favor…to ask," he said, despite the inappropriateness of doing so. "Two favors."

"All right. Ask."

"Would you tell the sergeant major that I'd like to talk to an army chaplain. Tell him I want to talk to one who has seen the elephant. Someone who's fought in battle and survived. Will you do that?"

"Yes," she said without hesitation.

"And I would consider it a kindness if you would find out whatever you can about Miss Eleanor Hansen—where she is."

He expected her to ask him for explanations, but she didn't. She nodded, and after one final cautious look into the hallway, she slipped away.

Chapter Four

What is wrong with me? Kate thought as she made her way to the kitchen. Hiding from a woman she had every right to challenge in her own brother's house. It wasn't like her to hide. Keep silent, yes. Endure, yes. But not this.

She gave an exasperated sigh. She knew perfectly well that it wasn't the hiding alone that had her so disconcerted. It was that she had willingly engaged in a prolonged conversation with a strange man—albeit a relative by marriage—in his—*her*—bedchamber.

She wasn't really certain why she'd tarried so long with Robert Markham—except that he wasn't like any man she'd ever met. He was literally her enemy, of course, an active participant in the war responsible for Grey's death and for Max's nearly fatal imprisonment, and yet there was something…else about him, something she couldn't begin to define. Perhaps it was the contrast between his rough physical appearance and his quiet demeanor. Or seemingly quiet demeanor. Even that was an intriguing puzzle to her. His eyes weren't quiet at all. They were so intense and intimidating—a look she thought he might have perfected in the prizefighting ring.

And yet he'd seemed perfectly willing to have her take refuge from Mrs. Kinnard at his inconvenience. She had immediately sensed that he would have given her whatever help she had required, if he could, whether he knew her or not. She decided that perhaps it was the knight-in-shining-armor quality Southern men were purported to have, but she had no experience in that regard and therefore couldn't possibly know with any certainty. All she knew of the group as a whole was what Maxwell and Grey had both told her—that they were worthy enemies and excellent horsemen, things soldiers—cavalrymen— apparently found time to note and admire despite their determination to kill one another.

"It is *Tuesday,*" Mrs. Kinnard suddenly announced behind her, once again making Kate jump. And the woman made it sound as if *Tuesday* was a very bad thing to be.

Kate waited as patiently as she could to be enlightened, but so did Mrs. Kinnard. And the impasse it created continued to the point where poor timid Mrs. Justice and the two orderlies who would have walked past them in the downstairs hallway immediately changed their minds and went back in the direction they had just come.

"How may I help you, Mrs. Kinnard?" Kate said finally, capitulating once again for Max's sake. But it wasn't just her need to keep the peace that made her try to be agreeable. She couldn't help but think of Mrs. Russell's lost son, and she intended, by keeping Mrs. Kinnard pacified, to be able to write her letter to Harrison at some point without interruption, a very long letter, whether John's parents would interpret it as intruding into his life or not.

John's parents.

She never thought of the Howes as Harrison's parents. There was a good chance that the trains would be running again after the heavy snow. If so, she wanted to make sure her letter would go out today. Her son was still in this world, and even if she couldn't be with him, couldn't see him, she could still have written contact and through his return letters know how he fared.

"I have had no communication from your brother," Mrs. Kinnard said, interrupting Kate's thoughts. "None. I should have heard from him by now."

"I'm afraid I couldn't say why you have not, Mrs. Kinnard. Perhaps the heavy snow has brought the telegraph lines down—or some other…incident regarding the telegraph has occurred," Kate added with enough significance to make her point. Diehard Rebels were still known to disrupt the telegraph messages in any way they could, and Kate had no intention of taking the blame for that or the weather. "Whatever the reason, he won't return until his military duties are satisfied."

"Well, I need to hear from him," Mrs. Kinnard said, clearly not placated by mere logic.

"And I'm sure you will. When he is able."

"And if Robert Markham dies without seeing Maria? What then?"

"He's awake now," Kate said. "Perhaps he won't die."

"Awake? Why was I not told!"

"I've just told you, Mrs. Kinnard. And I've carried out his request—"

"What request?" Mrs. Kinnard asked, immediately seizing on the remark as if something underhanded was afoot. And her tone suggested that she already knew she wasn't going to be happy with Kate's answer.

"He's asked to see the army chaplain—I've just advised Sergeant Major Perkins," Kate said—or tried to.

"What utter nonsense! Robert Markham has his own

pastor! If it's spiritual comfort he needs, I can send for Mr. Lewis right now!"

Mrs. Kinnard made an abrupt about-face and headed toward the main staircase—apparently because she suddenly realized she could go directly to Robert Markham's room and have this whole matter straightened out in no time.

Kate watched her go, feeling more than a little guilty that she'd unleashed the woman upon him without warning. Unlike Kate, he couldn't hide.

But the sergeant major intercepted Mrs. Kinnard at the bottom step and stood firmly between her and her obvious desire to ascend.

"I *will* see him, Mr. Perkins," Kate heard Mrs. Kinnard say.

"Yes, ma'am, you will. But not now. He's asked to talk to the chaplain and with us not knowing how much strength he's got at the moment, he's not going to use it up on anything but that."

"*She* says he has asked for *your* chaplain," Mrs. Kinnard said, swinging her arm around to include Kate.

"Yes, ma'am. He has."

"Well, I don't believe it! Clearly, he's not himself."

"Just the same, he's not going to be bothered until after we get him the kind of chaplain he says he wants—"

"And what kind is *that,* pray tell?"

"He wants one who's seen the elephant. He's the colonel's brother-in-law so that's what he's going to get. In the meantime nobody is going to be seeing him but the hospital orderlies assigned to look after him. I saw that tongue-lashing you gave him when he was down on the floor, Mrs. Kinnard. He doesn't need any more of that. He is going to be just as calm and rested as he is right now when the chaplain gets here. After that, *then* we'll see."

"Indeed we will!" Mrs. Kinnard said. "You should be mindful that Robert Markham is one of *our* people. He's not *yours* to direct as you please. Elephants, indeed!"

"And I remind you, ma'am, who won this war. It would be better for us all if you went somewhere and waited until I send for you. And right *now,* if you please. I don't want to take exceptional measures, but I have the authority to do just that if I see fit."

Kate stayed well out of the set-to, advancing only after Mrs. Kinnard had turned on her heel and headed for the dining room in a huff.

"How is it *I* have to maintain the peace for my brother's sake and you don't?" she asked the sergeant major.

"I am maintaining the peace, Miss Kate," Perkins said.

"It sounded more like you might shoot her."

"What I'm doing is trying to make sure that *Mrs.* Colonel Woodard finds her brother in the best state of mind and health possible when she gets back here. I'm thinking Mrs. Kinnard isn't going to be much help when it comes to either of those things. And I'm thinking if the colonel's lady is happy, then the colonel will be too. Which means, so will I. And probably you, too," he added for good measure. "If you remember, he's not going to be expecting to find *you* in the middle of all this."

Kate frowned at his annoyingly perfect logic. No. Max definitely wouldn't be happy that she wasn't where she was supposed to be. "As much as I hate to admit it, I think I have…things to learn, Sergeant Major," she said.

Sergeant Major Perkins was only too happy to take her at her word. "Yes, Miss Kate, you do," he said without even a token regard for her feelings. "For example, now would be a good time for you to go and apologize to Mrs. Kinnard for my very disrespectful behavior. Tell her your brother will hear of it, after which I'll be disciplined accordingly."

"I don't see how that will help."

"As you said, you have things to learn. It's time to start learning. If you please," he added respectfully.

"I am not going to lie, Sergeant Major," she said, despite having lived in a huge web of untruths for more than half her lifetime. The fabrication regarding Harrison's birth had been foisted upon her; she'd had no choice. In this matter she did.

"There is no lie in what I want you to do. I gave you the easy part. It's going to be harder to get the colonel's brother-in-law the chaplain he's asked for. It might take a while. We have to find him and then we're likely going to have to sober him up. The man gets into the O Be Joyful every chance he gets."

Kate frowned. "Then I don't think he's going to do."

"He's the only one we got who fits the bill," Perkins said matter-of-factly. "What would be very helpful now is for you to go and mend the fence I just knocked down. If you please," he said again, tilting his head in the direction Mrs. Kinnard had gone.

She didn't please. She didn't please *at all*. But she went.

"Miss Kate," he called as she reached the dining room door. "The company baker has made up a big batch of those shortbread cookies you like so much. They're locked in the pantry. Maybe you and the ladies would like some of them. They'd go nice with a pot of tea."

"You are bribing me with cookies," she said incredulously.

"That I am, Miss Kate."

She shook her head in exasperation, then took a deep breath before she opened the dining room door and went in. She was surprised to find Mrs. Justice and Mrs. Russell sitting at the long mahogany table, as well.

And the gathering felt more like a planned meeting than a happy coincidence. She wondered if she was to have been included, if that was the reason Mrs. Kinnard had been so determined to find her.

"What are you doing here?" Mrs. Kinnard said immediately, her rudeness causing Mrs. Justice to make a small sound of protest.

"This is my brother's house," Kate said calmly. "And if by *here,* you mean this room, I...wanted to ask if you might like some tea and shortbread cookies while we wait for Mr. Markham to see the chaplain—"

Mrs. Kinnard bristled at the mention of the clergyman she hadn't approved.

"Robert Markham has his own pastor, one who has known him since he was a boy," she said. "I can't imagine why he would want anyone else."

"He didn't say why. I believe he wants to speak to someone of faith, but he also wants someone who has been in battle, as he has. That's what 'seeing the elephant' means, that one has fought the enemy and survived."

The women looked at each other. Mrs. Kinnard must have more questions, but apparently she had no intention of asking Kate.

"I would like some tea," Mrs. Justice offered timidly from her seat at the far end of the table. "And cookies. I dearly love cookies. Mrs. Russell and Mrs. Kinnard do, too."

"I have no interest in...cookies," Mrs. Russell said, but Kate heard "*her* cookies."

"Nor I," Mrs. Kinnard assured her.

"Of course you do," Mrs. Justice said, stopping just short of blatantly insisting. "Remember when all three of us got into trouble for eating the cookies that were left cooling on the windowsill at old Mrs. Kinnard's house? I can still smell that wonderful aroma after all these years. Don't you remember? We were all three riding on my brother's decrepit old brindled mare. We got a whiff of those cookies and off through the spirea hedge we went. And we made the poor old nag go tree to tree and shrub to shrub until we got close enough to snap those cookies up—I don't know what that horse must have thought. Now *these* cookies we won't have to...um, borrow."

Incredibly, Mrs. Russell smiled. "We did do that, didn't we?"

"I don't recall any such thing," Mrs. Kinnard said. "The very idea. *I* certainly never took cookies from my mother-in-law's windowsill."

"Oh, for heaven's sake, Acacia," Mrs. Russell said. "She wasn't your mother-in-law then. We were only seven. You do remember being seven, I hope."

"Six," Mrs. Justice said. "And already well on our way to a highwayman's life—just as soon as we got a better horse."

Mrs. Justice and Mrs. Russell looked at each other, then burst out laughing, and Kate couldn't keep from smiling. Mrs. Kinnard, however, remained unmoved.

There was a polite knock—kick—on the door, and Kate went to open it. A young soldier stood in the hallway, struggling to hold on to a large silver tea tray laden with a matching teapot and a mound of cookies and mismatched china cups and serving plates.

"Sergeant Major Perkins asks if you would like tea and cookies, Miss Woodard," he said as if he'd rehearsed the line any number of times. Clearly, Perkins wasn't taking any chances that Kate wouldn't carry out his plans for fence mending.

"Do we?" Kate asked, looking over her shoulder at Mrs. Kinnard, giving her the final word.

"Wouldn't it be rude not to accept Miss Woodard's hospitality?" Mrs. Justice said behind her hand to Mrs. Kinnard—as if Kate couldn't hear her. "I believe all three of our mothers taught us how to behave in someone else's home, no matter what the circumstances might be."

"Oh, very well," Mrs. Kinnard said, clearly exasperated. "Since it's here. Bring in the tray," she said to the soldier. "Put it there. Will you pour or shall I?" she asked, clearly startling him to the point that even she realized it.

"Good heavens! Not *you*," Mrs. Kinnard snapped—to the young soldier's obvious relief. *"Her."*

"I would much prefer that you poured, Mrs. Kinnard, if you would be so kind," Kate said, assuming that she was the target of Mrs. Kinnard's remark. "Unfortunately I haven't had that much practice. My mother always chose to use the Woodard heirlooms rather than storing them, and she was always worried I would break something—with good reason." She was telling the truth, but she was also trying to do as Perkins wanted and lay some groundwork before she made an attempt to soothe Mrs. Kinnard's decidedly ruffled feathers. Besides that, she wanted to focus her attention on what was happening upstairs with Robert Markham.

"Indeed," Mrs. Kinnard assured her. Believing that a catastrophe would be imminent if anything breakable found its way into Kate's hands was clearly no hardship for her at all.

Mrs. Kinnard frowned at the mismatched cups and saucers on the tray, and for a moment Kate thought she was going to comment on it. But then she must have remembered what had likely happened to the set. "Maria went to such great trouble to hide her mother's things when the house was looted," she said. "We must do our best to preserve her tea service, after all."

"My thoughts exactly," Kate said, smiling. She understood perfectly that she was supposed to cringe at the insinuation that she had political and regional ties to the looters, and that as a hostess, she left much to be desired. But being able to preside over the pouring of tea didn't matter to her in the least and hadn't since Harrison was born. She gave a soft sigh at the sudden thought of him. She wanted desperately to be away from Mrs. Kinnard and the others so she could at least write to him. She had been so faithful in her correspondence to him that she liked to think he might even anticipate the arrival of her letters. She always tried to make them as interesting as she could in the hope that he would look forward to the next one. Perhaps she would tell him about the strange return of the man upstairs.

The tea pouring proceeded in silence and without mishap.

"Tell me, Mrs. Justice," Kate said at one point in an attempt to foster enough mild conversation to carry out her mission. "What other adventures did you have when you were a little girl?"

Mrs. Kinnard gave her a warning look. She clearly didn't want any more disclosures regarding her childhood. Kate tried not to smile again at the mental image of the three of them riding an ancient horse and trying to make it to those cookies on the window ledge without being seen. Somehow she couldn't get past imagining them dressed just as they were now.

But Mrs. Justice was saved having to answer by a loud commotion in the foyer. Kate thought for a moment that Mrs. Kinnard was going to get up and go see what was occurring for herself, lest the chaplain get by her without her having the opportunity to give him both his instructions and her opinion of his being brought here in the first place.

"Well, how drunk is he!" they all heard Perkins say.

Kate couldn't make out the reply. She worked on looking as if she had no idea what that comment might mean.

"Get him in here and sober him up! Stick his head in a bucket of snow if you have to!"

"Soldiers do seem to have unusual solutions to their predicaments, don't they?" Mrs. Justice commented mildly as the commotion intensified and moved past the dining room door toward the back of the house. She took another sip of tea and looked at Kate. "What did Robbie say, my dear? Did he mention where he'd been at all?"

"I didn't ask him anything about that," Kate said.

"Oh! Of course not," Mrs. Justice said, apparently alarmed that she'd dared suggest such a rude and thoughtless thing. "That wouldn't have been a good idea at all. But you did talk to him?"

"He had…questions. He didn't seem to remember what had happened to him." She took a quiet breath. "He didn't know his father had died."

"Oh, that poor, poor boy," Mrs. Justice said.

"And did he know about Maria's marriage?" Mrs. Kinnard asked.

"No. He didn't."

"I'm sure he was upset about *that,* as well."

"He is Maria's brother. He would naturally be concerned about her. Fortunately I could reassure him."

"Indeed yes," Mrs. Justice said. Mrs. Kinnard and Mrs. Russell both gave her a hard look.

They could hear a second arrival in the foyer and then heavy footsteps going up the stairs.

"That must be the chaplain, don't you think? Poor Robbie," Mrs. Justice said again.

"Poor Robbie, indeed," Mrs. Kinnard said, setting her cup down hard despite her desire to keep Maria's mismatched tea service safe. "He'll get no spiritual comfort *there*."

"Sounds like their army surgeon to me," Mrs. Russell said. "For a thin man, he has a very heavy tread. But then they *all* do."

Kate took a breath and tried not to consider what in the world could have been behind the remark. Her head was beginning to hurt, despite the tea and the excellent cookies. No matter what Sergeant Major Perkins thought, there were some things cookies just wouldn't fix.

"I'd like to say a prayer, if I may," Mrs. Justice said.

"For *whom?*" Mrs. Kinnard asked, as if prayers came under her jurisdiction, as well.

"For our Robbie, of course," she said. "If you would bow your heads please." She waited a moment for them to comply, then continued. "Dear Lord, we don't know where Robert Markham has been or what kind of trouble and heartache he's had, but we ask you—now that he's home again and safe—please guide us so we can know what to do for him, and please don't let us do anything to add to his worries and make them worse. Amen."

Mrs. Justice smiled and looked around at each of them. "There. I feel so much better now."

So do I, Kate thought. Incredibly, Mrs. Justice, with her gentle, forthright prayer, had reminded all of them that Robert Markham would likely need help—but none of them should arbitrarily decide what that help should be. She wondered if Robert had any idea what a staunch ally he had in this kind and pleasant woman.

Someone knocked softly on the door, and without

waiting to be admitted, Mrs. Kinnard's daughter Valentina swept into the room.

"Ah! Here you are, Mother," she said. She looked… stunning. She would have been perfectly at home in any salon in Philadelphia.

"Imagine my surprise when I arrived home—*finally*—the snow on the road from Mocksville was terrible—Aunt Matilda and Uncle Bart send their love, by the way. And here I discover you're nowhere to be found and the servants tell me you're in the middle of all this excitement about Robert Markham—and my word, there are soldiers all over the place. How is it that this house is *always* overrun with soldiers?"

"Perhaps because a colonel lives here," Kate said mildly.

"Oh. Well. Yes. Hello, Miss Woodard," Valentina said, smiling. "You're looking very…fine today."

Kate was well aware that she didn't look fine at all. She'd been alternating the same travel dress with a plain calico morning dress she kept at her brother's house specifically for getting down on the floor and playing with the boys. The fact that most of her wardrobe was likely sitting in the Philadelphia train station meant she might be alternating the two dresses for some days hence, turning whichever one she'd just worn wrong side out and hanging it on the rack in the airing room next to the nursery each night.

"You're very kind, Valentina, but I'm not at my best, I'm afraid. What a lovely dress and hat you have on," Kate said truthfully, openly admiring the bright orange shantung day bodice Valentina wore above a pale blue skirt with a pleated cream underskirt showing beneath it, and cream-colored lace at her throat and wrists. "Would you like some tea?"

"Yes—"

"No," Mrs. Kinnard assured them both.

"No," Valentina said dutifully. "I'm very apt to spill. Or break," she added, completely ignoring the look her mother gave her.

"So am I," Kate said. "I was only just telling your mother I ought not pour the tea because of it. Do you suppose there is anything we can do about it?"

"Perhaps there's hope for you, Miss Woodard," Valentina said. "As for myself—I am quite useless. Or so my mother tells me. You wouldn't believe the number of dresses and tablecloths and teacups I've wrecked."

Kate couldn't keep from smiling. For the first time in their numerous encounters since Max and Maria had married, Kate found herself coming very close to liking this young woman. Today she seemed to have no guile at all, despite what must have been her mother's diligent tutelage.

"So tell me. Is it true that Robert Markham has returned?" Valentina asked the room at large.

"Yes," Kate answered, because no one else seemed inclined to.

"Is he very changed— Oh, that's right. You wouldn't know. Is he changed, Mother?"

"I couldn't say. *I* haven't been allowed to see him," Mrs. Kinnard said, and Valentina actually laughed.

"Oh, dear. Someone is going to suffer for that." Valentina was openly teasing her mother—and somebody was going to suffer for *that,* too, Kate thought.

But Valentina didn't seem to be worried in the least. She was so different from the Valentina Kate had grown accustomed to, and she couldn't help but wonder why.

"Miss Woodard, I believe we were trying to ascertain

whether or not Robert said anything sensible. Are you or are you not going to enlighten us?" Mrs. Kinnard said.

"He said he was grateful to you, Mrs. Kinnard—and to Mrs. Justice and Mrs. Russell for establishing his identity," Kate said.

"As he should be," Mrs. Kinnard said, not about to give an inch. "Certainly we will have to find out where he's been all this—"

"Why?" Kate asked, daring to interrupt. "There's no need for him to justify his whereabouts to anyone, except perhaps Maria. She is the one he has hurt the most."

"Well, there's El—" Mrs. Justice started to say.

"And *that* is not fit for civilized discussion," Mrs. Kinnard snapped. "What she became is clearly what she always was." She looked at Kate. "Or perhaps things are done differently where you come from and there is no accountability for bad behavior."

I'm too tired for this, Kate suddenly thought. What little sleep she'd had had been on one of the boys' cots in the downstairs nursery wing of the house. Mrs. Kinnard had more than proved that she intended to go to any length necessary to be offended, and Kate just couldn't endure another round of verbal sparring.

She stood instead. "I believe I'll go see if the sergeant major can tell me what is happening with my brother-in-law," she said, hoping that the term "brother-in-law" would induce Mrs. Kinnard to understand whose claim on Robert Markham took precedence. This was a family matter. No one could pacify Mrs. Kinnard at this point, least of all Kate, and she had no intention of allowing the woman to meddle where she didn't belong. Kate had no intention of coming back, either, whether she gleaned any information from Perkins or not. She had to write her letter to Harrison and she had to get away from Mrs.

Kinnard before she said something to unravel Max's fragile hold on a peaceful military occupation altogether.

"I'll come with you," Valentina said.

"That's not necessary—" Kate tried to say, but Valentina ignored her and her mother's protests.

"Oh, but I want to. You must tell me about the dresses in Philadelphia—after you speak to Sergeant Major Perkins, of course. I get so lonely for my own kind sometimes. We can have a real conversation."

"Valentina. I require you here," Mrs. Kinnard said firmly as Kate stepped into the hallway. She could immediately hear raised voices coming from the upstairs. Sergeant Major Perkins stood at the bottom of the staircase, alert but not yet ready to intervene.

"What's happening?" Kate asked. "Is that the chaplain yelling?"

"Could be. Or it could be your brother-in-law," Perkins said. "Not sure who's preaching to who."

"Aren't you going to intervene?"

"Not until I hear furniture breaking," he said calmly. "Most of the time two soldiers yelling at each other won't mean a lot."

"Miss Woodard! Wait!" Valentina called behind her, and the sigh Kate had been suppressing for some time got away from her. Clearly her life would have been much simpler if she'd just gotten on that train.

Chapter Five

Where is she?

Robert kept listening for the sound of his sister-in-law's footsteps in the hallway outside his door. He had only seen her once since the hiding episode, when she'd brought him his Bible and his Confederate enlistment card, and that was two days ago. He didn't think she'd been driven to hide again because he hadn't heard Mrs. Kinnard's distinctive voice for some time now—or if she had concealed herself, she'd found a more obscure place to do it.

He was feeling much stronger; he was awake and dressed and seated comfortably in the rocking chair by the fire, like the old man he had seemingly become. His appetite had returned—much to Mrs. Justice's pleasure—but ever since he'd awakened from his laudanum-induced stupor, he'd found himself in the middle of a crossroad. Not a spiritual or an emotional one, but one that literally involved all manner of comings and goings in the house. People arrived in a steady stream at the front door, or they made their entry into the house at the back via the kitchen. However they managed to get inside, they all apparently had the same goal—ostensibly to deliver food and drink as a "welcome home" for him, but actually to satisfy their curiosity about his return. There was no surprise in that, of course; he had essentially come back from the dead. What surprised him was that the parade of would-be visitors continued despite the fact that none of them were ever allowed to visit. He had his brother-in-law's sergeant major to thank for that, and he was grateful. It was a great relief not to have to talk to anyone. Unfortunately the one person he actually wanted to talk to was prone to hiding.

Kate.

He had learned her given name by overhearing snippets of conversation in the house. "Miss Kate," the sergeant major called her. It would seem, too, that she actually did have a certain responsibility for keeping Mrs. Kinnard pacified, and he didn't envy her that.

He was also learning more about the soldiers assigned to the house—Bruno, who had cared for his father during his final illness and who clearly had a fondness for the old man. Private Castine, who was suffering the torture of being a young man surrounded by attractive Southern young ladies nearly everywhere he went, most of whom never deigned to speak to him and the ones who did weren't nearly so prized. Admiring someone from afar was a decidedly lonely pastime.

It came as a surprise to Robert that he rather liked Sergeant Major Perkins. The very first question the man had put to him had seemed offhand and innocent—even humorous—but it had been straight to the point: "Did you get the chaplain straightened out or not?"

It was a question for which there was likely no answer, but by asking it, Perkins had made it known that he—if not the entire household—had heard the heated exchange during what everyone had assumed was an occasion for giving and getting spiritual comfort. But he hadn't asked Robert for any details, as Robert had expected. Instead he had established that, at some point, he might, and at that time he would expect an answer.

Robert had managed to endure a short one-sided conversation with Mrs. Kinnard—she'd talked about the suffering she had endured at the hands of the occupiers; ostensibly, he listened. He'd also had a visit with Mrs. Justice, but she had cried so when she had seen him awake, sitting up and mostly himself again, that he couldn't find a way to ask her about Eleanor. Mrs. Russell didn't come to talk to him at all, and he supposed it was because he was too much of a reminder of Jimmy.

What with the influx of food into the house and the weeping, it was as if he'd died rather than come home again. He was certain of one thing, however. It had to be significant that Mrs. Justice did not once mention Eleanor. He was not so certain that Kate Woodard was going to be able to grant him his second favor and bring him the information he wanted.

He looked up at a sound out in the hallway. The sergeant major stood in the doorway.

"You sent for me, sir?" he asked.

"I… Yes. I was wondering if Miss Woodard was available. I'd like to speak to her."

"She's about to leave the house, sir, if she hasn't already," he said.

"Do you know when she'll return?"

"Couldn't say, sir. She had some letters she wanted to mail, and then Miss Valentina—Mrs. Kinnard's daughter, that would be—she kind of swooped in and pounced on her about wearing the same dress all the time. Anybody would have thought the fur would fly after a remark like that, but off together they went. Miss Woodard's got her hands full trying to keep the peace with the Kinnards. You probably already know things will run a lot smoother for a lot of people if she does," he added significantly, and Robert didn't miss his implication that whatever affected Colonel Woodard would also affect Maria, and ultimately her newly resurrected brother, as well.

"If Miss Valentina intends to address this wardrobe situation, she'll likely keep Miss Woodard hostage until she's got everything the way she thinks it ought to be. It's going to be interesting to see how this turns out, what with both of them being as determined about things as they are."

"Why is she wearing the same dress all the time?" Robert asked, commenting on the one thing in the sergeant major's report he found intriguing. He hadn't actually had the opportunity to notice her dresses, but he did understand enough about women to know that while such a situation might not be troubling to a farm woman who only had one everyday dress, to someone like Kate Woodard, it could be a catastrophe.

No, he decided immediately. It wouldn't be a catastrophe to her at all. Valentina might think it was the end of the world, but not Kate.

He frowned because he had no idea how he had arrived at that opinion.

"Well, she doesn't have much choice. All her trunks went on the train to Philadelphia. I guess you could say they went and she didn't."

"Are you saying she didn't go because I turned up?"

"No," he said bluntly. "I'm not. Anything else, sir?"

"Would you tell Miss Woodard I'd like to have a word with her when she comes back."

"I'll tell her—but I can't say for sure what she'll do about it. Like I said, she's a determined kind of woman."

"Sergeant Major," Robert said as Perkins turned to go. "Is there any word about my sister's return?"

"Not yet. Telegraph lines are down in places east of here. You would know how that goes."

Robert looked at him. It took him a moment before he understood what the sergeant major meant. In Perkins's opinion at least, and on some level, the war was still going on.

When Perkins had gone, Robert walked to the window and looked out. He didn't see Kate or Valentina—which likely meant that she was still here after all.

He took the back stairs down to the kitchen. Mrs. Justice was just putting loaves of bread into the oven.

"Dear Robbie," she said when she saw him. "Can I get you something?"

"I…was just looking for Miss Woodard."

"She's gone to army headquarters and then, I believe, on an emergency quest to the dressmaker's with Valentina. All her trunks went to Philadelphia without her, you know."

"Yes. I heard about that."

"It's terribly inconvenient," she said. "She has her valise, thankfully, but they only carry so much. I'm still not sure why she didn't go. The colonel had everything arranged. It was a good thing she didn't, though. Heaven only knows what might have happened if she hadn't been here to help you."

"Yes," Robert said, but the truth was that it hadn't occurred to him before, how timely Kate Woodard's being in the house that night had been.

"Robbie?" Mrs. Justice said, and she looked so troubled. He waited for her to ask the question she so obviously wanted to ask. She was frowning, something she rarely did in his experience.

"What is it, Mrs. Justice?"

"I— Oh, it's nothing. Here," she said opening the warming oven and taking down a plate. "Have a ham biscuit."

"You have such *adventures,*" Valentina said as they walked the distance to…Kate didn't quite know where. All she knew was that Valentina had insisted that they leave the house immediately and just go, that it wasn't too far for them to walk and that they would both enjoy an outing on such a sunny—if somewhat blustery—winter's day. Sergeant Major Perkins, in the meantime, had done some insisting of his own. He had assured Kate that she would not be going anywhere without being escorted, and he'd promptly assigned the same hapless and perpetually startled young private who had brought the tea and cookies to the dining room to trail along.

The sun was indeed shining—albeit a weak sun— but the snow was still on the ground and there were icy patches where it had melted and frozen again. The wind cut sharply at times, and the private's nose was soon red with the cold. He kept sniffing as they walked along. It was clear to Kate that he considered this duty to be some kind of torture, but she didn't think it had anything to do with the walk or the weather. She thought it was primarily because he wanted to admire Valentina openly and he couldn't, not with the firm knowledge of what Perkins would do to him if he were accused of gawking at Mrs. Kinnard's daughter. Valentina looked especially impressive this morning in her blue velveteen coat and pert little hat covered in black net and emerald-green feathers.

"I wouldn't say that," Kate said, turning her attention back to Valentina. *Adventure* was not a word she associated with any aspect of her life.

"Well, *I* would. I don't know *anyone* who ever got stranded without her dresses. You couldn't have worn any of Maria's, I suppose."

"Not and maintain any sense of propriety," Kate said, trying not to smile because the topic of conversation had apparently made the young private's ears turn as red as his nose. "I'm a good two inches taller than she is."

Valentina suppressed a giggle. "Can you imagine what my mother would say about *that?*"

Kate had no problem imagining it at all, but she didn't say so. "I must go to the army headquarters first. I want to make sure my letters get sent out on the next train. And then where is it we're going?"

"To the dressmaker's of course—Mrs. Russell's sister, that would be. She's the best dressmaker in town. She does beautiful work. I think her business is quite prosperous now that more of the officer's wives have come to share their husbands' occupation duty. I wonder if they find it lonesome here—hardly anyone talks to them, you know. Just at church and one has to be civil there. Anyway, we can hope Mrs. Russell's sister will have a few dresses mostly finished to carry you through until she can sew you some new ones. It's sad how her husband died in the war—not in the fighting—from the measles. It seems very inappropriate for a soldier, doesn't it? Dying of a child's disease, like that— Were you very afraid?"

"Afraid? When?"

"When you found Robert Markham in the house that night. I would have been terrified, especially since I thought he was dead."

"Well, he wasn't conscious long enough to be threatening, and I didn't know who he was."

They walked for a time in silence, and at one point,

because the ground was so icy, the young private had to offer them his arm as they maneuvered over the spot.

"What is your name?" Valentina asked him as she accepted his help—which caused his ears to redden again.

"Private Castine, miss," he said.

"Thank you, Private Castine. You are a very diligent escort—for a Yankee boy."

The private clearly chose to hear the compliment and not the insult in her remark, and blushed in earnest this time. Kate wondered if surviving an encounter with someone as dazzling as Valentina constituted yet another version of "seeing the elephant."

The closer they came to the wide main street and the army headquarters building, the more soldiers there were on the sidewalks and in the alleys and doorways. Some of them seemed to have a purpose in being there—keeping watch for signs of trouble around the saloons, guarding army supply wagons waiting to be unloaded, directing the movement of various buggies and carriages through the deep mud and fresh manure—and some did not. And those were the ones Kate dreaded to encounter despite having an escort. She knew that Max had strict rules regarding the military's behavior toward civilians, but she also knew Max was in New Bern and that even when he was not, there had been drunken incidents like the one involving the young officer who was in love with Mrs. Russell's now officially forbidden daughter. Since her talk with Robert Markham, Kate could almost understand Mrs. Russell's unyielding position. She had lost her beloved son to the war; she wasn't about to lose her daughter, too.

How hard this all must be, she suddenly thought—for ex-Rebels like Robert. His town, his very home—his sister—had been taken over by the enemy. And perhaps worse, all his suffering for the Confederacy had been for nothing. His prolonged absence had perhaps been driven by his need for solitude and freedom from other people's expectations. If so, it was much like her own decision to miss the train, only on a much grander scale.

How strange, she thought, that she and an ex-Rebel soldier, though their situations were profoundly different, might feel the same.

Kate and Valentina continued their way toward the army headquarters, and apparently Max's authority held fast today. Soldiers promptly stepped aside for her and Valentina whenever necessary, and none of them had anything coarse to say. She was able to deliver her letters to the sergeant on duty with no difficulty whatsoever.

When they came outside again, Valentina insisted on leading the way to the dressmaker's, which, as near as Kate could understand from Valentina's convoluted explanation, was somewhere near a church and less than a block off the main street. At least they were out of the wind much of the time now, and that made the going easier, but Valentina took so many shortcuts, Kate lost track of exactly where they were. Eventually she realized that the dressmaker was actually near the church she attended with Max and Maria every Sunday.

"I always wonder what kind of tree that is," Kate said of the tall, spirelike evergreen growing in the churchyard.

"Do you? I never wonder about things like that."

"What do you wonder about, then?"

"Oh, about husbands—finding mine, that is. Don't you do that?"

"No," Kate said truthfully. "Is there anyone in particular you have in mind?"

"Oh…no one suitable," Valentina said with such nonchalance that Kate wondered if someone had caught her eye who shouldn't have. "There aren't that many men to marry since the war. The ones who did come back are so...*changed*. Mother really wanted me to marry Colonel Woodard—she thought *he* was very suitable even if he did fight on the other side—but that didn't work out."

"No," Kate said, somewhat taken aback by Valentina's candor. She wondered if the girl had somehow forgotten that she was talking to Colonel Woodard's sister.

"I should like to pick my own husband," Valentina said wistfully.

"Perhaps you can," Kate said, despite the fact that they both knew Mrs. Kinnard wouldn't stand for such a thing—ever. She looked again at the unusual tree, but it was Harrison she was thinking about. Harrison would have wondered about the tree just as she had. He was blessed with such a wonderful curiosity about everything.

What are you doing today, my dear Harrison?

He was probably in the classroom, she decided. She wished she'd asked him about his daily schedule so she'd have a better idea of what his life was like now that he was away at school. It would be...pleasant to know what was happening in his world hour by hour.

Comforting.

She would ask him about it in her next letter.

"They say he's gotten religion," Valentina was saying.

"Who?" Kate asked because she hadn't been paying attention.

"Robert Markham, of course. He must have if he asked for a *chaplain*."

"Yes, but their meeting sounded more like an out and out argument than anything that had to do with his getting religion."

"Well, if he *is* religious now, I suppose it's because he was so wild before the war—he hardly *ever* went to church. Mother said at the time that a war was the best thing that could have happened to him—because his love of brawling might actually be useful for a change. But that was before Samuel was killed. Samuel was such a sweet, sweet boy. Robert was supposed to watch over him—and I'm sure he did—but poor Samuel was killed, anyway. That would make him sad enough to try to change his ways, don't you think? People used to say Eleanor Hansen would make him settle down, but look how that turned out."

Kate stopped walking. "How did it turn out?"

"Oh, dear," Valentina said, putting her neatly gloved hand to her mouth. "It's so confusing. I keep forgetting you don't know anything."

"Then tell me."

"I couldn't! It's one thing to mention such matters in the company of someone who already knows the particulars, but you can't discuss it with someone who doesn't— oh, no! There's my mother's carriage. I'm sure she's sent it to get me. I'm afraid we'll have to see about the dresses another time. I enjoyed our walk so much. Truly. We must do it again soon."

A carriage was indeed headed down the street in their direction. Valentina gave Kate a little wave and hurried to meet it, likely because Mrs. Kinnard didn't just send the carriage to fetch her daughter; she'd come along. Kate wondered if Mrs. Kinnard had approved an outing at all. Her best guess was that she had not. Mrs. Kinnard was nothing if not diligent in her quest to find Valentina a rich and prestigious husband, and once Max had married Maria, he was no longer important. Mrs. Kinnard certainly wouldn't want Valentina wasting her time and energy on an unavailable Yankee colonel's sister. Poor

Valentina. Kate and Valentina both were firmly ensnared by the expectations of society and family.

Kate gave a quiet sigh and wished yet again that Max would get home. Bearing even a small part of the responsibility for the federal occupation of this town was beginning to weigh heavily.

"I'm going to step into the church for a moment. I won't be long," Kate said to Private Castine, because the Kinnard carriage was still sitting on the street in plain view—much to the private's pleasure—but the last thing Kate wanted was yet another prickly encounter with Mrs. Kinnard.

Still hiding, she thought with a sigh.

She found the church unlocked, and she went quickly inside and took a seat on one of the back pews, thankful that the church had been so handy. She suddenly smiled. What must God think of the things Kate Woodard found to be grateful for.

But I am grateful, Lord, even when I'm not running away from something. Truly...

Her son was alive and well, even if she did worry about him, even if he was far away from her. It was only in one moment after Harrison's birth that she'd despaired so and wished herself dead. But she hadn't felt that hopeless since. She'd been sad and worried and afraid more times than she cared to count, but all of that had always been overridden by the fact that she was Harrison's mother.

She took a silent breath and looked around the sanctuary. No one else seemed to be about. It was so peaceful here. Despite her longstanding estrangement from God, she liked this church. Perhaps it was the extraordinary tree outside, or the pleasant smell of lemon oil and beeswax used to polish the pews and the wood paneling or the way the sun shone through the sparkling clean windows. She had always felt that church buildings had personalities, and this one had such a comforting air. She could almost feel the prayers and praise of generations swirling around her. After a moment she bowed her head and recalled the part of Mrs. Justice's prayer for Robert Markham that had resonated with her so.

But her prayer was for her son.

"Bless Harrison, Father, and keep him safe. And please—*please*—guide me so I can know what to do for him. And whatever situation he may find himself in, don't let me ever do anything to make things worse for him…" She stopped for a moment, then continued, "And watch over Robert Markham. Help him with whatever he needs to do to find his way home again. Amen."

The private was waiting where she'd left him when she came outside again. He kept glancing at her as they walked along the still snowy path toward Max's house. Clearly he had something on his mind, but she didn't say anything to push him into making a revelation.

"Thuya," he said finally.

"I beg your pardon?'

"Thuya. It's a thuya tree, miss. *T-h-u-y-a.* Thuyas come all the way from China. That's what Mr. Markham says—Mr. Robert Markham what's staying at the colonel's. He says it's planted in the churchyard to show that no matter where you come from, in God's house, you're welcome."

"That's…very interesting," Kate said, but she was thinking what a complex man Robert Markham was turning out to be.

"Yes, miss, it is."

The conversation ended, and by the time they reached the house, Kate was feeling the cold. Her toes and her fingers burned and prickled with it. She entered with nothing in mind but getting warm.

"Miss Kate," Perkins said as soon as he saw her. "Mrs. Justice saw you coming. She's got some good hot tea waiting in the dining room."

"Thank you, Sergeant Major," Kate said with a smile. She couldn't think of anything she would like better than tea with Mrs. Justice "Still no word from my brother?"

"No, Miss Kate. Not yet. I sent off another telegram. I don't know how much longer I can put off Mrs. Kinnard without having to lock her up."

Kate couldn't keep from smiling.

"What did you do with the other one?" she heard Perkins ask the young private as she walked toward the dining room door.

"Her mother came and got her—in this fancy carriage."

"How mad was she?"

"About like usual, I reckon, Sergeant Major. She didn't yell at nobody. Of course, Miss Woodard, she hightailed it into the church before Mrs. Kinnard got close enough. By the time she did, there weren't nobody left to yell at but me, and I had a couple turns yesterday. I reckon she decided to rest up before she gives me what-for again."

"Go see why that wagon's stopping out front," Perkins said, and Kate heard the front door slam again.

Mrs. Justice looked up from pouring the tea as Kate opened the dining room door and stepped inside. "You look frozen," she said. "Come sit close to the fire. I've got your cup ready for you."

"Bless you, Mrs. Justice," Kate said, removing her gloves and shawl and sitting in the chair closest to the hearth. She hesitated, then took off her wet boots as well, determined to savor the heat from the fire on her cold feet. It felt wonderful, and it reminded her again that she still didn't know precisely how to build one. "Is Mrs. Russell joining us?"

"No, she's overseeing the soldier who is cooking blancmange for the evening meal—or trying to. I believe he is balking at the addition of rosewater. Did you find yourself some dresses?"

"No," Kate said, taking the cup of steaming tea Mrs. Justice offered her, holding it in both hands rather than pretending she was a lady and not cold at all. "Mrs. Kinnard came and fetched Valentina before we got to the dressmaker's."

"Hmm," Mrs. Justice said.

"My thoughts exactly," Kate assured her.

"Did you see Robbie when you came in?"

"No, why?"

"He was asking after you earlier," she said. "He may still be in the kitchen. He was visiting with Mrs. Russell in there a little while ago." She gave a heavy sigh. "It was hard for them both."

"He told me about Jimmy Russell," Kate said.

"Did he?" Mrs. Justice said, clearly surprised. "I think Mrs. Russell had her hopes revived that Jimmy might turn up, too. But that's impossible, of course. A number of his comrades were with him when he died."

They sat for a time in silence, sipping their tea.

"I believe something is worrying him," Mrs. Justice said after a time. She looked at Kate. "Robbie."

"I— Mrs. Justice, Robert has asked me to find out what I can about Eleanor Hansen," Kate said, deciding to speak plainly. It was her first opportunity to actually talk to Mrs. Justice alone about the favor he had asked her to do.

Mrs. Justice frowned. "That seems— Why do you

suppose he would ask *you* to do that? You don't even know Eleanor. Oh, I know. Robbie trusts you to tell him the truth."

"Does he? I can't imagine why."

Mrs. Justice smiled. "You have a way about you, my dear. There is something you carry with you that inspires trust. It's probably the reason he talked about Jimmy Russell."

"I don't think Mrs. Kinnard would agree."

"Ah, well. Acacia and I have been friends since we were children so I can truthfully say—without malice— there aren't many things Acacia finds agreeable. I've always thought it was a sad and fearful way to live one's life. We should pray for her whenever we say our prayers, don't you think?"

Kate smiled without answering. She had just prayed for Robert Markham, whom she barely knew, and yet that hadn't seemed nearly as ill-fitting a task as the idea of saying a prayer for Mrs. Kinnard. She continued to sip her tea and stared at the fire in the fireplace, thinking about the train heading north sometime today. How many days would it take her letter to arrive? One could never be sure. A week? Or much longer? In her mind's eye she could see Harrison's shy smile when it was delivered to him. Or so she hoped.

Please watch over him...

"My dear," Mrs. Justice said gently, and Kate looked up at her. "It doesn't go away," she said. "The sadness. But it does get better."

Kate attempted a smile, to reassure Mrs. Justice if nothing else, but she couldn't quite make it. "Mrs. Justice, do you know where Eleanor is?" she asked, hoping to change the subject and to satisfy the quest Robert had given her.

"I know she left town. Warrie—her mother—doesn't talk about her. Even so, she is the one Robbie should speak to. Perhaps you could tell him that. She will have the information he needs."

"I can't remember meeting anyone named Eleanor. Did she come to Max and Maria's wedding?"

"She wouldn't have come to the wedding even if she'd been invited. It wouldn't have been…proper, and Eleanor would never have done anything to ruin Maria's lovely day. So you wouldn't have met her. And if you heard mention of her at all, you would likely have heard her called Nell."

"Nell—yes. I do remember someone named Nell. Oh," she said as her memories of the woman called Nell unfolded. "Oh," she said again.

"Just so, my dear," Mrs. Justice said.

There was a sudden sharp whistle outside the door, the kind one might use to summon a horse or a dog, and it heralded a great commotion in the hallway, a running and assembling of all the military personnel on the premises—along with Mrs. Russell, who was apparently still very concerned about the blancmange.

"Perkins! What are you doing here!" Kate distinctly heard her brother ask—demand.

"Sir! You didn't get my telegrams, sir!" Perkins said.

"I did not—why are these soldiers in my house?"

"Well, it's one of those long stories, sir—"

"The short version, Perkins!"

"Sir, I wish I could oblige, but this is going to take a while to explain. And we need to keep Mrs. Colonel Woodard out of the way somewhere until I do."

"Why? What are you talking about!"

There was an added disturbance in the foyer—the

boys and Warrie coming inside. And—surely not—Mrs. Kinnard and Valentina.

"Colonel Woodard, I will *not* be put off any longer!" Kate heard Mrs. Kinnard say.

Oh, please. Do not tell him the day of the week, Kate thought, remembering Mrs. Kinnard's earlier fit of pique when Max hadn't met her deadline for addressing her long list of complaints. It hadn't mattered to her in the least that he had been attending to army business in New Bern some two hundred miles away. Kate had worked too hard to preserve the occupation; she didn't want Max in his present state of mind to unravel it all.

"Our Maria's back," Mrs. Justice said happily, despite the escalating confusion beyond the dining room door.

Oh, no! Maria!

Kate scrambled to put her cup down and get to her feet, then ran for the door shoeless, but Mrs. Justice reached it ahead of her and threw it wide as she stepped into the chaos in the foyer. Kate was left staring directly into her brother's astonished face.

"Kate—?" he said incredulously. "Mrs. Justice—?" But whatever else he was going to say got lost in a long and terrible wailing sound coming from someone behind him. And it didn't stop. It went on and on. The boys began to cry, and in the sudden shuffling of people, Max ended up holding his youngest son. He thrust the baby into Kate's arms and turned to help Mrs. Justice ease Warrie Hansen down so she could sit on the bottom step of the stairs. Joe and Jake were clinging to her skirts, and Mrs. Kinnard kept insisting on having Max's attention.

And Maria—

Maria was standing just inside the front door, staring past Kate toward the rear of the house, her face ashen. And then her eyes rolled upward and her head tilted back.

She grabbed for Valentina's arm as she sank into a heap on the floor. Valentina's squawk of alarm added to the din, and Max moved her bodily out of the way so he could get to Maria. Perkins was barking orders, sending a runner for the army surgeon and the rest of his soldiers to either help clear the foyer of unnecessary people or get out of the way.

And Warrie Hansen was still sobbing.

"Joe! Jake!" Kate said to the boys, holding out her free hand. "Come here!" Surprisingly, they ran to her, and she took them back toward the kitchen, carrying Robbie, leading Joe and essentially dragging Jake, who held on to the folds of her skirt with both fists. Her only thought was to get them out of the melee, but Mrs. Justice and Mrs. Russell decided to bring Warrie Hansen down the hallway to the nursery wing so she could lie down. Kate and the boys were decidedly in the way. Mrs. Justice kept trying to soothe Warrie, but it was having no more effect than Kate's trying to soothe the boys. Their crying escalated, and Kate felt like crying right along with them.

Kate stopped short as she realized that Robert Markham was standing in the kitchen doorway, much as he had that snowy night he'd arrived home. But she knew more about him now, and when she saw his stricken face, she understood immediately what had happened. He must have been standing there when Warrie and Maria came into the house, and both women had seen him, not knowing anything at all about how he came to be there. Warrie was still so distressed, she didn't seem to know that she was passing right by him.

"Robert," Kate said, but he was looking at his sister being carried into the parlor. "Robert," she said again because she thought he was only a moment from going to her.

"This is my fault," he said.

"Yes," Kate said. "It is. But right now isn't the time for you to try to talk to Maria. My brother has to be told what's happened so he can prepare her. I told you how it is with them. He's not about to let you make things worse. Please," she said because he was clearly determined to handle this himself, but she knew her brother, and she knew she was right. "I need to get the children upstairs," she said, but he wasn't listening. She moved around to where she could see his face.

"I need to take them upstairs."

He finally looked at her. "Give me the baby," he said.

She hesitated, then handed Robbie over to him. He took the baby gently, skillfully, and held him against his shoulder. Kate managed to get Jake to release his grip on her skirts. She took him by the hand and led both boys through the kitchen and up the back stairway.

She looked over her shoulder at one point to make sure Robert was behind her. It suddenly occurred to her that he might be too unsteady still to carry a baby, but he seemed to be maneuvering the stairs without any difficulty. When she reached the big open upstairs hallway, she considered going into the sitting room on her right, but then she kept going, leading the way to the room Robert now occupied, primarily because she could hear what was happening downstairs better from there. Once inside she gave Robert a look of gratitude for being reasonable and tried to catch her breath, then she bent down and put her arms around both boys.

"It's all right," she whispered to them. "Don't cry."

"Maria fell down!" Jake wailed, and Kate could hear Robert's sharp exhalation of breath behind her.

Joe had nothing to say. At some point, as the older of the two, he had decided to leave the actual asking of whatever questions the two of them might have to Jake. For reasons known only to him, he didn't want anyone to know he might be in need of information. He especially didn't want to be laughed at because of something he didn't understand. Kate leaned back to look at him. He was trying so hard to stop crying and be brave.

"Max will come and tell us all about it just as soon as he can," she said, moving his hair out of his eyes. "We're going to wait right here so he won't have any trouble finding us."

Kate glanced at Robert again. The baby was still crying despite his gentle swaying and soothing words. Kate gathered the boys to her again.

"I found Robbie's horse. It's on the mantel in the sitting room. Will you run as fast as you can and get it?"

They both whirled around and ran out of the room, delighted in spite of their distress to have permission to run free *in* the house. They were back in no time, both of them clutching the horse and holding it out to her.

"Thank you," she said, smiling. "You were so quick! Robbie," she said softly, moving to where Robert stood so she could caress the baby's soft curls. "Robbie. Look what Joe and Jake found. See? Look, Robbie."

After a few more moments of crying he turned his head in Kate's direction, and seeing the horse, he took his fingers out of his mouth and reached for it. But he dropped it on Robert's chest in the process. Robert retrieved it and let him take it again, smiling slightly as the baby began to bite on the horse's head.

At least one problem is solved, Kate thought. Clearly she should address the few things she could actually accomplish. She began to help the boys off with their coats.

"Joe. Jake," she said. "Do you know who this man is?"

They shook their heads, still sniffling.

"This is…" She hesitated, ostensibly to help Jake get his arm out of his coat sleeve, but actually because she didn't know how she should explain Robert to them. He was Robbie's uncle, but she didn't know how he would feel about suddenly having two adopted nephews.

"I'm your uncle Robert," Robert said for her. Both boys looked at him doubtfully.

"We belong to Maria and Max," Joe said after a moment, his voice full of suspicion.

"Yes. And I'm Maria's brother, so that makes you my nephews—"

"Maria's brothers died. Everybody knows that. Maria cried and cried. Maria's brothers and my mama—they're all in heaven. Warrie said so."

"I was wounded in the war, but I didn't die," Robert said. "And I'm here now."

"Is my mama coming back, too?" Jake asked hopefully.

"No, Jake. What happened to me isn't what happened to your mama."

The boys looked at each other, and for once, Kate thought Joe might pose a question of his own. But then he sighed and said nothing, clearly disappointed that Robert was so certain that their mother wouldn't return.

"Papa went to Texas," Jake offered after a moment.

"Did he?" Robert said. He glanced at Kate, she thought for some kind of validation. He must have assumed that both the boys' parents were dead if Max had adopted them.

Kate gave him a slight nod. This was yet another change he didn't know anything about.

"I didn't know that," Robert said to the boys.

"And Uncle Billy, too. They couldn't stay here anymore—because of the Yankees. Have you been to Texas?"

"I have. Once, before the war."

"Do you know my papa and my uncle Billy?"

"*My* papa and *my* uncle Billy, too," Joe said, giving him a push.

"Yes, I know them. When Phelan and Billy and I were just about your age, we were best friends."

"Did *you* ever get in trouble?" Jake wanted to know despite Joe's pushing.

"Yes," Robert said. "I did."

"Papa and Uncle Billy, too?"

"Yes."

"Me, too," Jake said solemnly. "And Joe," he said, careful not to leave his brother out this time.

"Well, it's hard not to sometimes," Robert said, glancing at Kate again. She came and took the baby from him and moved to sit down in the rocking chair.

"We wanted to go to Texas, too," Joe said. "But nobody wanted any boys along. I could go to Texas. I could go right now. I could go *easy*."

"Can not," Jake assured him. "We like it *here*. Maria and Warrie would cry and cry if we—" He abruptly stopped, Kate thought, because current events had suddenly given him some insight as to what that might look like. Joe leaned forward and whispered something in Jake's ear.

"Where did *you* come from?" Jake asked, looking at Robert hard.

"New York City," Robert said. He sat down on the side of the bed and patted the folded blanket next to him as an invitation for both boys to join him—which they did, Jake sitting next to him and likely still full of questions, and Joe well apart from them both.

Kate looked down at Robbie. The rocking and the

quiet turn of the conversation seemed to have put him on the verge of sleep.

"Did you ride on the train?" Jake asked.

"No, mostly I walked," Robert said. "Sometimes I hitched a ride with a mule skinner."

"Well, *I* would ride on the train. I wouldn't be *walking* or riding with a mule," Joe assured him. "You should have thought of it. We rode on the train to Raleigh. Then we rode on another train to New Bern. I like New Bern. Warrie took us to see the boats. Boats and boats and *boats!*"

"I guess there were a lot of them."

"Yes!" the boys cried in unison.

"I think—" Robert suddenly stopped because Max stood in the doorway.

"I want to talk to you," he said. "Now."

Chapter Six

So. This is Maria's husband. Once his enemy, and perhaps he still was.

Robert got to his feet; he had no intention of letting the man tower over him. They stared at each other, and Robert found himself clenching and unclenching his fists as if he were about to step into the ring again, about to beat some hapless opponent bloody and reeling until he fell to the ground. He had thought he was done with all that, but how easily it had come back to him. He'd had to struggle hard to let go of his need to always respond with anger, and apparently he still did.

Watch ye, stand fast in the faith... Be strong. Blessed are the peacemakers.

"I think my brother means me, Robert," Kate said behind him. He thought she couldn't help but see the sharp contrast between the two of them—Robert raggedly dressed, disheveled and still in need of a shave, and her brother, all military spit and polish.

"Indeed," Max said. "But you'll have your turn, sir. I require at least some explanation as to why my house has been turned upside down."

Robert didn't actually flinch when Max Woodard said "my house," and he was grateful for that.

"Sergeant Major!" Max snapped. "Gather up these boys and see if you can find them something to eat."

"Yes, sir!"

"Come on, men," Perkins said to Joe and Jake. "You heard the Colonel. I happen to know we've got cookies around here someplace. If we can find them, I reckon you can put away one or two. What do you think?"

Both boys nodded vigorously.

"And take the baby to Mrs. Kinnard," Max said.

"Mrs. Kinnard, sir?" Perkins said, clearly thinking he'd heard wrong.

"Tell her I need her help. Say I know she's very busy, but I've asked if she'll take Robbie into the dining room and keep him there for a bit. Say I'm sure she'll know what to do for him."

"Yes, sir. If anybody can settle that woman down, I reckon our Robbie can. Come on, Little General," he said, taking the baby from Kate. "Let's go see the elephant."

"Kate," Max said, holding his hand in the direction he wanted her to go

But Robert had her attention now, and he thought his brother-in-law knew it. Kate was looking at him with such…concern, but he saw no pity in her eyes. It was more a kind of understanding, and he was grateful for that, as well. But there was something else, something he recognized easily because of his wild younger days and because he'd had a sister like Maria. Kate Woodard was fervently hoping that the men around her—her brother and he—would at least make some effort to behave in a civilized manner.

"I trust you'll stay here—where I can find you," Max said to him. And while the statement, on the surface, was at least somewhat cordial, it was by no means a request. This Yankee colonel didn't want him doing anything without his knowledge and approval, and the two armed soldiers standing in the hallway assured that he wouldn't.

"You do know the war's over," Kate said to her brother as she passed by him on her way out.

"Only for a select few," he said, and Robert certainly knew the truth of that. The Reconstruction held both sides captive and would for the unforeseeable future. And then there were the individuals like himself and like the colonel, if he had been a prisoner of war—soldiers for whom the war would never end.

Surprisingly Kate and her brother didn't move very far down the hallway, and Robert could hear them both quite clearly. He made no pretense that he wasn't listening, standing where both the soldiers left to keep him in line could see him. Neither of them apparently considered overheard conversations any of their concern.

"What are you doing here?" he heard Max ask his sister bluntly. "How did you get tangled up in all this?"

"One thing doesn't have anything at all to do with the other," Kate said. "So don't suppose that it does."

"Perkins told me what he knew about *him* being here, but he was less clear about how it is you're not in Philadelphia."

"I didn't go," Kate said.

"Yes, I can see that. The question is *why?*"

"I didn't want to go. So I didn't."

"Just like that."

"Exactly like that," she assured him.

"And why would that be, I wonder?"

There was a long pause.

"Sometimes..." Kate said as if searching for the right

words. "Sometimes one gets weary of other people's arrangements." Her voice was calm yet full of significance. Robert had no idea what she might have meant, but the silence that followed suggested to him that the colonel did.

"Kate, you can't just—"

"That's all I have to say about it, Maxwell," Kate interrupted. "I mean it."

"You do understand that I worry about you."

"Yes. And I appreciate it—sometimes. Now tell me what's happening with Maria."

"The doctor and Mrs. Justice are with her."

"And?"

"And I was ordered out of the room. So I came to find out what kind of cataclysm I've walked into."

"Perhaps it's not that dire," Kate said.

"Any situation that has Perkins wearing his sack and burn face *and* Mrs. Kinnard firmly established on the premises is dire. If this man really is Maria's brother—"

"He is. Mrs. Justice, Mrs. Russell and Mrs. Kinnard have all vouched for him."

"Which counts for nothing with me."

"Then Maria will settle it."

"Yes. She will. And assuming he is who he says he is, then what? Is he going to stay around or is he going to go off and play dead just when she's used to the idea that she has the last of her family back again? She loved her brothers, Kate. If what I've heard of this one is true, his staying isn't going to do much for Maria's peace of mind—"

Robert had heard enough. He stepped out into the hallway, causing both the soldiers standing by to move toward him.

"I want to see my sister," Robert said. "Now."

"And I want you to stay put until I tell you otherwise.

I would hate to have to shoot you, Markham," Max said in response.

"I've been shot before," Robert said.

"So have I—"

"Oh, for heaven's sake!" Kate said sharply. "What is wrong with the two of you! It doesn't matter what either of you wants. I know you're used to being in charge, Max, and you, Robert, you need to make things right with Maria—but she—and Mrs. Hansen—have had a terrible shock. At least give them a chance to get their footing before you start squabbling over who's going to do what when. Honestly! Sometimes I can't—"

"All right!" Max said, holding up both hands. "Your point is well taken. Any particular reason why you're so...prickly?"

"Yes," Kate said.

"I don't suppose you'd care to enlighten me."

"Very well. *I* am not a member of your occupation army—and I don't have any dresses."

"Or shoes, either, from the looks of it. If I'm meant to understand that remark—" Max stopped because Maria was coming up the stairs.

"Here you all are," she said calmly, but she was looking directly at Robert. Her mouth trembled slightly, and she bit down on her lower lip to stop it.

How pretty she still is, Robert thought, realizing that he hadn't expected her to be. He'd seen too many Southern women completely worn down by the war, their youth and their health gone. She looked...fine, like the grown-up woman she was meant to be. But she was yet another one of the many with sad eyes, and the difference this time was that *he* was directly responsible for the sorrow he saw there—and the disappointment.

A sudden cascade of memories filled his mind. Maria,

the happy and smiling baby sister who'd toddled around after him just so she could give him hugs and kisses and who'd had him wrapped around her little finger from the day she was born. Maria, dancing the evening away in her white summer dress with gardenias in her hair— while he had made certain her enthusiastic beaus knew precisely whose sister she was and what he would do to them if they happened to forget. Maria, standing on the upstairs veranda, her heart breaking as he and Samuel rode blithely off to war.

Maria.

Sweet. Funny. Strong. He'd always been so proud of her.

Yet he had deliberately let go of his life here just so he would never have to face her again. His throat ached as he realized, perhaps for the first time, what he'd given up. She was all he had left, and he could see how hard she was struggling now to rise above the pain *he* had caused her.

He stepped forward, and so did his brother-in-law.

She held up her hand. "I want to speak to Kate," she said, looking directly into his eyes.

"Me?" Kate said, clearly surprised.

"Mrs. Justice told me you were here when Ro—when my brother arrived," she said, still looking at him.

"Yes—"

"Maria, I'm the one you need to talk to," Robert said with every intention of pushing past his guards to get to her.

"No," Max said sharply. "Not until I know how you are, Maria."

"Max, I am myself now. Truly. And I know you won't understand this, either of you, but sometimes a woman just needs to speak with her own kind."

Robert looked at his brother-in-law. He strongly suspected that in this one matter they could agree. They didn't understand, not in the least.

"Will you just…stay here, please?" she asked. "Or go spy on Mrs. Kinnard. She has our boy giggling in the dining room. This is apparently a day for…extraordinary events."

"Maria," Robert said, and she looked at him for a long moment. Then she shook her head and went down the stairs.

Kate didn't wait to hear what her brother and Robert decided. She maneuvered around them and followed after Maria, despite being in her stocking feet. Halfway down the steps Kate realized what Maria had meant by "her own kind." It wasn't just that they were both women with a common interest—Max. It was that they were women with exasperating older brothers. Surprisingly they had been able to sit together on the upstairs veranda on warm summer nights after her marriage to Max and compare their experiences as "little sisters" on more than one occasion—until her sadness at Robert's loss came rushing back again. No one in the house would understand what Maria was feeling at this moment better than Kate.

Maria put her hands to her face as soon as Kate closed the parlor door.

"Oh, Kate," she said, close to tears. "My brother is back from the dead and all I want to do is—*shoot* him! What's happened to him? His face— I don't—"

"Sergeant Major Perkins thinks he's been fighting—prizefighting."

"Prizefighting! Well, why not! That's so much better than coming home to the people—who—love—you—"

She was weeping now, and Kate came closer and put her arms around her.

"We—*I*—needed him. And my poor father—he loved Robert so, Kate."

"I know," Kate said. His warrior son.

Maria took a deep breath and stepped away, crossing the room to open a box on the writing desk. She removed a small, framed daguerreotype and brought it to Kate. It was of a Confederate soldier—Robert Markham, Kate realized after a moment, before his features had been battered so.

"You see? You see how much he's changed? Mrs. Justice says you've talked to him. What did he say?"

"I did most of the talking, I'm afraid—he didn't seem to have any information about what had occurred while he was gone or after he collapsed in the hallway. I told him you and Max were married. I told him about your wedding—how much I thought your father had enjoyed it—and that he'd likely managed to sneak at least one cigar."

"He smiled at that," Maria said, but it was more a statement of hope than one of fact.

"Yes," Kate said truthfully. "He did."

"But where has he been?"

"I…didn't ask him. He told the boys he'd come from New York City."

"New York City. Prizefighting—"

"The army surgeon says the wounds he received at Gettysburg were severe. He had to have spent a long time recovering."

"But all this time he let us think he was dead!"

There was nothing Kate could say to that.

"Perhaps…"

"What?" Maria asked.

"He must have had a reason, don't you think? And it must have been…unbearable."

Maria wiped at her tears with her fingertips and began to pace around the room, apparently lost in her own thoughts until she suddenly stopped and took a deep breath.

"I thought I was ready to see him, but I'm not, Kate. The boys—Perkins is good with them, but they're so afraid something is going to happen to me like it did with their mother. I've gotten myself together enough to reassure them, but if I see Robert now, I'm just going to—come—undone. I'm going to stay down here. Will you tell Max I'm in the parlor? And tell Robert—oh, I don't know what to tell Robert. It's— I just—"

"I'll tell him you need a little time before the two of you talk—but I don't know if he'll listen." She offered the daguerreotype she was still holding.

Maria nodded and wiped her tears from her cheek again before she took it. "Tell him—ask him—if he'll wait for my sake, then. I can't bear to have him and Max at each other, and you know they will be if I can't be calmer than I am now."

"If it comes to that, Perkins will step in."

"Perkins. Yes. I forgot about Perkins. Kate," she said as Kate opened the parlor door. "Has Robert…asked about Eleanor Hansen?"

"Yes," Kate said.

"Did you tell him anything?"

"I don't really know anything to tell him. Nothing firsthand."

Maria gave a heavy sigh and looked down at the daguerreotype as if she didn't quite know how she happened to be holding it.

Kate hesitated, then stepped into the hallway and

closed the door quietly behind her. And she didn't have to worry about telling Max anything. He was already coming down the stairs. He went into the parlor without stopping, brushing past her without saying anything.

Kate stood in the middle of the now empty hallway, at a loss as to what she should do next. She suddenly looked down. Shoes. First things first.

She walked quietly to the dining room, remembering that Mrs. Kinnard and Valentina were in there with Robbie only after she'd opened the door.

"I...need my boots," she said because she had no choice, quickly crossing the room to get them.

Mrs. Kinnard was sitting near the fire. Robbie stood happily in her lap, bouncing from time to time on her crisp, dark blue taffeta skirts and making them rustle in a way that was clearly appealing to an almost-ready-to-start-walking baby boy. Valentina opened her mouth to say something, but Mrs. Kinnard cleared her throat sharply, and her daughter stayed silent. Kate braced herself to hear a lecture on being seen in her stocking feet and her utter—but typical—lack of social decorum.

"Is Maria all right?" Mrs. Kinnard asked instead.

"She's...distressed."

"Yes," Mrs. Kinnard said. "And she will remain so until she's had a real opportunity to speak with Robert without interruption. This won't do. This won't do *at all*." She stood and handed the baby over to Valentina, who was surprisingly pleased to have him.

"Hello, handsome," she said to him. "*Where* have you been? I've been looking for you *everywhere*. Yes! I have!"

Robbie grinned and removed his fingers from his mouth and tried to stick them into hers, making Valentina laugh. "No, thank you, young master Woodard," she said. "I've had my baby fingers today."

"Mrs. Kinnard—I don't think—" Kate tried to say. She was more than alarmed that Mrs. Kinnard had apparently decided to execute one of her heavy-handed plans—when the situation was precarious enough already. The last thing any of them needed was an unfettered Mrs. Kinnard in the middle of it.

"Miss Woodard, I am sure you will agree that there are some things about us here that you cannot begin to understand. I will be back in a moment," Mrs. Kinnard said firmly.

Kate sighed. Short of trying to restrain her bodily, there was no way to stop the woman. She would just have to leave that to Max.

And she still needed to find Robert and tell him as tactfully as she could that his sister was refusing to see him. She sat down heavily in the chair close to the hearth and reached for her boots, but she didn't put them on.

"You're tired, aren't you?" Valentina said after a moment.

"I… Yes."

"Well, it's been a very tiring hour."

Hour? Kate thought. Had no more time passed than that?

"Valentina, what do you think your mother is going to do?"

"Why, something for Maria, of course."

"I'm not at all sure that's a good idea."

"My mother knows what she's doing," Valentina said, smiling again at Robbie, who wanted to bounce. "Believe me. My mother *always* knows what she's doing."

Kate looked at the dining room door, listening hard in an attempt to determine in which direction Mrs. Kinnard had gone, but the exasperating woman would pick now to go about quietly.

"My guess is she'll be talking to Maria and the Colonel," Valentina said. "Where are they?"

"The parlor," Kate said. She sat for a moment longer, then began putting on her boots, but she stopped every few seconds to listen again for Mrs. Kinnard. The house was so *quiet* given the intense emotions that had just been unleashed. There was nothing, no sound whatsoever to tell her what was happening.

"Sergeant Major Perkins thinks of everything, doesn't he?" Valentina said suddenly.

"I think he has to," Kate said, but she had no idea what had precipitated the comment and no desire to learn.

"Mother thinks I should know how to do all sorts of things for babies. The War, you know. She said there was a lesson in that terrible event for all of us—one never knows when one will have to fend for oneself."

"Yes," Kate said. She had already realized the wisdom of that, especially if one happened to deliberately choose to go it alone. "You're very comfortable with Robbie."

"Mother thinks she taught me how to handle him, but she didn't. She'd be very surprised if she knew who did. It was Sergeant Major Perkins," Valentina said, whispering now. "He told me not to drop him and to just *talk* to him like I would anybody—as if he actually understood. He said babies like that because they don't know they're babies— Ups-a-daisy!" she said suddenly, because Robbie began to bounce in earnest. "He told me about this, too. He said be ready for the jumping—babies Robbie's age love to jump. That's what he said," she added to Robbie, who grinned.

Kate turned her head sharply because she thought she heard rustling in the hallway. But if it was Mrs. Kinnard, she kept going, past the dining room toward the rear of the house.

Kate looked at Valentina, who was preoccupied with Robbie and apparently hadn't noticed anything.

"I wish there was a rocking chair in here," Valentina said. "Robbie is ready to nap, I think."

But in lieu of rocking, Valentina began to walk around the room with him, humming softly—and telling him all about a new dress Mrs. Russell's sister was making for her, down to the last detail. In a short time Robbie began to rub his eyes and his head began to nod. He fretted for a moment, then lay his head down on her shoulder. She made a few more rounds, then walked over to Kate and turned around so she could see Robbie's face.

"He got very heavy all of a sudden. Is he asleep?"

"Quite asleep," Kate said. "That was nicely done."

"Oh, I think it's Robbie, not me. Or so Mother says. She says young master Woodard is 'unusually pleasant.' I understand I wasn't like that at—"

There were distinct footsteps in the hallway now—a lot of footsteps. Kate moved quickly to open the door and peer out. Perkins was getting the boys' coats on, and Mrs. Russell was coming along the hallway supporting Warrie Hansen, whose eyes were red from weeping. Mrs. Justice and Mrs. Kinnard followed directly behind them; Mrs. Kinnard was clearly in charge.

Maria stepped out of the parlor just as Warrie reached the front door.

"I can't stay here tonight, honey," she said to Maria. "I just can't. He ruined my girl. I can't stay here."

Maria didn't say anything. She reached out and briefly clasped Warrie's hand, then she bent down and kissed both boys. "Be good for Warrie and Mrs. Russell. I'll see you tomorrow," she said, and kissed them again.

"Is Warrie going to cry again?" Jake asked, frowning.

"I don't think so," Maria said. She reached into a

pocket and took out a neatly folded handkerchief. "But if she does, you can give her this."

He nodded solemnly. Having a remedy of sorts in his hand and ready if he needed it seemed to give him courage.

Kate moved out into the hallway closer to Mrs. Justice. "Where are they going?" she asked quietly.

"Warrie and the boys will stay at Mrs. Russell's house tonight. Mrs. Kinnard thought it would be better for them if they weren't here while Maria talks to Robert. Better for Maria, too. I imagine that's how she put it to Colonel Woodard."

And apparently Max had been convinced. He picked up both boys and carried them out to Mrs. Kinnard's carriage—an exciting prospect apparently. Her carriage hadn't reached the eminent status of a train or a New Bern boat, but as far as the boys were concerned, it clearly had its merits.

"Valentina!" Mrs. Kinnard called loudly. "Let's get this baby bundled up. Mr. Perkins! Where are his things?"

"He's all packed and ready to go, Mrs. Kinnard."

"His cup? He will only drink from his silver cup, you know."

It also happened to be the cup Mrs. Kinnard had given him at his christening, and Robbie's eventual fondness for her gift had probably done as much to keep the peace in this town as anything. It was Max's droll opinion that he liked it because he could see himself in it.

"Yes, ma'am. It's in the basket."

"Valentina!" Mrs. Kinnard called again. "Take Robbie and let his mother kiss him good-night."

"Yes, Mother," Valentina said. "Just let me get my coat."

"Robbie is going with the Kinnards?" Kate whispered

to Mrs. Justice as the sergeant major, Johnny-on-the-spot as always, helped Valentina into her coat.

"Yes—and the sergeant major, too," Mrs. Justice said. "Just to make certain all goes well. I'm staying here in case Maria needs something. Or you, my dear," she said kindly and, incredibly, Kate felt the sudden prickle of tears behind her eyelids.

She stepped back out of the way as Mrs. Kinnard and her entourage trooped out into the cold winter dusk. After a moment Max came back inside. He stood with Maria, but they weren't talking, his unhappiness with the entire situation clearly visible on his face. Kate continued to wait by the dining room door. It seemed as good a place as any until she determined where she should go to be out of the way. But as strained as the atmosphere was, she was grateful that Mrs. Kinnard hadn't decided she should be relocated to another house, too.

Even so, Kate had to fight down the urge to wring her hands and pace. It wasn't as if she hadn't experienced a family crisis before—indeed, she'd even been the cause of one. But this was different. This had nothing to do with trying to stay ahead of a monumental scandal. This was about hurt and anger and forgiveness—and who knew what else.

"Sergeant Major Perkins has put a campaign table and the latest army dispatches in Bud's sitting room," Mrs. Justice said. "He thought there should be some tea and buttered bread on hand as well—just in case you and the Colonel find you're hungry while you're waiting."

It seemed that the Sergeant Major truly did think of everything. It wasn't difficult to guess what he likely had in mind. Max would be both out of the way and close by in the sitting room—and occupied if he chose to be.

"Oh," Kate said without meaning to when she saw

Robert coming down the stairs. He looked tired, so much so that she wondered if he were up to this. He stopped near the bottom step.

Max barely looked at him. Instead he said something to Maria and caressed her cheek, then walked in Kate's direction.

The sack and burn face, Kate thought. Clearly Perkins wasn't the only soldier who had one. She looked past him to where Maria stood waiting for her brother to come the rest of the way down. Tears were running down her cheeks, but she made no attempt to wipe them away. Maria had earned her tears, and thanks to Mrs. Kinnard's impromptu rearrangement of the entire household, she didn't have to hide them from her sons.

"I'm going to sit myself down by the fire in the kitchen and do some knitting now, Colonel Woodard," Mrs. Justice said softly. "If you need anything, that's where I'll be."

"Thank you, Mrs. Justice. You have been a great help to me this day," Max said, but Maria still had his attention. He clearly didn't want to leave her on her own to hear whatever Robert Markham was about to tell her.

"You're welcome, Colonel Woodard," Mrs. Justice said. "Maria is as dear to me as if she were my own. Don't forget the tea," she added as she walked away.

"It's upstairs," Kate said to Max. "I think perhaps we should go drink it."

Max took a deep breath, stood for a moment then led the way toward the back stairs.

He's too used to being in charge of everything, Kate thought. She glanced over her shoulder as she was about to follow him. Robert was looking in her direction. She gave him the barest of nods, hoping he would understand that she wished him the best in his endeavor to make amends.

Hoping.

And praying.

Please help him, Lord. And help Maria and my brother. Help them all to put this family back together.

She turned and quickly followed Max up the back stairs. When they reached the sitting room, he looked at the campaign table and the leather pouch full of dispatches, but he made no attempt to read any of them. He sat down in the nearest rocking chair instead.

"This—homecoming—has been the—"

"I know," Kate interrupted, hoping to keep him from dwelling on the chaos he'd found on his arrival, not to mention her presence in the middle of it.

He sat and stared at the fire. After a moment Kate poured two cups of tea. Serving tea informally—with a brown glazed pottery teapot instead of a monstrously ornate silver one—she could handle. But neither of them drank it. They sat in silence, listening for some sound that would tell them what was happening in the parlor downstairs.

At one point Kate got up, intending to walk the length of the hallway to the head of the stairs to see if she could hear anything.

"No," Max said. "I gave Maria my word I wouldn't interfere. I think eavesdropping is included in that."

"Oh, all right," Kate said with a sigh, sitting down again. She looked at her brother, then at the dispatches. He didn't take the hint. He continued to sit, and so did she. Despite their extreme attentiveness, the only noticeable sound in the house was Mrs. Justice stirring around in the kitchen below from time to time.

Kate leaned her head against the back of the rocking

chair and closed her eyes. Every now and then she sighed. With the last one Max kicked the rocker on her chair with the toe of his boot, startling her enough to make her jump.

"Max!" she said in annoyance, and he gave her a hard look.

Then he stared at the fire again—and she had to suppress another sigh.

"What do you think of him?" he asked after a moment. "Robert Markham."

"I think he wants what's left of his family back," Kate said without hesitation.

"He abandoned Maria when she needed him most."

"There must have been a reason."

"He's asking a lot of her!"

"He's her brother," Kate said simply, because that particular kinship would erase a lot of sins. "He's yours, too, regardless of how this turns out."

Max made a noise of annoyance and moved to the campaign table, apparently deciding to read dispatches after all. He dumped them all out, paying no attention to the ones that slid off the pile and landed on the floor. He read. He stopped to sign his name from time to time. Then he read some more, but like Kate, he was still waiting.

Kate closed her eyes again, only to promptly open them.

Someone—Maria—was playing the pianoforte—or attempting to. There were several false starts and stops before Kate could recognize the song. It was "How Firm a Foundation."

Chapter Seven

"Oh! I'm sorry. I didn't know you were—anyone—was— I'll go," Kate said.

Robert was sitting there in the dark—the last person she expected to find in the nursery. Both her hands were full, and she struggled to keep from dropping everything.

"Wait," he said as she turned to leave, apparently without considering whether her brother might object to his having a conversation with her, too. Kate strongly suspected that Max would do just that because, thanks to the events of the evening, he was now set to object, without rhyme or reason, to anything associated with Robert Markham, no matter what the situation might be.

She stood there, unsure whether or not she should stay or go. It seemed that she was destined to keep losing her space in the house to him.

"I don't want to disturb you," she said.

"You aren't. I was just thinking about a passage from Isaiah."

"Isaiah?" Kate said, and he actually smiled.

"Yes. I'm not as unchurched as I might look, Miss Woodard."

"No, I—didn't mean—"

"You aren't the only person who would be surprised," he said, still smiling.

He stood and crossed to the fireplace to add another log and waited until the sparks had settled. Kate looked around the room for a place to put the unlit candle and candlestick she was holding without dropping her book, some paper, an inkwell and a pen.

"I'll light the candle," he said.

She managed to hand it to him, and the candlestick, but she dropped the book on the floor in the process. He bent to pick it up and her *carte de visite* of Harrison fell out. He retrieved that as well and held them both out to her. She took them from him quickly, clutching them tightly while trying to put the rest of the things down on the small, well-used oak table in the middle of the room.

"My mother brought that table with her when she married my father," he said. "It wobbles. See?" He reached out to show her how uneven the legs were. "It was a keepsake from her girlhood, her 'something old.' I suppose it's a place for Maria's boys to have their meals with Warrie Hansen now—and whatever else little boys might want to do with their books and toys and treasures." He looked around the room for a moment as if he were searching for something else familiar.

"I see you're writing another letter," he said as he lit the candle and set it securely in the candlestick. "When I was looking for you earlier today, Sergeant Major Perkins told me you'd gone to mail some letters," he added.

"Oh," Kate said. "I…didn't feel sleepy, so I thought I'd just have this handy—in case—" She stopped because she was running out of inane things to say. She had no idea what had passed between him and Maria tonight, but whatever it was, seeing him now, she didn't think he was the better for it.

"It's good that you keep in touch."

"I…suppose so. What was the passage?" she asked, hoping to steer the conversation to a better topic. "From Isaiah."

"'This is the rest wherewith ye may cause the weary to rest. And this is the refreshing,'" he quoted. "I think I need that—the refreshing."

"Why were you looking for me?" she asked when he didn't say anything more. She thought that it likely had something to do with his request that she find out whatever she could about Eleanor Hansen. She did have some information now, most of which she wouldn't share. She could tell him that Mrs. Justice had said that Eleanor left town, but she wouldn't say that Mrs. Justice had also told her—without actually telling her—that Eleanor Hansen was Maria's childhood friend Nell, the one who had lost her honor and reputation—or had thrown it away. And, based on Warrie Hansen's remarks as she'd left the house tonight, in her mind at least, Robert Markham was the one responsible for her daughter's downfall.

"Is it very late?" Robert asked instead of answering. "I don't have any idea what time it is. The big clock in the hallway seems to be missing."

"I understand it didn't fare well—when General Stoneman raided the town." Kate paused, but he seemed disinclined to make any comment regarding the fate of the Markham grandfather clock. "It's just after midnight, I think," she said.

She could feel Robert watching as she moved the sheets of paper on the table a little to the left with her free hand.

"Would you…stay for a while?" he asked. The request was simple enough, and he made no attempt to justify it.

"Yes, all right," she said after a moment.

Kate sat down in the other rocking chair, which was closer to the one he had been sitting in than she would have liked. But she didn't want to make a point of moving it. She really didn't mind the proximity. What she minded was Mrs. Kinnard somehow finding out about it. Kate could hear him sit down in the other rocking chair, but she didn't look at him. She stared into the fire instead. The log he'd just put on the andirons began to pop and hiss. She wouldn't ask him about his talk with Maria. She would just leave him to his thoughts.

They sat in silence; the silence was not uncomfortable—at least not for her.

"This was Samuel's room," he said after a time. "Our father decided to take out a wall here and there to make a bigger space for one of us. We played poker for it—much to our mother's dismay. Or she would have been dismayed if she'd found out about it."

Kate turned her head to look at him. "And you let him win."

"What makes you think that?"

"Phelan and Billy Canfield's Harvard cousins make me think that."

He smiled. "How did you know about them?"

"You told me."

"I don't think I remember."

"You were heavily dosed with laudanum at the time."

"Ah. That would explain it then," he said.

"You were a good brother," Kate said, daring to glance in his direction. She wanted to know how he was. She had been too direct in her conversation with him before, and now she couldn't seem to find that kind of directness at all.

"Not good enough," he said, his voice flat. "I'm not

very good at putting the things I've broken back together again."

"You were—are—a good brother," Kate said firmly. She believed that to be true even without knowing whether his remark pertained to his distant past or to whatever had happened when he'd talked to Maria tonight.

Once again the silence between them lengthened. Somewhere in the distance a dog barked. Kate held on to her book and waited, thinking of Harrison and of Joe and Jake and Robbie, all of these boys asleep tonight in a place that was not their home.

"I...don't know where Samuel is," Robert said, his voice quiet and devoid of emotion. He might have been telling her the day's date or the correct time. She could see that his hands were clenched tightly on the arms of the rocking chair.

"I know he died," he continued. "I was with him when he died. I saw the wound. I saw the light...go out of his eyes. It was there, and then it wasn't. He was gone and I knew it, but I still couldn't...

"I tried to get him to the rear, but I couldn't carry him. I couldn't get him up off the ground. I kept trying and trying. Somebody dragged him away from me. Somebody else carried me the way I was trying to carry him. I thought he must have been brought off the field, too. But he wasn't. I kept asking, but no one could tell me—" Robert stopped, and Kate could almost feel him struggling to remember. "And then I was on a wagon full of wounded men, in retreat with our tails between our legs. We couldn't believe it—Bobby Lee had let us down. It rained for days after the battle, and Samuel was still out there. In the rain. I don't even know if he was...buried. I remember the rain, but after that, it's all blank. I just—can't remember. I try but I can't. It's…gone."

"You can't blame yourself when you were wounded, as well," Kate said. She had heard the army surgeon tell Perkins how severe Robert's wounds had been. But she knew the moment she said it that he wouldn't accept that reason as an excuse for whatever had happened, no matter how rational it was.

Grey's last letter, the one that had arrived weeks after she knew he was dead, suddenly came to mind.

If you ever feel sorry for me, don't let me see it…

She took a hushed breath. Why was she feeling his loss so strongly tonight? "Perhaps some of the men in your old regiment will know, men who were there," she said.

"I think not. Samuel was—" He stopped for a moment before he continued. "He was the company favorite. Everybody loved him. They would have told our father and Maria where he was, if any of them had known. Father would have moved heaven and earth to get Samuel home so he could be buried here beside our mother. I… was supposed to take care of him and I…"

"Did you tell Maria any of this?"

He didn't say anything. "Yes" would have been an easy enough answer had he done so, and from his ensuing silence, she could only conclude that he hadn't. She felt instinctively that this one event was at the heart of everything, the prize fighting, his not coming home and perhaps Eleanor Hansen, as well. And not telling Maria about it now could only prolong both their misery.

"Don't—" Kate began, than stopped.

"What? What were you going to say?"

Kate leaned forward in the chair so she could see his face. "I was going to say don't spare her. She won't thank you for it. You said you weren't any good at putting the things you'd broken back together. If you can't find the solitude you need to sort all of this out—if it gets too difficult being home when it's not home anymore, and you can't find the…courage to tell Maria the worst of what happened to you and Samuel—don't just up and disappear again. At least tell her that you're going, even if you can't say why."

He was looking back at her. "Are you always so certain about things?" he asked.

"No," Kate said. "But when I am, I don't want to ever regret not having said so." She stood. "I'll take my leave now. Good night, Mr. Markham."

"I'm not going anywhere," he said when she was in the hallway. "You can tell your brother that."

Kate kept walking.

"Miss Woodard," he called, and she stopped and turned to look at him.

"Thank you."

"For what?"

"For praying for me."

"I—I'm afraid I'm…not someone who offers prayers on behalf of other people very often," Kate said, not quite denying that she had done exactly that.

"But you prayed for me. I could feel it. I want you to know I'm grateful. I'm often in need of prayers. I hope you will keep it up."

She stood for a moment longer. "Good night," she said without acknowledging his gratitude, and she continued down the hallway.

"My dear," Mrs. Justice whispered as she passed the kitchen door. "Will you join me?"

Kate hesitated, then followed Mrs. Justice into the kitchen. She was surprised that Mrs. Justice was still up and dressed. At this late hour she would have expected that the woman would have been fast asleep by now in the room off the kitchen she'd been sharing with Mrs. Russell ever since Mrs. Kinnard had essentially ordered them both here.

The kitchen was warm and quiet and still smelled of the bread that had been baked earlier in the day—yesterday. She was so hungry suddenly; her stomach rumbled.

"You've been neglecting yourself," Mrs. Justice said. "I don't believe you've eaten all day. Sit down at the table. I'm going to find you something. We can't have you getting sick on top of all this upset."

Kate would have protested, but she was too hungry. "Thank you, Mrs. Justice," she said instead. "Bread and butter would be nice."

"We've plenty of that. And some nice strawberry jam. One of the soldiers brought it—young Private Castine, I believe. I'm not going to wonder where or how he got it. We'll just open a jar and have a bit of a feast. Sit—sit," she urged.

Kate sat. In no time at all Mrs. Justice had the strawberry jam on the table and had fetched the milk and butter from the cold shelf in the cellar and then sliced some bread she took from the warming oven in the cookstove. She sniffed the jug before she poured them each a glass.

"Hasn't turned. *Eat,*" she insisted. "No need to wait for me."

Kate began to eat, while Mrs. Justice went into her bedchamber. The bread was warm, warm enough for the butter to grow soft and delicious. Kate's face was sticky with jam by the time Mrs. Justice returned.

"I've made up another of the beds," she said. "You must come in with Mrs. Russell and me—at least until… the house is more settled."

Kate looked at her. Mrs. Justice had said "house," but

Kate suspected that wasn't what she meant at all. She meant Robert Markham.

"I don't—"

"We must do what is proper, my dear. It's late. You can't sleep in the nursery while Robbie is sitting there—he may be in there some time. And you can't go to the room you normally use because he's so at loose ends he may turn up there, as well. You'll find the room down here warm and comfortable. There's hot water in the ewer, and I've laid out a fresh nightgown for you—one of mine, so it'll be too big, of course, but still comfortable enough for sleeping. I believe tomorrow may be every bit as trying as today has been. If it is, you will need your rest."

"Mrs. Justice, I—" Kate hardly knew what to say in the wake of the woman's kindness. "Thank you."

"You're welcome, my dear. I'm only acting in dear Bud's stead. He would want you to be comfortable in his house despite everything that's going on. Of that I am certain. Run along now, if you're finished. I want to speak to Robbie before I retire—if he'll let me."

Kate hesitated, thinking she should at least help Mrs. Justice clear the table, but the woman shooed her away.

"Sleep well, my dear," she said. "And don't forget your prayers."

The gentle reminder made her sigh heavily.

"What is it, my dear?"

"I— It's— I want to pray but I'm so—" Kate shook her head. "What do you do when everything is just a—"

"When your worries are all jumbled together and you don't know where to start?"

"Yes," Kate said. "That's it exactly."

"Well," Mrs. Justice said. "For me, two words always take care of it."

"What two words?"

"Thy will. *Thy* will. And then you take a deep breath and...let go." Mrs. Justice smiled, and Kate couldn't keep from smiling in return.

"Thank you, Mrs. Justice."

"You're welcome, my dear. Good night now."

Kate waited, listening as Mrs. Justice walked toward the nursery wing. It was good that she was going. Perhaps she could give him the emotional comfort Kate had been too afraid to offer.

"Afraid," she whispered. And she only just this moment realized it. She couldn't say why exactly. She only knew that she was and that she shouldn't have been. They had no connection beyond Max and Maria's marriage. Yes, Robert had confided in her, but it didn't mean anything. Their long conversation, when she was hiding from Mrs. Kinnard, had set some kind of precedent, she supposed. And it was always easier to tell a stranger something because they couldn't be hurt by the revelation. He was simply—

Kate gave a sharp sigh. She didn't know what he was doing, and perhaps he didn't, either. Her only certainty at the moment was that she was exhausted and she wanted to go to sleep. But first she crossed the kitchen and quietly looked into the hallway. She didn't see Mrs. Justice, but she could hear a quiet murmur of voices coming from the nursery, and she felt at least a little hopeful.

She had never been in the room the Markham family apparently kept available for visiting friends and relatives or, as in this case, people like Mrs. Justice and Mrs. Russell, who came to help when some emergency arose. Kate had always used the room upstairs whenever she'd stayed here, the one she now knew had been Robert's. When she opened the door, she could see that a fire burned brightly on the hearth. There were four beds of varying sizes, one against each wall, and a braided rug had been placed on the floor beside each of them.

Warm. Comfortable. Just as Mrs. Justice said.

Kate walked to the bed she assumed was hers—the one with a nightgown draped across the foot. She sat down on the edge, trying to gather her wits enough to get undressed. She really wanted to lie down just as she was and feel sorry for herself. She had presumed too much in her remarks to Robert. He had revealed to her something terrible, something personally devastating, and she'd given him no real words of comfort at all. She'd only heavy-handedly suggested that no one—*she*—didn't particularly expect him to follow through with what he'd started by returning home, and that Maria would be the worst for it if he didn't.

She gave a heavy sigh and moved to the washstand despite the impulse to forgo everything but sleep. There was indeed hot water in the pitcher, and Mrs. Justice had laid a clean piece of flannel, a towel and some rose-scented soap next to the basin. Kate made some attempt to wash away the stickiness of the jam from her face and fingers. She would have liked to wash away the worry she felt as well, but there was nothing she could do about that or about the ache in her heart. She couldn't stop thinking about Robert Markham and what had happened to him and to Samuel.

The warrior and the poet.

What would she do if something like that happened to Harrison? Mrs. Russell—and Grey's mother—how did they bear the loss?

She pushed the thought out of her mind and finished washing up. She took the pins out of her hair and shook it loose, then put on the nightgown. It smelled of sunshine and fresh air and lavender sachet, and it was decidedly too big—but comfortable, just as Mrs. Justice had predicted.

"Bless Mrs. Justice's heart," she said aloud, borrowing the phrase she'd heard many times during her visits here and never once heard in Philadelphia. For the first time she actually thought she understood what it meant. She climbed into the bed and stretched out, savoring the lavender smell of the crisply ironed sheets, as well. It felt so good to lie down.

I laid me down and slept; I awakened; for the Lord sustained me.

She closed her eyes, but her mind raced from one worry to another unabated.

Don't forget your prayers...

She kept thinking of Harrison. Was he lonely? Worried? Afraid? And then she thought of Robert again.

Robert.

What a struggle it must have been for him to get this far; she believed that, *knew* that, she supposed, the same way he had known she had asked God to help him. It was so disconcerting to have him know that she had prayed for him—when she hadn't the right to pray for anyone except Harrison. She was Harrison's mother, and offering prayers on his behalf was perhaps the only privilege she had where he was concerned.

Don't forget your prayers...

"Thy will," she whispered. "But please help him."

And she lay there listening to the sounds of the house settling and the wind outside, knowing the prayer she had just spoken had been as much for Robert Markham as it had been for her son.

Chapter Eight

"I wouldn't go up there," Perkins said.

Kate wasn't close enough to put her foot on the bottom step of the staircase, but the sergeant major still presumed to know what her immediate plans were. And, of course, he was right—but at least he didn't know the nature of her business, *why* she was in such a hurry to see her brother this morning.

She had awakened sometime during the night thinking it was dawn, but a full moon had lit the room, not the sunrise. She'd lain there in the moonlight, and she had finally acknowledged something she had been well aware of for some time. She was becoming far too involved in Robert Markham's troubles. She was simply too…concerned about him, and she didn't want to be. She didn't want to worry about where he was. She didn't want to look into his eyes and see the anguish there. And she could only think of one remedy for all those things she *didn't* want. She would have to leave and return to Philadelphia as soon as possible.

Having made that decision, she had slept very late, and she felt the better for it. She'd had a quiet breakfast with Mrs. Justice—Mrs. Kinnard, thankfully, wasn't yet on the premises. The last thing Kate needed was to squander her newfound energy crossing swords with her.

Or with the sergeant major, for that matter.

"Why shouldn't I go see my brother?" she asked him anyway.

"Your brother-in-law's up there. With the Colonel."

"Whose idea was that?" Kate asked, trying to ascertain just how distressing this encounter might turn out to be—for everyone.

"Your brother-in-law's."

"Do you know why?" Kate persisted.

"Well, Private Castine said he went out early this morning—the sun was barely up. He stayed gone a long time, and when he came back, he went out there to the summer kitchen and he was banging around in there for a while, doing nobody knows what. Then he wanted to see the Colonel, and he wouldn't take maybe for an answer."

Kate frowned. "Has he been up there long?"

"Not long. I reckon they're still in the staring each other down stage."

Kate had no doubt that Perkins was right. It occurred to her—belatedly—that he was no longer at Mrs. Kinnard's house, and she wondered if that was good or bad.

"Have you seen Mrs. Woodard this morning?" she asked, trying to discover yet another aspect of the situation if she could, hopefully without seeming to do so.

"I have. She sent for the Little General first thing. They're in the parlor."

"Thank you, Sergeant Major," Kate said. She headed to the parlor, then immediately changed her mind. She was far more concerned about what was happening upstairs between Max and Robert at this particular moment. She walked as quickly as she dared toward the rear of the house instead, through the kitchen to the back stairs, looking over her shoulder at one point to see if Perkins might have guessed that she was all but running because she was about to shamelessly eavesdrop. He apparently hadn't, and she quietly climbed the steps to the first landing.

She could hear Robert quite plainly.

"—to ask a favor."

There was a long pause before Max answered.

"What kind of favor?"

"Permission to live in the summer kitchen. I want to be here—on the premises—it's my family home. But I don't want to distress Maria by being underfoot when she's not…used to the idea of my being back. I think it would be better for both of us."

Again, there was a long pause. She could almost feel Max considering the consequences of having Robert out of the house, but still so close, good and bad.

"I'll speak to Maria about it," Max said finally.

"I've already spoken to her," Robert said.

"When in blazes did you do that!"

"When she was waiting downstairs for Perkins to bring the baby home. I didn't think I needed your permission to have a conversation with my sister."

"Well, think again!"

"Maria doesn't need you to tell her what to do!"

Kate hurried up the rest of the stairs, but Perkins was already there ahead of her.

"Excuse me, Colonel Woodard. Urgent dispatch," he said, stopping just short of breaching military protocol by barging all the way into the room and putting himself between the two men.

Kate couldn't see her brother, but she could imagine the look Perkins was getting about now. She didn't doubt that the dispatch was "urgent," but she wondered if Perkins had been holding on to it longer than he should have in case he needed to derail an impending brawl.

"It's urgent, sir," Perkins reiterated in the unlikely event that his superior officer hadn't heard him the first time. "I'll handle this," he said under his breath to Kate, but it was apparently loud enough to cause Robert to look in her direction.

Oh, Kate thought. He looked so sad and so weary. She had been asleep when Mrs. Justice had returned from her attempt to talk to him, and she wondered how late their visit—if it could be called that—had lasted. Or perhaps they hadn't talked at all. Perhaps, after Mrs. Justice had left, the candle had burned down and once again he'd sat in the dark until he'd left the house this morning.

She sighed and turned to leave the way she'd come. Clearly this was not the time to talk to her already annoyed brother.

"Kate!" he said loudly.

"Yes, Max," she answered.

"Did you want something?" His tone suggested that he wasn't likely to be receptive if she did.

"I did—do—but I'll wait until you're a little less... truculent."

"I'm a colonel," he said. "I'm *supposed* to be truculent."

"Indeed you are. And the nonmilitary members of your family find it ever so endearing. I'll be back later."

"I need to talk to you, Kate!" he called after her.

"And so you shall!" she called back as she reached the first landing. She didn't go any farther. She stood there, assuming that he meant for her to wait her turn.

It's worse than I thought.

Looking into Robert Markham's eyes just now, she was more convinced than ever that she should *not* stay here. Robert Markham seemed to want her company, but even that might be more than she could give. His body had been seriously wounded—and so had his soul. That aside, he couldn't find the woman he obviously loved, and when he did, he would likely be gone again, hopefully not in the dead of night without Maria knowing.

Eleanor.

She could still hear the longing in is voice that night when, in his delirium, he had thought she was Eleanor Hansen.

But none of that was any of her concern. Her focus needed to be on her son and not on her unbridled curiosity about her brother's family situation, a curiosity that was piqued every time she encountered this enigmatic ex-Rebel...*prizefighter.*

She looked around at the sound of footsteps behind her. To her dismay Robert was coming down the stairs. She thought he would just go on by, but he didn't. He stood on the landing with her, apparently giving no thought to decorum or her brother's current mood.

She looked at him with all the directness she could muster, hoping to seem calmer than she felt.

"Did Max say yes or no?" she asked, making no attempt at pleasantries.

"Neither. He gave me a curt nod. I'm taking that to mean he's handing the summer kitchen over to me—against his better judgment."

She couldn't help but smile. In her opinion that was exactly what the nod meant. She continued to look at him, and she was beginning to regret this direct approach. She couldn't seem to look away, and if he had second thoughts about having spoken to her so frankly about Samuel's death, she couldn't tell it.

"I think I've remembered something else," he said after a moment. "About the night I got here."

"What is that?"

"I remember hearing you say that you had to learn how to build a fire. It's rather a strange comment, especially given the circumstances, but nonetheless the memory seems real. Is it?"

She frowned, not wanting to say.

"That's what I thought," he said, despite her silence. "You don't have to worry about it anymore. I intend to teach you. It's the least I can do for someone who saved my life."

"I didn't save your life."

"Mrs. Justice maintains that you did. She thinks something very bad would have happened to me, had you not been here. I'm inclined to agree."

"I was only—" She stopped because it occurred to her that he could be teasing her, despite the seriousness of his face. There was something different in his eyes now. Amusement? Mischief? She didn't quite know.

"So, Miss Woodard, prepare yourself to learn. I'll let you know where and when."

With that, he continued down the stairs into the kitchen.

"I don't think my brother's nod included that," she called after him, and she actually thought she heard him laugh.

"Kate!" Max suddenly barked at the head of the stairs, making her jump. Between his *and* Mrs. Kinnard's penchant for abrupt summoning, it was a wonder she had an ounce of serenity left.

"I need to talk to you," she said ahead of whatever pronouncement he was about to make. She climbed the stairs and edged past him to lead the way into old Mr.

Markham's sitting room, and she closed the door firmly as soon as he was inside.

"I'm going home," she said without prelude.

"I want you to stay here," he said at the same time.

"What?" she said.

"I said I want you to stay here."

"No. I'm going home to Philadelphia—"

"You're not listening to me."

"You haven't said anything!"

He sighed. "No. I guess I haven't. It's…Maria."

Kate waited for him to continue, but he now seemed disinclined to do so.

"What about Maria?" she said to prompt him.

"I have to go back to New Bern. I think I'll be there for…a while. I want you to stay here with her."

"Max, I'll be in the way. Maria needs to reconcile with her brother and not have to deal with one of her in-laws perpetually underfoot."

"No," he said firmly.

"What do you mean, *no?* I was headed home, anyway."

"We'll get to that at a later time," he said. "I want—" He stopped and took a breath. "I *need* you to be here. Maria's going to have another child—"

"Oh, Max," Kate said, smiling. "Maybe a little girl this time. You need a little girl."

"I'm leaving Perkins behind again—because of this brother situation. But there's only so much he can do where Maria is concerned. I need you here to make sure she doesn't…overdo."

"Did her talk with her brother go that badly?"

"I honestly don't know. She was…upset afterward. She didn't really give me any of the details. If there are more talks, I may need you to referee—I have no doubt that you can handle it."

"Well, I'm not sure I like that remark. You make me sound like Mrs. Kinnard."

"I meant it as a compliment, Kate. You're very…astute. I think you will see early on if things aren't going well and intervene. I won't be easy about leaving if Maria is here alone. Will you do this for me?"

Kate looked at him, more than a little amazed that he was actually asking rather than telling.

"Kate?"

"Yes, all right. I'll stay until you get back," she said, watching yet another of her so-called plans dissipate.

"You just found out about this, didn't you?" she asked, because she was certain that Max would never have allowed Maria to confront her brother last night if he had known.

"The army surgeon told me this morning. It seems my wife is very…persuasive when it comes to when I may and may not know what I ought to know."

Kate couldn't help but smile.

"This is not cause for amusement," he said pointedly, and her smile broadened.

"She loves you," Kate said.

"She loves that wayward—prodigal—ex-Rebel brother of hers," Max countered.

"Yes. She does. And that's what makes her Maria."

"I can count on you, then?"

"I'll do my best. I don't think I'm very good at refereeing. My first impulse is always to flee."

"That's not what Perkins tells me. He said you did a fine job placating Mrs. Kinnard and keeping her in hand."

"Oh, yes—except for the small fact that Perkins and I both have been ready to shoot her—on several occasions. Besides that, he doesn't know about the times I went into hiding— You won't go yelling at the lieutenant who was supposed to see me to Philadelphia, will you?" Kate suddenly asked. She thought she had seen him in the house earlier, and it seemed the least she could do for the man—intervene on his behalf since she'd deliberately put him in an untenable position with his superior officer.

"I expect I will," he said. "Why? Feeling guilty?"

"Just a bit," she said. "He tried his best to dissuade me. He and his wife."

Max was looking at her steadily. She could tell the moment he decided that despite the opportunity she'd inadvertently given him, he didn't want to discuss her refusal to board a northbound train when she was supposed to.

"It's been a long time since you've seen Harry," he said quietly, indicating perhaps that he understood more of the situation than she thought. She looked away. Max was making an observation, not asking a question, so she said nothing.

"Does he write to you?"

"Sometimes," she said, deliberately keeping her response to his question to a minimum. She didn't trust herself to be able to enter into a conversation about Harrison, not even with Max, who knew everything there was to know about her downfall. "He…sent me a *carte de visite*."

She wanted to tell Max how worried she was that he might be unhappy at his boarding school and how unsuitable she thought that particular institution would be for a quiet boy like Harrison, despite its being the alma mater of the Howe men. But she didn't. Max had enough worries of his own.

"Perkins has retrieved your trunks, by the way," he said after a moment. "They may have already been delivered to the house."

"Hmm. I think I can see how disingenuous your 'request' for me to remain here was just now."

"I can assure you it was sincere, Kate. No matter how it sounded, I was asking, not ordering. But I admit I was willing to do whatever it took to get you to agree to do this for me. Now. Go away. I have things to do."

Whatever those things were, Kate soon realized that it required a good deal of military activity. Max apparently had chosen not to go to army headquarters. Instead he had headquarters come to him. Soldiers—officers mainly—arrived en masse and congregated noisily in Mr. Markham's sitting room. Kate had no idea where Robert had gone. He wasn't in the house as far as she knew, and she didn't see him anywhere around the summer kitchen whenever she looked out the window—which was more often than would have been seemly had anyone noticed.

Truthfully she was glad he wasn't here at the moment; the last thing he needed to see was how completely his family home had been taken over, not just by Union soldiers, but by her, as well. Apparently she had already been reinstated as the occupant of the bedchamber upstairs. Max had lost no time taking Robert at his word that he wanted to move out of the house. Sergeant Major Perkins informed her on her way back downstairs that the room had been "readied," and that her trunks would be taken there as soon as they arrived from the depot.

She couldn't keep from smiling. The thought of having more than two things to wear was pleasurable indeed. She went looking for Maria. If Kate wanted to know how her sister-in-law's meeting with her brother had gone last night, she was clearly going to have to ask the source—if she could figure out a tactful way to do it.

As she headed for the parlor, she encountered Maria and the baby coming in the opposite direction. The baby immediately reached for her, and she took him gladly, smiling as she remembered Valentina's remark regarding Mrs. Kinnard's opinion of him.

"Yes," Kate told him earnestly. "You are definitely pleasant."

Maria gave her a quizzical look, but Kate didn't explain.

"Are you all right?" she asked instead, watching Maria closely for some indication of her well-being, regardless of what she said.

"I'm...better," Maria said. "In fact, I was looking for you. We're all going to have a special dinner in the dining room tonight—in honor of Max's last night home."

"All?" Kate asked, a bit taken aback by the idea.

"Yes, all. I've told Robert I expect him to be present, as well."

"And what did he say to that?"

"Actually he asked me if someone had dropped me on my head while he was gone."

Kate didn't mean to laugh, but her amusement got away from her. It was so like something Max might have said. She was beginning to think that these two men were far more alike than she—or they—might have realized.

"Does that mean he'll be here?" Kate asked.

"I wish I knew. All I can do is set a place for him and hope for the best."

"What about the boys and Warrie?"

"They'll be at Mrs. Russell's another night. I was afraid Mrs. Russell would find Joe and Jake being there too much of a reminder of her lost boy, but that doesn't seem to be the case. She asked to have them another night and they were begging to stay, so I agreed—for Warrie's sake as much as anything. Mrs. Kinnard and Valentina are also invited here tonight."

"Max's idea, I imagine," Kate said. She couldn't help but marvel at his presence of mind when it came to maintaining his peaceful occupation. She had shared a sit-down meal with Mrs. Kinnard before, on the occasion of Max and Maria's very rushed engagement announcement, and she could do it again if she set her mind to it, only this time she understood the necessity of preserving Mrs. Kinnard's sense of her own importance better than she had even a few days ago. No, it wouldn't do at all for Colonel Woodard to have a farewell dinner without her present, especially after all she'd done for him in his absence by maintaining a semblance of propriety in his household.

"Max's soldiers are doing the cooking—he was adamant about that. I hope we won't have a table full of army food."

"If one of the cooks is the soldier who makes the cookies Sergeant Major Perkins keeps bringing, I believe you need not worry."

Robbie was becoming rambunctious, and Kate handed him back to his mother.

"I think I'd better see about my trunks," Kate said.

"And we are going into the nursery. This young man's mother needs for him to take a nap."

Maria turned to carry him to the back of the house, but then she stopped.

"Thank you, Kate," she said.

"Whatever for?" Kate asked, returning Robbie's uncoordinated but very enthusiastic wave goodbye.

"For…being here when Robert came home. Things might have turned out very differently if you hadn't been."

"I didn't do anything, Maria. Truly. Sergeant Major Perkins and Mrs. Kinnard are the ones who—"

"That's not what Robert says. You're the one w talked to him so straightforwardly. He says your cando helped his state of mind a great deal."

Kate didn't know what to say. "I...like your brother," she said finally, because it was the truth. "It was no hardship."

Maria smiled. "Anyway, I thank you for that, and I'm glad you're going to be here while Max is gone," she said, switching her wiggling baby boy to her other arm. "I—" She stopped, apparently because of the commotion on the back stairs—soldiers leaving, and from the sound of it, Max was among them. Apparently he was going to headquarters after all.

"They sound like boys being let out of school," Kate said.

"Don't let Max hear you say that," Maria said, and Kate laughed.

Maria continued toward the nursery wing, and Kate stood for a moment, trying to decide whether or not she was annoyed that her brother's wife had assumed she would be staying even before Max had asked her. But of course she would. Kate was the Woodard family's official spinster. Still, there was a lot to be said for being needed. Max and Maria and the boys were her family, and she would just have to work around the growing concern she had for Robert and for Harrison. It occurred to her that Mrs. Justice would likely be staying here during Max's absence as well, and she was comforted by that thought. Mrs. Justice's presence in the house was as soothing as Mrs. Kinnard's was unsettling.

The dining room door was slightly ajar, and as Kate passed by, she could hear voices—Mrs. Justice's and Robert's. He was here in the house after all.

She hesitated, concerned for a moment that he might

...ve overheard the admission she'd made just now. It was better that he didn't know what she'd said about liking him. She didn't look in, and as she passed the door, she realized too late that one of Max's officers—a major whose name she didn't know—was coming down the front staircase instead of following the rest of his fellow soldiers out the back way. When he saw her, he immediately headed in her direction rather than the front door.

"Miss Woodard!" he said with far more enthusiasm than was appropriate. "What a pleasure it is to see you again. May I be the first to offer you whatever assistance you may require while the Colonel is away?"

The major continued to advance, crowding too closely for her liking. She tried backing up, but it didn't help the situation. She glanced over her shoulder. Except for Mrs. Justice and Robert in the dining room, the downstairs was completely deserted.

"Thank you, but that won't be necessary. Excuse me, sir," she added firmly, but he didn't seem to register that she meant for him to get out of her way.

"I will plan to stop by every day," the major persisted. "You are a stranger here, just as I am. I'm sure you will enjoy the company of a fellow Northerner."

"That won't be necessary," Kate said again. "Mrs. Woodard and I will be well cared for." He was close enough now for her to smell the whiskey on his breath.

"Just in case you require anything of a more personal nature," he continued, reaching out to put his hand on her arm. "I feel it's my duty—"

"Actually it's *my* duty," Robert said behind her.

"And who are you?" the major asked, truly overstepping his authority now.

"This is Robert Markham," Kate said. "Mrs. Woodard's brother. My brother-in-law."

She watched the major's face as it occurred to him that *her* brother-in-law would also be the brother-in-law of his commanding officer.

"I'm afraid I don't know your name, Major," she said, hoping to defuse the situation before it got any further out of hand. "I must tell my brother how…accommodating you are."

The major looked as startled as she hoped he would, and as she expected, he didn't offer to identify himself.

"Kate, where is Maria?" Robert asked, using her given name, she thought to establish that he was indeed her family—and her protector—and therefore he had the right.

"She's in the nursery wing, putting the baby down for his nap."

Kate briefly met his gaze, and she was not reassured by it. He was working hard again to control his emotions, his rage at one of the enemy.

"I believe you know your way out, Major," she said, but she made no attempt to leave the two men unattended in the foyer. She knew enough of how the occupation worked to know that the unsubstantiated word of an ex-Rebel soldier wouldn't count for much against that of a Union officer—whether he had been drinking or not. She wasn't about to walk off and leave Robert without a witness. Max had assigned her the task of "refereeing," but she doubted that even he thought she would need to begin this soon and under these circumstances.

The major stood for a moment longer.

"Miss Woodard," he said finally—with great formality. He gave Robert a hard, narrowed-eyed look meant to intimidate him, then he turned and left by the front door.

"Why did you do that?" Robert said as the major slammed the door behind him—hard.

"Do what?"

"You know what. Did you think if you didn't inter-vene, I'd be in the stockade about now?"

"Only if you'd hit him."

"I wanted to."

"Yes. I know."

They stared at each other. It suddenly dawned on her that he was actually angry that she *had* intervened. "You are my duty as well, Mr. Markham. As I understand it, a peaceful occupation is the utmost priority in this house. You'd do well to remember that."

She walked away, without looking back, and she went straight into the parlor for no reason whatsoever, closing the door behind her and leaning against it for a moment. It was incredible to her that he couldn't see where an al-tercation with an officer in the occupation army would have led, regardless of the circumstances. It wasn't that she didn't appreciate his stepping in on her behalf. She did. The fact that she'd encountered this kind of behavior in her brother's house suggested that the major wouldn't have been daunted by her protests, no matter how firmly she'd made them.

She heard Mrs. Justice say something and Robert answer. Then she heard the front door slam again. She moved to look out the window. Robert was striding down the gravel path toward the street—but then he apparently changed his mind and veered off to his left. He disap-peared from her view, and she moved to a window on the side of the house to look out. She could see at least part of the summer kitchen without difficulty, and after a while, she could see Robert, as well. He was carrying an ax, and after some preparation, he began splitting logs and stacking the pieces near the summer kitchen door, working in his shirtsleeves despite the winter cold. She wondered if this was a necessary chore or if it was something he needed to do in lieu of hitting a Union officer.

And here he was again, she suddenly thought—in the forefront of her mind where she didn't want him to be. She tried to convince herself that it didn't matter whether he was present at the dinner table tonight or not—except that it did, and she knew it. She just wanted him there. She wanted to be able to talk to him if she felt like it. And she could do that without consequence—socially. It would be quite safe because a table full of people and her brother would be present.

Safe.

Because Robert had abandoned Eleanor Hansen and was therefore untrustworthy and unsuitable? Or because his loving Eleanor meant Kate wouldn't have to keep up her guard? It wouldn't matter what *she* might feel when there was no chance of such feelings being returned. It would be pleasant to be his friend—if he weren't still annoyed with her. Pleasant. Uncomplicated. Meaningless.

And safe.

She looked out the window again. He was still chopping wood, but he had to stop and rest from time to time, as if his strength had been quickly depleted by the exertion. The house was quiet; Kate was free to go see about her trunks, but she didn't. She continued to watch him work. He was no longer the man who had collapsed in the hallway, but he was not yet as strong as he wanted to be perceived. And he was troubled. He was also, by all accounts, wild. Had the war and Samuel's death taken the wildness out of him? She knew that love had changed both Max and John Howe, but did sorrow have the same effect? She didn't know.

She gave a quiet sigh. She had told Maria the truth.

She did like him, regardless of the fact that she barely knew him.

Private Castine came trotting up and handed him a piece of paper. Robert read it, imbedded the ax in the chopping block and left, apparently with no intention of returning any time soon. It was only then that she finally quitted the parlor to go upstairs.

The sergeant major had once again thought of everything. There was no sign whatsoever that Robert Markham had ever occupied this room. It was completely hers again. Her trunks were sitting at the foot of the bed—with the keys in the locks. The small tables that had been removed to give the hospital orderlies room to carry out their duties had been returned, as had her books. She unlocked the trunks and then removed from the large one the brassbound mahogany writing box Grey had given her. He had teased her that he wanted to make sure she would have no excuse for not writing to him, but he had also known that she was…scholarly, that she liked to read and make notes, and he had simply wanted to give her something she would enjoy.

She smiled slightly at the memory, touching the fine wood of the box with her fingertips. But that memory was fleeting at best, and she was suddenly thinking of Robert Markham again. That he had lived here in this house, grown up here, left here most likely in the same flurry of duty and patriotism that Max and John had left their own homes. And he had loved his family, just as they had; she was certain of that—which made his choosing not to come home all the more inexplicable.

"What is *wrong* with me?" she said out loud.

What with her recent penchant for hiding and her preoccupation with a man who had been her country's enemy *and* a prizefighter, she hardly recognized herself.

She began lifting her dresses out of the trunks and spreading them on the bed until she decided which one she would wear to dinner tonight. Her anxiety regarding the upcoming evening seemed to be growing, likely because neither sequence of events was desirable—that Robert wouldn't come, and his chair would sit there empty for the entire meal, or that he *would,* and she would see the look in his eyes and likely feel a pressing need to worry about him even more than she already did.

She eventually decided on a dress, a plain pale beige one with a blue iridescence to the fabric and blue edging on the collar, cuffs and bustle. No ruffles. No pleats. No lace. It would do nicely. She had no doubt that Valentina would arrive in all her splendor, and in this dress, Kate could all but disappear into the background, where she would happily remain for the duration of whatever social torture was about to unfold. She knew Max would try hard for Maria's sake, and she thought that Robert—if he came—would, as well. But they were, after all, men, and bitter enemies at that. Who knew what would happen, especially with Mrs. Kinnard in the mix? It would be so easy for any one—or all—of them to take offense.

She took a long bath and even longer to arrange her hair and dress. She ultimately decided on leaving her hair "careless," pulling the front and sides back into a topknot and allowing the blond tresses to fall free down her back. The simplicity of no padding and no false hairpieces suited the dress and her mood.

It was growing dark outside, and the noise level in the house rose as did the aroma of baked bread, apples and roasting meat coming from the kitchen. She continued to look out the window from time to time for some sign of Robert, but she didn't see him.

She stayed upstairs as long as she could—until it was

absolutely necessary that she be on hand to greet Mrs. Kinnard and Valentina when they arrived. As she headed downstairs, she smiled slightly to herself, wondering if Private Castine would be on hand somehow to see Valentina.

Max was standing in the foyer, resplendent in his uniform.

"Very handsome and military," she said as she reached the bottom of the stairs, knowing her teasing him about the way he looked would annoy him.

"I see you're not wearing *your* uniform this evening."

"No," she said, trying not to smile. "I am not." For a moment it was like the old days, she, joyfully on the verge of becoming the woman she hoped to be, and he, the big brother who teased her unmercifully and yet was always kind.

"You look very nice, anyway," he said, making her smile in earnest. She was on the verge of asking him if Robert had returned, but then she didn't. Having *all* the women in the house fixated on Robert Markham would do nothing for his mood this evening.

She turned her head sharply at some commotion on the porch, but it was only Private Castine, stamping his feet to stay warm. She left Max with a sympathetic pat on the arm and went into the parlor, leaving the door ajar and sitting were she had a good view of the foyer. Maria stood by the window, tense with the effort it took not to wring her hands.

"I don't believe Robert will be here," she said. "He's gone off somewhere, and I have no idea where that might be."

"Private Castine brought him a note earlier. Maybe he would know."

"I'll ask," Maria said, heading for the door.

"He's on the veranda," Kate called after her.

Maria was gone only a moment.

"He says the note was from Reverend Lewis, but he doesn't know what it was about. Max told me about Robert asking for an army chaplain. I simply do not understand my brother's sudden interest in the clergy."

"Surely there are worse things he could be doing, don't you think?"

"It's the *reason* he's doing it that worries me. It's not like him. At all."

Kate looked at her without comment, thinking how changed Max had been when he'd come home. She thought it was to be expected, but she didn't say so.

They sat for a time in silence—until Kate suddenly made up her mind to ask what she wanted to know.

"Maria, when you and Robert talked, were you able—"

But the question was interrupted before Kate could finish asking it. Mrs. Kinnard and Valentina were arriving, much to Private Castine's obvious delight. Kate could see him through the window as he bounded off the veranda to hurry and open the door of Mrs. Kinnard's carriage.

But his obvious pleasure must have been short-lived. Valentina had no time to pay him even a backhanded compliment this evening. She disembarked from the carriage and swept past him with barely a glance in his direction.

"What a chilly evening," she said to Max as she entered the foyer. "But I'm sure it's colder in Philadelphia."

"Much colder," Max said. "Miss Kinnard, Mrs. Kinnard—and Mrs. Russell—I am very glad you could join us this evening."

He might be glad, Kate thought, but there was something in his voice that suggested he hadn't known Mrs.

Russell was on Maria's guest list. Somewhere along the way, Kate suspected, it had become Mrs. Kinnard's guest list. If there were any more additions, Max was going to be decidedly outnumbered at the table.

"I understand there are *soldiers* cooking the meal," Mrs. Kinnard said bluntly.

"Yes—and I would be very glad if you would give me your opinion of the food. Secretary of War Belknap—when he was here making his inspections—found their efforts too Southern for his liking."

"Too *Southern?*" Mrs. Kinnard said in a tone that all but guaranteed that whatever showed up on the dinner table tonight, it would be—in her opinion—exceptional.

"I'm afraid so," Max said. "Thanks to Maria's fine cooking, I am quite partial to Southern cuisine, myself."

Kate could hear that Private Castine was still attending to his duties and was now on hand to take the ladies' wraps. He carried them to the chairs that had been brought from somewhere and placed in the hallway just for that purpose and carefully draped each one over the back as if his life depended on it.

"Miss Woodard!" Valentina said as soon as she spied Kate. "You have dresses! Or a dress, at any rate." She was wearing a bustled frock in a shimmering blue color—"Independence Blue," it would be called in Philadelphia, and likely "Bonnie Blue" here. It had a ruched overskirt with a smooth long skirt beneath it. Two rows of deep ruffles adorned the hem. There were ribbons of a lighter shade of blue at her wrists and a large bow of the same color over white lace at her throat. Her hair was elaborately arranged in two large chignons. She was—as always—stunning.

"I do. My trunks have found me again," Kate said, but she was thinking, *Poor Castine.* She was also listening for some sound inside or outside the house that would indicate that Robert had returned.

"Everyone, please do sit down," Maria was saying. "Valentina, what a beautiful dress. You look lovely. If you'll excuse me, I must check on our dinner—"

"Kate can do that," Max said over Valentina's demure thanks, looking at his wife hard. In her condition and after the emotional upheaval of last night, he did *not* want her tiring herself out—and that was that. "Kate?"

"Yes, of course," Kate said, happy to have a reason the leave the gathering in the parlor. She walked quickly down the hallway, thinking as she went of the leather-bound, handwritten book of etiquette her mother had made her read—study—so that she could at least supervise the running of a household. She remembered a particular notation that said that the number of dishes served at a sit down meal with guests didn't need to be many—but they did need to be excellent.

She wasn't the least bit worried about Max's soldier-cooks; it was the atmosphere at the table that concerned her. According to the book, such a meal wasn't to be hurried on any account—and that alone was a major drawback to her way of thinking. The sooner this evening was over, the better. But the worst departure from the rules was that one should make certain that the invited guests were "compatible." Mrs. Kinnard and Mrs. Russell, because of their strong personalities, were barely compatible with each other, despite their highwayman history, and if Robert managed to get here in time, even a modicum of harmony would be unlikely, if not impossible.

Kate stood for a moment in the kitchen doorway before she interrupted the bustle of food preparation that seemed to be going on everywhere at once. Every soldier in the room seemed to be busy at some cooking task, except for the one who held a happy Robbie on his knee while he ate a mashed up…potato, it looked like—with the wrong end of a spoon.

Little General, she thought. She doubted he would have any of the prejudices associated with the war that must afflict both his father and his uncle.

"Good evening," she said, startling everyone except Robbie, who waved his backward spoon in her direction. "Is your spoon broken, Robbie?" she asked him, making him grin.

"Aye, miss," the soldier holding him said. "I believe it is. He doesn't like the big end, and he's a clever lad. He finds his own way."

"The Colonel's lady would like to know when you will be ready to serve," Kate said to the group at large because she didn't really know which of them held the highest rank. A grizzly-looking man with a large piece of food-stained muslin wrapped around his waist stepped forward.

"Twenty-five minutes, miss," he said. "No sooner. No later, if it's all going to come out right."

"Excellent," Kate said. "Thank you…Sergeant. Is that apple pie I smell?" she asked.

"It is, miss."

"My very favorite," she told him. "I shall look forward to it."

On her way back to the parlor one of the lower ranked soldiers called to her. "Miss!" She stopped and waited for him to catch up.

"Mr. Markham says for you to come to the summer kitchen, miss," he said in a rush. "Now, if you please."

"What?" Kate said, thinking she'd heard wrong.

"Brother to the Colonel's lady, miss. He says for you to come now—and hurry, if you please."

Kate frowned because it was disconcerting to realize that she wasn't even going to hesitate. She immediately followed the soldier back into the kitchen, sidestepping the cooks, and boxes and baskets, and waving to Robbie again as she made her way to the back door.

A lantern hanging from a post lit the slate path that led to the summer kitchen door. She had no difficulty seeing where she was going. *Why* she was going was something else again.

She didn't knock, and she didn't stand in the cold and wait for Robert to open it. She pushed the door open and went inside. There was a fire burning on the hearth, and the stone structure was not nearly as frigid as she might have expected. There was also a man lying flat on his back on the long harvest table Maria must use for food preparation and preserving.

"I need you to bring me some things from the house," Robert said immediately, standing in her way as if he didn't want her coming any closer.

She could still see the man, and the most significant thing about him was that he was obviously in the Union army.

"Who—?" she began.

"It's the chaplain," he said, heading her off.

"The one who's 'seen the elephant'?"

"Yes. He's in a bad way."

"Drunk, you mean," she said because she could smell the whiskey on him from where she stood.

"No— Yes. And he's used up all his second chances. They'll put him in the stockade this time. He's a friend of Reverend Lewis's— they were in the seminary together. Reverend Lewis doesn't think the man is well enough to be hauled off to the stockade. Mrs. Lewis is temperance in the extreme and won't have him in the house. He's asked me to hide him until he sobers up."

Kate stared at him. "Well, you picked the worst possible place I can think of to do it," she said. "Mrs. Kinnard's in the house. And Mrs. Russell. I don't know where Mrs. Justice is—"

"Will you help or not?" he asked, apparently trying to hurry this along.

"Yes, I'll help. What do you want me to do?"

"Can you get out of the house with some coffee and blankets?"

"No," she said with some trepidation. "But I will. Somehow."

And that turned out to be much harder than she anticipated. When she opened the summer kitchen door, Valentina, in all her blue shimmering splendor, fell into the room.

"What's happening?" she asked as she righted herself, clearly not concerned that she had been caught spying. She kept bobbing up and down on tiptoe, trying to see for herself.

"There's a problem," Kate said, and she knew from experience that there would be no getting rid of Valentina now. It would be impossible to fob her off with some concocted story, even if Kate had been so inclined— which she wasn't. The only thing left was to recruit her. "I have to get some hot coffee and some blankets out of the house. It's important that my brother doesn't see me," she said, keeping the details to a minimum.

Valentina kept trying to see the man on the table. Clearly this was not what she'd expected to find.

"We have about twenty minutes before dinner is served. I will need you to either help me or stay out of the way," Kate said, and Valentina finally stopped bouncing up and down.

"Oh. All right. Yes. I'll help," Valentina said. "What do you want me to do?"

"Go back to the parlor, tell everyone that dinner will be ready in fifteen minutes time. And don't look like there is anything going on."

"I can do that," Valentina assured her. She suddenly grinned. "This is wonderful! I can't tell you how long I've been waiting to have adventures like you do."

"Then hurry," Kate said, shooing her out the door.

Kate glanced at Robert. He was almost on the verge of smiling.

"You have adventures?" he asked.

"So it seems to Valentina."

"She knows about the hiding, then."

"No, she does not," Kate said pointedly. "No one knows about that."

"I do," he said. The man was teasing her, she suddenly realized. In the middle of all *this*.

She exhaled sharply and turned to go.

"Kate," Robert said, and she looked back at him.

"What?"

"I…appreciate your help."

"I haven't done anything yet."

"Maybe not, but you've kicked over the traces."

"Is that another…soldier saying?" she asked. "Like the elephant?"

"It is."

"Well, I'll have to wait to find out what that one means—and hopefully you and the chaplain won't end up in the stockade. The chaplain is stirring," she added, looking at him for a long moment before she hurried out the door.

I'm doing this for Max, she told herself on the path back to the house. So he won't have to step on an urgent request from Reverend Lewis. It would mean nothing to Mrs. Kinnard and Mrs. Russell if he put a drunken chaplain in the stockade, but for the Reverend.

She had formed a plan of sorts by the time she got to the house, one that involved Private Castine. But just as she was about to corner him, the sergeant major stepped into the foyer, and her hope that Private Castine would likely do anything if he thought it was for Valentina evaporated.

"Is there something you need, Miss Kate?" the sergeant major asked, looking at her closely. Kate was trying hard to hide her agitated state, but from the expression on his face, she knew it wasn't working.

In for a penny, in for a pound, she thought.

"Yes," she said hurriedly, whispering to keep anyone in the parlor from hearing. "The chaplain—the one who has 'seen the elephant'—is drunk in the summer kitchen with Mrs. Woodard's brother—*he's* not drunk, just the chaplain. Reverend Lewis and the chaplain were friends in the seminary, and the Reverend wants the chaplain hidden until he's sober because this time he's going to end up in the stockade and the Reverend thinks he's not well enough for that kind of punishment. I need coffee and blankets and somebody to mind him—so Ro—Mrs. Woodard's brother can sit down at this dinner—so *my* brother won't have to risk the occupation peace by having to address any of this with Mrs. Kinnard *and* Mrs. Russell here—because it all comes down to Reverend Lewis's request, you see, and they will surely take exception if it isn't carried out. And we definitely don't want Mrs. Woodard all upset because her brother's in the middle of it." She stopped to breathe and found she didn't have anything more to say.

"Miss Kate," he said after a long moment. "I can tell you right now, I'm going to think long and hard before I ever ask you a question like that again. Castine!" he whispered sharply, making the private jump despite a much-less-audible-than-usual summons. "You and Giles get coffee and blankets out to the summer kitchen *now*. Send Mrs. Woodard's brother back to the house and you two stay there with this…problem until I tell you different. Go!"

Castine scurried toward the kitchen just as the dinner guests poured out of the parlor on their way to the dining room.

"There you are," Valentina said as if she hadn't just seen her. "It's time to be seated." And she followed Max and Maria to the table with a great sense of importance— and mischief—which was not lost on Max.

He gave Kate a pointed look; she ignored it. She lingered in the hallway, trying to see if Robert was going to come back to the house.

"Kate? What are you doing?" he asked when she didn't immediately join the rest of the guests.

"Oh…nothing," she assured him.

"Then could you do it in here? Somebody's got to sit between Mrs. Kinnard and Mrs. Russell," he added in a whisper.

Kate smiled sweetly and took her place between the two women, noting with some dismay that Robert—if he came—would be seated directly across from her. As usual the table was set in mismatched china. It immediately set Mrs. Kinnard and Mrs. Russell to reminiscing about the occasions they'd attended when this set or that set in its entirety had been used—Maria's christening,

Samuel's birth. There seemed to have been no occasions regarding Robert.

Kate made the mistake of looking at Valentina, who raised her eyebrows and looked at the empty chair next to her, then back at Kate—with the subtlety of a broad ax. Kate wasn't quite sure whether Valentina was simply enjoying her "adventure" or whether she was trying to ask a question—which Kate could not have answered because she had Max's full attention. She sat there, trying her best to effect a certain air of nonchalance and hoping that for once, his reputation for knowing everything wouldn't hold.

Soldiers began bringing the food in and placing it on the sideboard—beef, pork, chicken, buttered potatoes, shell beans, sweet and sour beets, cooked cabbage, pickles, bread and butter, cold milk and coffee. Everything looked and smelled wonderful, and the soldiers selected to do the actual serving clearly had had practice. Kate accepted a few spoonfuls of everything, but she had to force herself to eat. It didn't help that she could see Sergeant Major Perkins walk past the open dining room door carrying Robbie more than once.

Kate looked down at her plate and concentrated on the food, bite by bite. Neither Mrs. Kinnard nor Mrs. Russell seemed interested in conversing—with her—to Kate's relief. Maria included all three of them in conversation from time to time, as a good hostess should, but Mrs. Kinnard stayed disengaged, until Max introduced the topic of civic pride, especially the possibility of beautifying the area around the train station where visitors gained their first impression of the town.

Beautification, after so many years of hardship and deprivation, was obviously dear to Mrs. Kinnard's heart, and she was full of ideas and suggestions—and criticisms of the occupation. Valentina, who had likely heard them all before, fidgeted in her chair and looked at the ceiling from time to time.

Kate glanced toward the dining room doorway again, thinking she had caught a glimpse of someone in the hallway.

It wasn't Perkins pacing to keep Robbie happy. It was the baby's namesake himself. Robert stood just in the doorway until he caught his sister's attention.

"Robert!" Maria said, as surprised as she was pleased.

"I apologize for my lateness," he said. "I thought it better to be tardy if it meant showing up presentable."

There was at least some truth in that. He'd clearly been to see the town barber at some point, something Kate hadn't noticed in the dimly lit summer kitchen, and he was wearing a white shirt and a dark suit, both of which looked new.

Yes, Kate thought. *Presentable.*

He greeted Mrs. Kinnard and Mrs. Russell; they both seemed pleased to see him.

"Miss Woodard," he said as he took the seat across from Kate. "Are we missing Mrs. Justice this evening?" he asked, causing Mrs. Kinnard and Mrs. Russell to look at each other despite Kate's being in the way.

"She is visiting someone in need," Mrs. Kinnard said after a moment.

"That sounds very much like Mrs. Justice," he said, finally glancing in Kate's direction. Once again she looked down and concentrated on her plate.

The meal continued pleasantly enough, punctuated by succinct but informed comments regarding the weather—from Mrs. Kinnard and Mrs. Russell—and how the recent snow affected train travel— from Max. Maria kept staring at her brother, as if she still couldn't believe he was here.

Kate thought that Max was making every effort not to say something that might lead to the topic of wars lost and subsequent martial law and reconstruction. Robert chatted with Valentina, asking her where the little girl Samuel used to tease so had gone. Kate could sense the tension in Maria at the mention of Samuel's name, but it soon passed, likely because of the gentleness with which Robert spoke of him. There was no evidence of the agonized pain Kate had witnessed last night, but she would have guessed that it was not easy to mention him. Perhaps Robert's talk with Maria had helped after all, even if Kate still suspected that he hadn't told her the full details of Samuel's death.

When the dessert—apple pie, as promised—arrived and had been served, there was a slight commotion in the foyer, but it was loud enough to catch everyone's attention.

"Just the mail pouches," Max said, looking at Kate, because he knew the degree of her expectancy when a train bringing the mail from the north arrived. She took a quiet breath, aware that Robert was looking at her as well. She didn't count on there being a letter from Harrison, but she hoped for one all the same.

"I would like to make a request—it's more of an invitation, actually," Robert said. "To all of you."

Neither Mrs. Kinnard nor Mrs. Russell had finished eating, but his remark caused both their half-lifted forks to return to their plates.

"What is it, Robert?" Maria asked, clearly wondering if this was going to be something worrying. She glanced at Max in what Kate thought was a request of her own.

Whatever it is, let him be.

"I want to ask all of you to be in church tomorrow," Robert said.

"I am *always* in church on Sunday, Robert," Mrs. Kinnard said. "Surely you remember that."

He smiled. "Yes, ma'am. So I've always heard. And you must remember that despite my dear mother's best efforts, I *wasn't* always there in the Markham family pew on Sunday."

"I believe *never* would be the more apt word for it," Maria said, and his smile broadened. Kate watched as it quickly faded. It was as if he couldn't—wouldn't—let himself enjoy even the smallest pleasantry, and if sometimes the enjoyment overtook him, he had to push it quickly away.

He doesn't think he deserves it, Kate thought. And no one understood that better than she.

"Even so, I wanted you all to know that I am extending my personal invitation, and I earnestly hope you'll be on hand."

"*Your* personal invitation," Max said.

"Are you going to tell us why?" Maria asked.

Robert looked around the table and then directly at Kate.

"I'm preaching the sermon."

Chapter Nine

Robert watched their faces. If he had to assign an emotion to each of the people present at the table—the ones who had known him before the war—it would have been the same emotion—incredulity. And he would have to include his brother-in-law as well, because the Colonel, who had likely heard a great deal of what Maria's brother had been like, was nothing at the moment if not incredulous.

"And who has approved this?" Mrs. Kinnard wanted to know, clearly intending to interrogate him, as was her self-appointed duty.

"Reverend Lewis," he said. "I had a long talk with him. It's all arranged," he added.

Mrs. Kinnard opened her mouth to say something, but then didn't. She was clearly undecided about the appropriateness of such an event. She, like everyone else in the town, knew that he had lived "a man's life" before the war, and "all arranged" was not a term she was inclined to recognize, especially when she had had no part in the arranging.

"Well," she said after a moment. "I simply do not know what to say."

"It won't be my first sermon," Robert said. "If that helps."

Clearly, it didn't because she looked even more startled than she had at his initial announcement. And Maria. Maria was openly bewildered by it all, and he couldn't fault her for that. He was still somewhat bewildered himself.

"I take it you have had some kind of Saul-on-the-road-to-Damascus experience, then," Max said finally. The remark was rude; everyone at the table recognized that fact, just as everyone wanted to hear Robert's response.

"Nothing nearly so dramatic," Robert said, looking at his brother-in-law directly. "I will talk about that tomorrow in church."

"I see," Max said.

There were no more comments and the silence at the table grew more and more uncomfortable.

Robert looked at Kate. He couldn't read her expression at all—because she was avoiding his eyes. He expected her to be surprised—and doubtful. Given their conversation last night, *doubtfulness* was the one emotion he was most prepared to see. But when she finally did look at him, he saw neither. What he found there in her eyes was understanding, as if the things he'd just said, to her way of thinking, explained everything: his coming home again, the effort he was making to mend his relationship with Maria—and the chaplain in the summer kitchen.

Two are better than one, he suddenly thought. *For if they fall, the one will lift up his fellow...a threefold cord is not quickly broken.*

He gave her a slight nod and stood, and he thought for a moment she was going to ask him to sit down again. It was clear to him that she didn't want him to go, not yet, and that she was a woman with questions, who apparently saw no reason in this world why he shouldn't answer them.

"If you'll excuse me now," he said. "I'll take my leave. Maria—Max, thank you for inviting me. The meal was excellent. The best I've had in a very long time. Ladies, it was a joy to spend this time in your company. I am most grateful."

He shot a look in Maria's direction.

See? I haven't forgotten everything our mother taught us.

"Robert—" Maria began, but then she seemed to realize that whatever she needed to say, she couldn't say here. "Good night."

He smiled and left the table, waiting until he was out of sight to sigh in relief. It was over. He had done it, and now he was committed to this new life he was about to embark upon.

Be strong and of good courage...for the Lord thy God...He will not fail thee.

I'm trying, Lord...

He looked around at a sound. Kate had come out of the dining room. He watched her now as the sergeant major approached her, holding a letter in his hand. She thanked him and took it, barely glancing at it, as if she had no real interest in where it had come from or who had sent it. But then, when the sergeant major was walking away, she looked down at it and, holding it with both hands, briefly pressed it to her lips.

"Oh!" Valentina exclaimed as she came into the hallway. "There was a letter for you in the mail pouch! I love to get letters. I don't care to answer them, though," she said with a laugh. "It's so tedious. Is it from someone special?"

"Just a young friend of the family," Kate said. "He's... away at boarding school."

"Not that exciting, then. Not like when it's from an admirer."

Kate said nothing to that. She put the letter carefully into her pocket. Robert had hoped to speak to her—about what, he hadn't decided. He just wanted to look into her eyes again. He wanted to know if he had been mistaken earlier and perhaps to ask if she would be at tomorrow's service. It would help him a great deal if she were, but he wouldn't tell her that. To do so would be inappropriate, and he'd done enough inappropriate things where she was concerned already. Valentina's presence precluded any exchange between them at all, but Valentina wasn't the only reason. Standing here and being privy to that one intimate and heartfelt gesture regarding her letter had suddenly made Kate unapproachable. He wondered suddenly if the letter was somehow connected to the photograph she kept hidden in her book. She was such a mystery to him, and he had no wish to intrude.

He turned and left the house, heading down the slate path to see how the chaplain fared. If the man was sober enough now, he would likely either be belligerent or embarrassingly remorseful, neither of which would be a true measure of the man. In any event Robert would have done all that Reverend Lewis had asked him to do—with Kate's help. She had taken care of what he couldn't—at least not without a stint in the stockade. It was possible that the chaplain could be sent back to his barracks now, hopefully in the company of soldiers who wouldn't let him make any detours along the way. Or he might still be deep in his whiskey-induced oblivion. Either way Robert had a sermon to write. He would do that and he would not think about Kate Woodard.

* * *

"Robert's leaving," Valentina said. "It takes some getting used to, doesn't it?"

"What does?" Kate forced herself to ask. It would perhaps be another hour before Mrs. Kinnard and the rest of them left, and it was all Kate could do not to go upstairs now, without a word to anyone, and read Harrison's letter. But Valentina was here, forcing her to participate in what was supposed to be an enjoyable evening.

"The way he looks— Oh, I keep forgetting. You didn't know him before."

"Maria showed me his photograph," Kate said, glancing at Max and the rest of the guests as they passed by on their way to the parlor. "I could see that he is…changed."

"He's still handsome, though, don't you think? In a rough and dangerous kind of way—like a *pirate* or a *highwayman*. I wonder how the man is?"

It took Kate a moment to realize that Valentina likely meant the chaplain.

"I was so surprised when Robert came to dinner, weren't you? This evening has been more exciting than any evening I've ever had—well, except when there was a bread riot during the war. Or when the prisoners broke out of the stockade—Mother and I both were quite afraid. Oh, and when General Stoneman raided the town. But those involved *everybody*. They weren't very…personal. Not like tonight when I was able to actually participate. I've decided I quite like adventures. It will be hard to go back to the dull everyday things. Excitement seems to follow you, Miss Woodard. I must visit you every single afternoon in case there is more."

"No, I don't think so," Kate said, meaning the daily visits as much as the idea that events like tonight's escapade somehow followed her about.

"Oh, dear," Valentina said, looking past her. "Mother wants us. We'd better go in."

Us? Kate thought. But she didn't argue. She followed Valentina dutifully into the parlor, her hand resting on the pocket where Harrison's letter lay safe and hidden.

"Play for us, please, Valentina," Mrs. Kinnard said.

"Of course," Valentina said with the assurance of someone who was completely secure in both her appearance and her accomplishments.

Valentina sat down at the pianoforte and began looking at the piece already open on the music stand. Kate intended to take the chair by the window, regardless of the cold draft.

"Remember where you are," Kate whispered to Valentina, who looked at her blankly for a moment before she realized that it wouldn't do to play either Southern or Northern songs.

"I brought these with me from Philadelphia," Kate said, retrieving a stack of sheet music from the bookshelf nearest the pianoforte.

Valentina looked through them. "I don't know any of these—'Little Brown Jug'?"

"They're quite new," Kate said. "I believe you'll enjoy playing them."

Valentina looked at them doubtfully, then selected one.

"'Sweet Genevieve,'" she said over her shoulder to her mother and began to play as easily as if the song were part of a well-rehearsed repertoire.

Kate sat down by the window. She could see that a lamp burned in the summer kitchen and that from time to time someone—Robert, surely—moved about.

Valentina worked her way through the sheet music, and after being cajoled into an encore, began to sing the lyrics the second time through. She even managed to get Mrs. Kinnard and Mrs. Russell to join in on "Little Brown Jug."

Kate might have found this a most enjoyable evening if she hadn't had Harrison's letter in her pocket. And she felt a little sorry for Private Castine because he couldn't hear Valentina play and sing. Mrs. Kinnard had clearly done her work well in preparing Valentina for whatever bride fair she might find herself participating in.

Kate glanced out the window again. The moon was high, and the night cold and still. She saw the lamp in the summer kitchen go out, and someone leaving, but she couldn't tell who. All must be well with the chaplain, she thought. For now at least. But despite the Reverend Lewis's good intentions, it seemed to Kate that they were only delaying the inevitable.

Out of respect for Max's departure tomorrow, the evening ended early despite Valentina's desire to keep playing. Kate said her good-nights to the women, and she intended to go straight upstairs to her bedchamber.

"We're almost all accounted for," Maria said when Kate was about to take her leave. "Sergeant Major Perkins says Robbie is fast asleep in the nursery, but Mrs. Justice hasn't returned yet."

"I'll stay down here and let her in," Kate said. "I'm not sleepy and I want to read awhile." She was telling the truth on both counts, and it didn't matter to her where she read Harrison's letter, only that she be alone.

She waited for a little while after Maria had gone because she wanted to make sure that she wasn't interrupted. When the house was quiet, she removed the letter from her pocket and turned it over to read her name in Harrison's painfully meticulous handwriting. Mrs. Howe had insisted upon that, that he achieve the penmanship of a gentleman. Kate had seen him practicing many times—struggling—to accomplish what Mrs. Howe had asked of him.

Miss Kate Woodard.

She took a deep breath and opened the envelope.

Dear Kate, it began.

She looked up because of a slight rustling in the hallway. Mrs. Justice was standing in the doorway, and she was clearly distressed.

"What is it?" Kate asked immediately.

"My dear," Mrs. Justice began. She gave a heavy sigh. "I need your help. I've done a terrible thing."

"What?" Kate said, growing alarmed now.

"I've been at Mrs. Russell's house—talking to Warrie. It didn't help. It didn't help at all. She blames Robbie for everything that happened to Eleanor. Mrs. Russell told her that he's going to preach tomorrow, and she's—she's—oh, she is just not herself. I think she's going to disrupt the service. I couldn't talk her out of it—and poor Robbie—I thought he should know, so I told him."

"About the disruption?"

Mrs. Justice stood wringing her hands. "And about—Eleanor, too," she said, her chin trembling. "Oh, my dear—I just didn't know what else to do. And now I've made things worse. Now he's so— Will you talk to him?"

"Me? Mrs. Justice, I couldn't possibly."

"You have such a good effect on him—"

"How could I? I barely know him."

"I don't know how. I just know that you do. He knows it, too."

"Mrs. Justice—"

"You're the only one who can help. Please, my dear. He's in the kitchen."

"The lamp isn't lit in the summer kitchen."

"No, no. Not out there. The kitchen in here. Just…go.

Sit with him for a time. Let him have someone to talk to if he needs to—the way you did before. It will help him. I know it will."

Kate closed her eyes and sighed. She did *not* want to do this. If she was certain about anything, she was certain that he would much rather be alone.

"Hurry, my dear!" Mrs. Justice whispered, looking down the hallway. "Please!"

Kate folded Harrison's letter and put it back into her pocket. Then she took a deep breath and stood.

"I'll…go," Kate said. "But I don't think I'll stay."

"That's all I ask, my dear," Mrs. Justice said. "Even if it's just for a moment, it may be all in this world he needs."

Kate walked steadily down the hallway, the soft-soled shoes she was wearing making very little noise. She saw him long before he saw her. He was sitting at the worktable near the cookstove. He looked up sharply when he realized someone was there.

"Go or stay," she said bluntly.

He looked at her for a long moment before he answered.

"Stay," he said finally.

Kate walked to the stove and looked into the coffee pot. It was half full, so she got down two cups from a nearby shelf, poured them each a cup and brought them to the table.

She sat down in one of the chairs at the side of the table so she wouldn't be across from him.

"Did Mrs. Justice send you?" he asked.

"Yes," Kate said, and he nodded.

He didn't say anything more, and neither did she. After a time he picked up the coffee cup and took a sip.

"Did you make this?" he asked, for the sole purpose,

she knew, of making her smile. He already had at least a notion of her domestic shortcomings.

"I pour it much better than I make it," she said, smiling.

"Something to add to the list."

"List?"

"The one with learning to build a fire on it."

"Oh. *That* list. How…is the chaplain?" she asked, thinking it was a safe enough question.

"He's sober and able to walk on his own two feet. He is likely to fall down at some point, but Castine is in charge of monitoring that."

"I've been wondering…" she said, tentatively taking a sip of coffee. It wasn't bad at all. She'd had much worse in some of Philadelphia's best restaurants.

"About what?"

"About the day the chaplain came here to see you. I've been wondering what you were arguing about."

"I had the impertinence to comment on his highly inebriated state. Men who already know they drink too much don't like having the fact that they aren't sober when they should be pointed out to them. It didn't help that I was in the wrong army."

"I see," Kate said.

"Did you…know?" he asked quietly, and Kate looked at him, knowing full well that they were on a different topic now.

"Yes and no," she said. "I knew about the woman, Nell. But I didn't know until just recently that she and your Eleanor were one and the same."

"Would you have told me about her?"

"No."

"Why not? I've come to think of you as being straight-forward."

"Because I only knew some of the details and those were secondhand."

"Do you know if they…drove her out of town? Mrs. Kinnard—did she make Eleanor leave?"

"Not that I know of. It helped a lot that she—"

"She what?"

"Max told me that Eleanor…made sure Maria got her earrings back. The ones you and Samuel gave her. The previous military commander had confiscated them as contraband of war."

"And how did she do that?"

Kate looked at him directly. "I don't know," she said truthfully. "I think that her being shunned by the people here was more…self-imposed, at least where Maria was concerned. Maria didn't—wouldn't—cross the street to the other side if she saw her, and Eleanor wouldn't let her sacrifice her own reputation to keep up their friendship. Thinking about it now, I seem to remember that the reason Max and Maria hired Warrie to help with the boys was because Eleanor asked them to—because the fire that killed the boys' mother happened when Warrie was away from the house and she was taking it very hard. Eleanor didn't want her mother to know that it was her idea."

"Yet another broken thing that can't be fixed," Robert said, more to himself than to her.

"Are you ready?" Kate asked. "For tomorrow's service." She meant for Warrie's interruption, but for all her straightforwardness, she couldn't quite bring herself to say it.

"No. I expect it to be…difficult."

"Because of Warrie Hansen?" she asked after all.

"No. Because I need to…speak to the congregation first—before I presume to speak to them about God."

Kate looked at him thoughtfully.

"What?" he asked after a moment.

"Maria—and Valentina—say you were never…interested in religion."

"I wasn't. But when a man goes to war, it changes him. I've seen two things happen. He can either lose his faith or he can find it. I found mine."

"Yes," Kate said, because she believed him. She thought this must be the explanation for his being…comforting, despite his warrior-like intensity. She looked toward the windows. The bright moonlight was no longer in evidence. It was raining.

"I've been wondering something, as well," he said.

"What is that?"

"I was wondering who wrote the letter Perkins gave you this evening."

The remark took her completely by surprise, and after a moment, she decided there was no reason why she couldn't tell him the same thing she'd told Valentina.

"A young friend of the family. He's away at boarding school. His name is Harrison. Some people call him Harry."

"But you don't."

Kate looked at him, wondering what had made him decide that.

"No," she said. "I don't. He's always seemed like such an old soul to me, even when he was a little boy. Harry just didn't fit."

"So what does Harrison have to say about boarding school?"

"I don't know. I haven't had a chance to read his letter."

"Read it now," he said. "You won't be interrupted."

Kate could feel him looking at her. There was no reason why she couldn't do that. She felt perfectly comfortable here—with him—despite her early reluctance. But she still hesitated until finally she removed the letter from her pocket, smoothing it carefully and leaning toward the lamp hanging over the table so that she could see it.

She had to force herself to read slowly, to make it last. She couldn't keep from smiling at the familiar handwriting, but then—

She shuffled the pages to backtrack and started over, reading quickly now, straight through to the end. Then she sat there, holding the letter in her hands, trying to understand. After a moment she held it up to the lamp in an attempt to decipher crossed out words at the bottom of the last page.

"What's wrong?" he asked

"I can't tell what this last part is," she said, hearing the tremor in her voice despite her determination to sound calm and in control.

"Maybe he didn't mean for you to."

"And that is why I need to see it. Something isn't right with him. He said the same thing twice."

"Boys sometimes lose track, I think."

"Not this boy. But it's not just the repetition. It's what he said. He said that being there was good for his character and he would be strong when it was over, as strong as his brother was when he escaped from the prison here. And then a few paragraphs later, he wrote the same thing again, as if he'd forgotten—only I know he didn't." Kate stopped. She could feel him trying to understand her concern—and failing.

"John—his brother—wasn't strong at all. He was half-starved and his mind was—if it hadn't been for his love for the woman he married, I think he would have never recovered. Harrison knows that. This is not like him. It's not like him at all," she said.

"His is the photograph you carry in your book," Robert said. It wasn't a question.

"Yes." She held up the letter again. "I think the last word is *me*."

"May I?" Robert asked and she handed it to him. "The word before that would likely be *for* or *to*. Perhaps *with*." He held it up to the light as she had done. "Three words," he said. "Something ending in the letter *y* and then *for me*. I think I know what it is."

"What?" Kate asked. "What is it?"

"I think it says, 'Pray for me.'"

"Pray for me? Oh!" Kate got up from her chair and began to pace the room.

This! This is what it feels like to be a mother, she thought wildly. *This is what it feels like to love your child and be able to do nothing to help him.*

"He crossed it out—"

"Yes, but why? *Why?* That's the question. Maybe he was afraid he'd said too much—because of what he wrote about John. It simply wasn't true, and he knew I would realize it. John was in terrible shape when he came home. And maybe he—oh, I don't know what to do!"

"What kind of school is he in?"

"A legacy school. All the Howe men went there—he's not like the Howe men."

"What kind of boy is he?"

Kate looked at him. "Quiet. Scholarly. Sensitive."

"An old soul," Robert said.

"Yes! I don't know what to do!" she said again.

"Is there no one who might understand your concerns?"

"No," she said. Then, "Yes. His…brother might."

"Then you must let him know. Can you do that?"

"I could write to him. I can't explain this in a telegram without making him think I'm—" She stopped and forced herself to take a deep breath. She was close to weeping and that wouldn't help anything. "John lives here, but he and his family have been in Philadelphia for several months—some kind of family legal business that had to be dealt with—and then his mother fell ill. The letter would go out on the train tomorrow—yes. I'll do that." She took another deep breath. There was something she could do after all.

Robert stood and moved her chair around. "Sit down," he said.

"No—I must write the letter."

"I think it would be good if you—we—did what Harrison asked first."

She looked at him blankly.

"I think we should pray for him."

"I— Yes," Kate decided immediately. No matter why the words had been marked out, Harrison had written them.

She sat down. Robert moved his chair facing hers and sat down as well.

"Give me your hands," he said.

Kate hesitated, then she bowed her head and placed her hands in his outstretched ones, feeling their warmth and strength, seeing the scars. It was raining still; she could hear it beating against the kitchen windows. She took a wavering breath.

"Kate needs Your help, Lord," he said quietly, and she looked up at him. This was not at all what she was expecting. There was none of the formality she was accustomed to. It was if he were speaking to someone there in the room.

Robert's eyes were closed; she bowed her head again.

"She's afraid for Harrison. You already know that, just as You are privy to his situation, while we are not. I know You are always with us, but if there is cause, if he's in trouble, I ask that You help him to know that You are there. *Help* him. And help her—us—so we can be ready to do whatever we can for this boy who means so much to her."

In spite of all she could do, Kate could feel a tear sliding down her cheek. She watched as it fell onto the back of his hand.

Chapter Ten

Kate was late for church. Robert had all but relinquished his hope that she was coming when he saw her standing tentatively in the vestibule, as if she still hadn't made up her mind as to whether or not she would attend this morning's service. He thought she hadn't slept because she looked so pale, so weary. He had no doubt that her letter to young Harrison's brother had been written—he'd seen the lamp burning in her window late into the night. It was likely already in the mailbag, awaiting the next northbound train.

Kate waited until the ushers were taking up the collection before she came into the sanctuary. The Yankee major who had accosted her in the hallway was sitting next to the aisle midway down, and he watched her intently as she passed by him. Joe and Jake, who were sitting with Maria, did, as well.

"Kate!" one of the boys called, only it sounded more like "Cake!" She smiled at them and put her forefinger to her lips, a gesture both of them returned, grinning from ear to ear all the while.

The only vacant places were on the front pew, and Kate continued her way down the aisle to take a seat.

Robert watched as she took a deep breath and then looked up at him. He gave her the barest of nods, and she returned it with such subtlety that he might have only imagined that she had.

She's nothing like Eleanor.

And yet she was. They both had this...fierce quality about them that was not in the least offensive and definitely to be admired.

Eleanor.

He had to believe what Mrs. Justice had told him, albeit without her actually saying the words that would have left no doubt in his mind as to what she meant. But the fact was, he didn't. He couldn't. Eleanor was...*Eleanor*—laughing, headstrong and defiant. She was his first love. Some part of him, no doubt, would always love her. He simply didn't understand what could have made her become what people—Mrs. Justice—hinted she had become. What he did understand was that Eleanor would let the good people of this town think whatever they wanted to think, whether it was actually true or not, and enjoy the joke, no matter the consequences. He realized now that Warrie Hansen believed that he was the cause of her daughter's supposed downfall, despite the fact that it was Eleanor who had ended their engagement. He could only suppose that she had never told her mother about the letter she'd written to him.

But no one knew better than he did how a person could do things they never thought they'd do and then find themselves trapped in the consequences with no way out—and never once understand how they had gotten there.

He gave a soft sigh.

Bewildered again, Lord.

He looked out over the congregation. This morning's

service was well attended, and he didn't doubt that he was at least one of the reasons. It surprised him that his brother-in-law was here. Apparently he had delayed his departure, most likely for Maria's sake if this church service proved too upsetting for her. Robert hoped that that would not be the case, but if it was, then he would be glad that Max was here.

Aside from his brother-in-law, the military was well represented—officers, mostly—and the decidedly openhearted Private Castine. He liked Castine—because he reminded him of Samuel.

He saw people he recognized from his childhood— Mrs. Kinnard and Valentina, Mrs. Russell and Mrs. Justice, of course, but many others, as well. How long ago it all seemed now. A number of his comrades had come. As boys he'd led them on more than one foray into what they all considered a lark and what Mrs. Kinnard considered the end of civilization as she knew it—the turning over of any number of residential privies. When they were young men, they had gone drinking and gambling together, and eventually, full of patriotism and pride, they had gone off to war.

And look at us now...

Until this day he had lost track of all of them.

The Reverend Lewis accepted the offering and blessed it; the choir sang the doxology. Mrs. Kinnard scowled at one of Max's officers, who was openly staring at Valentina. Then Reverend Lewis said a few words of introduction, and suddenly it was time.

Robert rose to his feet and walked to the lectern, surprised that his hands didn't shake. He felt the familiar restlessness, the kind he always had before a bareknuckled fight in the ring, but he was not afraid.

He stood quietly looking down at the open Bible on

the lectern. He could hear the creaking of the pews as people shifted in their seats. He could hear the whispers. Before he spoke, he wanted to give them enough time to look at him, to satisfy their curiosity about whether it was really Robert Markham standing up there and whether he did or didn't look like himself.

"There's Wah-but!" Jake called out, as if he'd only just that moment realized that his brand-new uncle was standing where the pastor normally stood. He had no doubt that Maria would put her finger to her lips just as Kate had done.

He looked up, first at Kate, and then slowly at the rest of the congregation. He didn't see Warrie Hansen.

"What am I doing here?" he said, his voice strong. "I believe that is what everyone is wondering—including me."

There was a ripple of laughter through the congregation. He waited until it subsided.

"I had a conversation with a friend last night. In this conversation, the fact that I was never known for my church attendance came up."

He could see Mrs. Kinnard straighten up and sit taller as she concluded that the friend he referred to was she.

"I said the rumors were undeniably true," he continued. "I didn't go to church as I should have. As my mother wished. But I also said then that when a man has been to war, he is changed. I said that I had seen two things happen. Some men lose their faith, and some men find it. I am here today to tell you that I have found mine.

"My experience was nothing like Saul's on the road to Damascus. It was more like Cleopas's on the road to Emmaus. Cleopas and another disciple did not recognize the resurrected Jesus as He traveled along with them, I think, because they weren't looking for Him.

"And so it was with me. I was not looking for Him. I was too lost in my own guilt and rage. I had failed the people I loved in the worst way possible. My brother, Samuel, was killed on the battlefield when I had promised my father to keep him safe. Samuel, with his poet's heart, was the best of us hardened soldiers, you see—"

"Amen," someone in the congregation said—a comrade who had been at Gettysburg.

"And yet it was he who died. It was beyond my understanding. All I knew was that I had broken my promise—"

"We all did, Rob," another veteran said. "Not just you. We *all* did."

Robert hesitated. It had never occurred to him that there might be men in the company who had felt the same sense of responsibility for Samuel that he had. He looked at the man who had spoken, and nodded, grateful for his candor.

"I was wounded, and it was many weeks before I knew where I was. My only strong memory of what had happened on the battlefield that day at Gettysburg was Samuel—alive and then dead. I know that there were men who pulled me to safety, but all of that is a blur.

"My wounds were such that I was thought to be dying as the army retreated back to Virginia. I'm told that when that was the case—when the ambulance wagon or whatever conveyance was being used—had a dying man in it, the driver would stop at a house along the way and ask the people who lived there if they would give the dying soldier a decent burial. A Maryland family—one that did not believe in war, but did believe in the parable of the Good Samaritan—took me in, with the intention of giving me whatever ease they could and then a place in their family cemetery. Living—dying—it didn't matter to me—but it must have mattered to God. I tried to let go of this life, but He wouldn't let me. When I became aware enough, I realized no one there knew my name. My identity had gotten lost in the battle and in that terrible retreat south. In my shame and in my rage at Samuel's death, I didn't tell them who I really was." He paused to look at Maria, who was openly weeping now.

"I said there was no one they could write to. It was a way out, a way to escape from a thing I could not bear, and I took it. I took it and I *lived* it, until the day came when I couldn't live it any longer.

"There is a church mission in New York City—in an often violent and unruly part of the city known as the Bowery. The mission is called Rising Hope, and it is their vocation to reach out to men like myself. The lost ones. The hopeless ones. The war-scarred ones who survived but know they don't deserve it and can't understand why.

"I was making my living by prizefighting there in the Bowery—illegal, bare-knuckle fights on the river barges beyond the reach of the law, where poor men and powerful men alike—and their women—came to gamble on my ability to beat another human being into the ground. I was good at this…trade, but I was not good at anything else. I knew that what I had become was despicable, but I didn't stop.

"A man can live by the sword only so long, and then he will die by the sword. Men who had bet heavily on one of my opponents took exception to my ability to win, and they did their best to keep me from ever winning again.

"The churchmen from Rising Hope found me. They picked me up out of the gutter, and they took me in. They looked after me until I could look after myself. And all they asked in return was that while I was there, I try to help the men around me who were worse off than I was.

"And so I did. Little by little. I helped in the kitchen at first, because I couldn't bear the company of others. And then one day I saw a man there who was trying to hide from his pain just as I had been trying to hide from mine. I *knew* what he was feeling—his despair and his anger—because I had felt the same. I was also coming to realize how pointless running away from it was. It was always there. Nothing took it away. Not drink. Not violence. Nothing.

"I spoke to him. Later, I spoke to another despairing man. Then another and another, until—

"It was like the hymn. I 'was blind, but now I see.' In reaching out to others, I found a way to live again. I had been on a long and terrible journey to get to that very place without even knowing it, and I thought I was alone every step of the way. But I wasn't alone. *He* was there— and had been all along. He was on the battlefield when Samuel died. He was on the river barges and He was with me in the gutter. Only I couldn't see Him because I wasn't looking for Him. My awareness of His presence came so slowly that I barely noticed—but it was no less profound to me than Saul's having been struck blind. Like Saul, I had been traveling this world with death in my heart until one day it was gone.

"I have asked God for His forgiveness for my many sins, and I believe I have received it. But before I can begin my new vocation, before I can presume to help others, I need to ask for your forgiveness as well. I want all of you to know—especially you, Maria—that I am truly sorry for the pain my weakness and my deception has caused you. And I want to thank those of you here who helped to take care of my family when I could not. I'm home now—truly home in body and in spirit—and it is my hope that I can begin to repay the debt I owe.

"For the time being, I will be staying in the summer kitchen—" he looked at Max "—on Colonel Woodard's property. We have all suffered through a terrible war, and we must continue to help each other as best we can. I want you to know that my door will be open.

"Now I want to ask you to remember God's words from a passage from the Book of Joel," Robert said, knowing that for some present in the congregation, what he was about to quote would no doubt border on an act of sedition. He looked at Kate again before he read it. She was looking up at him and clutching her handkerchief. Had the sad tale of his past seven years affected her that much? No, he decided. He could hear the long wail of a train whistle approaching, and her letter was waiting.

"'And I will restore to you the years that the locust hath eaten…'" he said, his voice once again strong. "'And ye shall eat in plenty, and be satisfied, and praise the name of the Lord your God…and my people shall *never* be ashamed.' May all of us recall these words and have hope."

Robert stepped down from the lectern, but instead of taking his seat, he walked down the center aisle. He had said what he wanted to say, and he had every intention of leaving now, but men and women alike reached out to him as he passed. Some of the women were crying. Maria came out of the pew where she was sitting and embraced him. Joe and Jake grabbed him around his legs.

And Warrie Hansen stood in the vestibule.

He would have gone to her, but more and more people left their seats and crowded around him. He shook hands, accepted the pats on the back and received, with as much dignity as he could muster, the unrestrained hugs from people who still saw him as the boy they'd once known.

When he finally reached the vestibule, Warrie was no

longer there. He could hear Reverend Lewis hurriedly end the service, which for all intents and purposes had already ended. Maria waited just outside the church doors with Joe and Jake chasing each other around and around and Robbie soundly asleep on her shoulder. He expected to see his brother-in-law as well, because the Bible passage from Joel must have sounded to him like a call for the South to rise again. But it hadn't been that at all. He had wanted to encourage the people he'd known all his life to have hope and to let go of the past and build again on the ruins of the country they had loved.

Maria reached up to touch his cheek. "I'm very proud of you," she said. "Father would have been, too."

He nodded, but he was still trying to see if Warrie was somewhere in the crowd.

"Will you escort Kate and Mrs. Justice home?" she asked. "The children and I are going to wait with Max at the train station until he leaves."

She was looking at him so hard.

"What is it?" he asked.

"It's going to be better now," she said. "For us both."

"I need to talk to Warrie," he said. He was not yet ready to consider "better" as a possibility.

"Yes, you do. There's Kate. I think you'd better catch up with her."

He gave her a half smile. "And I think you're afraid I'm in trouble with your husband and you want me several yards in the other direction."

"Robert Markham," she said in mock surprise. "Whatever do you mean?"

He kissed her cheek, and walked toward Kate and ultimately Mrs. Justice. The weak sun that had been evident earlier this morning had completely gone. The sky was heavy and gray, and a cold wind blew out of the north.

Spring would come quickly here, once it gained a foothold, but that time clearly hadn't arrived yet.

"Are you not going to see your brother off?" Robert asked Kate when he caught up with her.

"No, I've said my goodbyes. He needs some time with Maria and the children before he goes."

They both stopped to wait for Mrs. Justice, but she shooed them on, and they began walking again. In silence.

"Thank you," Kate said when they were nearly in sight of the Markham—now Woodard—house.

"For what?"

"For not asking me...anything. I don't think I could bear any questions."

"There's nothing I need to ask," he said. "I can see how you are."

She looked at him quizzically.

"You haven't slept. And you aren't going to rest easy until you know how Harrison is."

She gave a hushed sigh. "It was a job well done," she said after a time. "Your sermon."

"Well, it wasn't quite a sermon. It was more a belated confession."

"It must have been very hard for you."

"I've done harder things."

"I doubt that," she said.

"Does Mrs. Justice know about Harrison's letter?" he asked quietly.

"No one knows—except you."

Kate didn't say anything more. She walked along, completely lost in her thoughts. She dreaded the long afternoon that stretched before her. She dreaded the slow crawl of days it would take for her letter to reach John in Philadelphia and then to hear something in return. All she could do in the meantime was worry—that John wouldn't take her seriously, that something bad was happening to Harrison and her letter would arrive too late to prevent it. And all the while she was completely aware that just being with Robert Markham brought her a kind of ease and that it would be much worse for her if he were not here.

She realized that he had dropped back to speak to Mrs. Justice, and she stopped and waited for them both.

"It's time," Robert said when he and Mrs. Justice caught up.

"Time?" Kate asked.

"For you to learn to build a fire."

"What?" she said, thinking she had to have misunderstood.

"It's time for you to learn to build a fire. Right now—when the boys are out of the house. We wouldn't want to give them any ideas. Mrs. Justice agrees. Don't you, Mrs. Justice?"

"I do, Robbie," she said, smiling at them both.

"See?" he said. "If you would both be so kind as to bear with me, you, Miss Woodard, will soon learn everything there is to know about managing a hearth. The cookstove comes later."

"I think not," she said, certain that she wasn't about to participate.

"It won't take long."

"Robert—"

"I believe learning something is the best way to pass the time when it hangs heavy. And…"

Kate waited for him to continue. "And what?" she asked.

"And this is something you yourself said you needed to learn."

Kate looked at him, then frowned. "I think I'd do better learning not to talk to myself around seemingly unconscious men."

"I agree," Robert said. "But since you did, and I now know about this terrible shortcoming and I am fully prepared to remedy it, what else can you do?"

"What, indeed," Kate said. "Where will this fire building take place?"

"Where do you think, Mrs. Justice?"

"I think Bud's sitting room would be a good place. The logs have burned out and need to be redone and a new fire started. Maria will likely want to be in there once the Colonel has left for New Bern. It gives her comfort, you know."

Yes, Kate thought. *And Mrs. Justice, as well...*

The three of them trooped into the house and up the stairs to old Mr. Markham's sitting room.

"Come over here," Robert said, motioning for Kate to come close to the hearth.

She took off her hat, her coat and gloves and did as he asked.

"It looks as if the fire is out. But it isn't. That's because the embers were covered in ashes, so when I stir them up again, I'm going to find they're still smoldering and will flame up when I—you—add kindling. Pay attention now. This is how a fire should be laid. Ashes at least an inch or two past the andirons—you don't want a draft of air getting under the logs."

"Why not?"

"A draft of air will make the logs burn through too fast. That's better than no fire at all, but you have to keep tending it. You want a fire that will burn slow and steady and keep the room warm without making it too hot and risking a fire in the chimney."

"What if there aren't any ashes?"

"Then you use sand. Not dirt—sand."

Kate had no idea where to find sand, but she didn't say so. She heard the train whistle suddenly give one long blast, and her thoughts went immediately to Harrison.

"You see the logs here in the wood box are different sizes? Kate?" he prompted because her attention had wandered and she wasn't listening.

"Yes. I do," she answered, forcing herself to look at the contents of the wood box. The train whistle blew again.

"A large log goes in the back, up against the brick. A smaller one goes on top of it. A third log, one that's not as big as the big one or as small as the small one, goes in the front, as far forward as you can get it and still keep it on the andirons."

"Wait!" Kate said when he was about to lay the logs on the hearth. "If I'm the one learning, I'll do it."

"You'll get your dress dirty," he said.

"I have more than two now. Kindly move aside."

She had to struggle to get the largest log into place— somehow she'd never realized how heavy wood could be. But she managed. Placing the other two was much easier.

"Now what?" she asked.

"Now we start the fire—between the back log and the fore log. Get some kindling—those small flat pieces there. That's kindling. Take the shovel and uncover the coals, put a few pieces of the kindling on it. Give it a puff of air from the bellows. Keep adding kindling, a little at a time, until the fire is burning well enough to add a small log. Then place some more kindling so the log will catch fire. Then situate another log. Let it catch fire, too, then put on another one until you've got several logs burning in the middle. And that's it."

"How do I keep the fire going?"

"Just add whatever size log has burned up—that will be the ones in the middle mostly. Then the fore log and the small one on top of the back log. It'll take a while for the back log to go. Use the poker to get a new back log into place so you don't get burned."

"Anything else I need to know?"

"Don't set the house on fire?" he suggested.

"What an excellent idea. Anything else?"

"Wash your hands after you've handled the logs. Sometimes they've had poison ivy vines wrapped around them and it will get on your hands. You don't want that."

Kate looked at him. "No," she said, agreeably. But she realized suddenly how sad they both were. She also realized what he'd been doing by insisting that she have this household lesson. He was trying to keep her occupied, trying to give her at least a few moments respite from her worry about Harrison. She abruptly looked away, and she began to follow his instructions to the letter, cajoling the flames with kindling until she had four small logs burning brightly in the center. When he was satisfied that everything was as it should be, they both stood.

"That's a very fine—"

"Robbie," Mrs. Justice interrupted from where she had been standing by the window. "There are men waiting at the summer kitchen. There must be a dozen."

Robert looked out. It had started to rain steadily. "I said my door would be open. I'd better go down."

"Wait, Robbie," Mrs. Justice said. She pointed off to the side.

When he looked out the window again, he could see

Warrie Hansen standing among the trees, the rain beating down on her.

"I'm going to go speak to her," he said, but Mrs. Justice caught him by the arm.

"You wait here," she said. "If she's here to talk to you, I'll bring her to you."

Mrs. Justice gave Kate a worried look and hurried away. In a moment Kate heard the front door open and Mrs. Justice calling Warrie Hansen's name.

"I'll go let the others into the summer kitchen," Kate said. "Before they follow Warrie in."

"Yes. Good," Robert said. "And build them a fire."

"What?"

"You know how, so do it."

Kate stood looking at him. He was challenging her to put her brand-new skill to good use—already—and she was going to take him up on it.

"All right, I will."

"And don't forget to wash your hands."

"I'll remember," she said. She hesitated a moment longer, then went downstairs; Warrie Hansen was just coming in the front doorway with Mrs. Justice, her face haggard, her eyes red from weeping.

"I'm wanting to talk to him," she said to Mrs. Justice, and Mrs. Justice nodded.

Kate stood out of the way as they walked toward the stairs.

"Maria and the boys will be home before long," Mrs. Justice said.

"I ain't planning on taking long."

"I think you should take as long as you need, Warrie," Mrs. Justice said with a firmness that was surprising. "And I think you should plan on staying. You have a job to do here with those rascally boys. I just wanted you to know that the children aren't here now. Robbie is in Bud's sitting room. Close the door when you go in, if you will."

Kate could hear Warrie's progress down the hallway, and Robert must have come out to meet her.

"What about my girl?" Warrie said. "I didn't hear you say you was sorry for what happened to her. Why ain't you sorry for *that,* Robert Markham? When you decided you'd play dead, you all but took her with you, you know that, don't you? And you don't say one thing."

The door closed, and Kate couldn't hear any more. She stood for a moment, then headed for the back of the house. She hurried through the back door to the path that led to the summer kitchen, all but running because the rain was coming harder.

The men were clearly surprised to see the colonel's sister running around in the rain. She opened the summer kitchen door for them. "Do go in," she said. "Please," she added when they hesitated. "Robert should be here soon. I hope you won't mind waiting."

"No, miss," one of them said. "Being in the army gets a body used to that kind of thing."

Kate followed them in. There were only a few chairs, but the men didn't seem to mind. After a moment most of them began sitting on the floor. Kate looked around as Mrs. Justice came in with a bag of coffee and a tray full of stacked tin cups.

"The coffee grinder's over there on that shelf, Wiley," she said to one of the men. "If you'd fetch it for me." She sat the cups and the sack on the table where the chaplain had lain earlier. "I understand soldiers have their own way of making coffee, so I'm going to turn it all over to you. Here are the beans. Wiley's got the grinder—"

"He don't know what to do with it, though, do you, Wiley?" one of the men said, making Wiley grin.

"The pot is over there," Mrs. Justice said, smiling. "And there's the water bucket and plenty of cups..."

She gave Kate a pointed look, and Kate went immediately to the hearth. She recognized the configuration of the logs and ashes immediately. She could do this; she was certain.

Mostly certain.

She supposedly didn't have to worry about anything but resurrecting the smoldering embers that were presumably under the ashes.

And so they were. There was plenty of kindling, and in no time at all she had a blaze burning. She smiled to herself, feeling more useful than she had since—ever. But her sense of satisfaction only lasted a moment until her worry about Harrison returned.

"Now," Mrs. Justice said. "There's a nice fire for you. If you'll excuse us, Miss Woodard and I will go back to the house now. Robbie should be here soon."

"Much obliged, Mrs. Justice, Miss Woodard," they said, more or less in unison.

"I made a big batch of buckwheat cakes yesterday," Mrs. Justice said as they walked down the slate path to the house. "I'll give them time to get their coffee going, then I'll take a platter and some molasses out to them."

"No, I'll do it," Kate said. "You shouldn't be out in the rain."

"Oh, thank you, my dear. I would appreciate that. This kind of weather makes these old bones ache."

They both stopped just inside the kitchen and listened. Kate could hear a murmur of voices coming from old Mr. Markham's sitting room, but no actual words.

"I hope—" Kate said. She stopped, because she didn't know quite what she hoped. She could only imagine what a difficult day this must be for him, and it was far from over. She sighed. She just wanted everything to work out all right for him.

And Eleanor, she thought. She had no business forgetting about Eleanor.

She realized suddenly that Mrs. Justice was watching her closely.

"Come let's sit in the kitchen," Mrs. Justice said. "It's warm there, and we'll be out of the way. There's coffee left from breakfast on the stove. And my buckwheat cakes are in the warming oven. Let's have ourselves another feast."

"Yes," Kate said, forcing herself to smile. "Let's."

After they'd eaten, Kate took the remaining buckwheat cakes—a heaping platter—more than enough for the men in the summer kitchen to have at least one—and headed out the back door, struggling to hang on to a jug of molasses as well. She could smell the aroma of hot coffee before she was halfway down the path.

Fire must still be burning, she thought, pleased.

One of the men saw her coming and held the door open for her. All of them were clearly happy to see her bringing something for them to eat.

"If you see Robert, you can tell him to take his time," one of the men said as she set the buckwheat cakes and the molasses on the table, and she and the others laughed.

She was still smiling as she made her way back to the house. Robert was standing by the well, apparently waiting for her. He looked so…resigned—she supposed that would be the best word for it. It was as if he had encountered a formidable situation he could not change, and he had no choice but to accept it.

She didn't ask him if he was all right. She didn't ask him about Warrie or if she had told him where Eleanor had gone.

"They're still out there, I take it," he said when she was close enough.

"Yes. They're eating Mrs. Justice's buckwheat cakes and molasses."

He gave a slight smile. "We used to talk about her buckwheat cakes on the march sometimes. Hers were the best in the county. We'd remember all about when and where we'd eaten them and how many we had—and make ourselves miserable."

He looked toward the summer kitchen. Kate could feel him trying to gather his thoughts—or perhaps let go of them. Whatever had happened with Warrie Hansen, she thought that he didn't want to take it with him when he talked to the men who were out there waiting.

"Thank you for doing this, Kate," he said quietly.

"I built a fire," she said, hoping to make him smile.

He did, and Kate felt as if he had given her a small but incredibly special gift.

Then he took a deep breath and stepped out into the rain. She watched him go, waiting until he went inside the summer kitchen. In only a moment a loud cheer went up. Robert Markham was home at last, and he'd gotten a hero's welcome.

She was on her way upstairs when the carriage bringing Maria and the children home arrived. Sergeant Major Perkins came in carrying the baby in one arm and the civilian mail pouch that would contain the family's personal mail in the other. Private Castine had Joe and Jake slung over each shoulder as if they were sacks of flour, running the last few steps to the door to make them giggle as only little boys can.

"Send them young'uns over here to me," Warrie Hansen called from the far end of the hall. "We got to get them out of their Sunday best while we still can."

Castine deftly put both boys on their feet, and they dashed down the hallway to Warrie.

"Sergeant Major, bring that one along, too," Warrie called.

Maria was just coming in the door, and she stopped dead.

"What?" Kate asked.

"Well, I hardly know where to start. Warrie's here, for one thing..."

"She came and talked to Robert a little while ago. I didn't realize she hadn't left—he's out in the summer kitchen."

Maria was still looking at her. "And you're..."

"I'm what?"

"Well, you don't look like you did at church," Maria said, trying not to grin.

"Why?" Kate asked. There was no mirror in the downstairs hallway where she could see for herself.

"You haven't been shoveling coal, have you?"

Kate looked down at the front of her dress. It was heavily streaked with wood ash.

"Face, too," Maria advised her, grinning openly now.

"It's your brother's fault. He has been teaching me how to build a fire," Kate said.

"Why?" Maria asked.

"Mostly because I didn't know how—and please don't look at me as if my sanity was suspect. It's not my fault I was brought up useless."

"Kate, you are the least useless person I know," Maria said kindly.

"Then I've certainly got you fooled. Anyway, a vote was taken and I lost. Robert and Mrs. Justice outvoted me, so I had a lesson. I'm happy to say I can now officially build a hearth fire."

"I should hope so," Maria said, still teasing. "Given the way you look."

"Actually I've lit not one but two fires since the church service," Kate said. "And the fire brigade hasn't had to be summoned—so far," she added in an effort not to tempt fate, and they laughed together when—Kate was certain—neither of them felt like it. But she and Maria knew the importance of at least trying to find a better humor. Doggedly making the effort had likely gotten them both through difficult times in their lives. This would be a somber house until Max came home and until Kate knew for certain that her letter had reached Philadelphia.

A train whistle sounded in the distance, and they both turned their heads in that direction, the brief respite from the disquiet that threatened to overwhelm them rapidly fading.

The boys—shoeless and half-undressed now—came racing down the hallway despite Warrie's objections. It was clear that they had no intention of returning to her. They ignored her as long as they dared, giggling as they circled Maria and Kate both, and then running back in the direction they'd come. Kate couldn't help but smile at the audacity of young male children. Had Harrison done things like this when he was their age? Had he ever had the opportunity for exuberance? She had always wondered. John very likely had, because he was as recalcitrant as they came, but Harrison was nothing like John. Mrs. Howe had wanted him seen and not heard and he would always have done his best to please her—until now.

"I think I'd better put on my play clothes, too," Kate said, and she went upstairs to repair what damage she could to her face and her dress—but not before she checked on the fire in old Mr. Markham's sitting room.

It was burning just as Robert said it would—slow and steady—and the room was warm and comfortable.

She smiled slightly when she returned to her room. A fire burned there, as well. Castine had beaten her to it.

Kate washed her face and hands, then she changed her clothes, deciding she really would put on the dress she always wore whenever she played with the boys—or whenever her trunks went somewhere without her. She stood for a moment looking at her sad reflection in the washstand mirror, then closed her eyes.

"I'm afraid again," she whispered. "I want to believe You're here, just the way Robert says You are. He believes You're always with us, no matter what. I want to believe that, too. Help me."

She sighed, and turned away.

The house had grown quiet, and Kate assumed that Mrs. Justice, and Warrie and the children, were all settling down to take their customary afternoon naps. Maria would likely be napping, as well. She was going to have another child, and Kate knew from experience how fatigued Maria must be in these early days.

Kate moved to the window where she could see the summer kitchen. After a moment she thought she could hear…singing.

Yes, she decided. Robert and the men in the summer kitchen were singing a hymn—"Amazing Grace." She could hear the melody quite clearly now, if not the words. They had sung together before, she thought. Perhaps as boys, and as young men and as soldiers.

She took a deep breath, her mind suddenly filled with the most disturbing aspect of Harrison's letter.

Pray for me.

"I am, sweet boy," she whispered. She moved to the bed and stretched out. She had been so long without sleep that it was a relief to lie down, and yet she still wanted to get up and pace the room, as if that would somehow help. Eventually she reached for the quilt at the foot of the bed and pulled it over her, and—incredibly—she slept.

Chapter Eleven

"Robert has company," Mrs. Justice whispered to keep Warrie from hearing her.

Kate kept stirring finely chopped onion and bacon into the cornbread batter Robert had Mrs. Justice teaching her to make. Kate was fully aware that Robert was bent on keeping her busy as a way of making time pass, and in the interval since her fire-building lesson, she had learned all manner of things pertaining to the kitchen and the household. Or so it would seem to the casual onlooker—and there were several. The most diligent observer had been Valentina, who seemed to pop up at the most unexpected times without ever saying why. It seemed to Kate that she only wanted to know what Kate was doing, and where Robert was while she was doing it.

Kate didn't have to ask Mrs. Justice who Robert's company today might be. Men came to the summer kitchen all the time, sometimes just one and sometimes a half dozen or so. She had even seen the chaplain arrive under his own power—twice. Robert always spoke with them, and when he did, Kate and Mrs. Justice would bring coffee. Today it looked as if some of the men's wives or sisters or mothers had come along, as well. Robert's reputation was growing, and so was the strain on the household schedule. There were constant disruptions to the sergeant major's routine—and therefore everyone else's—despite Robert's best intentions. After the second week he sat up specific times for prayer meetings—Thursday and Saturday early evenings so as not to conflict with the other churches in town. And, aside from just bringing the refreshments, Kate found herself staying to hear him speak, keeping well in the background so as not to be a distraction. Her brother was the occupation commander, something very few people in this town would be able to ignore if she were too obvious.

Thanks to Mrs. Justice, Kate was beginning to know, at least by sight, many of the people who showed up—and how they figured into Robert Markham's early life. They were merchants he'd run errands for after school, church friends, distant relatives by marriage, old classmates, Sunday School teachers who had thrown up their hands more than once at some of his antics, but all of them were apparently finding some degree of comfort and good sense in what he had to say.

Surprisingly—or perhaps not—Valentina had shown up for a recent meeting, but whether it was for a personal spiritual need or whether she was bent on finding herself another "adventure," Kate couldn't say. Or perhaps Valentina had come on her mother's behalf, to keep Mrs. Kinnard informed so that she would know if—when—she needed to put a stop to all this.

A much bigger surprise was the evening Mrs. Russell came. After the service many of the Confederate veterans who were present gathered respectfully around her, speaking to her of James Darson and their regard for him. It was as if they had been wary of doing so before, because of her intense grief, but now that she had come to hear Robert—and in her lost son's absence—she would henceforth belong to all of them.

Kate made a point of spending time with Maria in old Mr. Markham's sitting room in the evening because she had promised Max she would be available to his wife, and because—if she were truthful—she knew that Robert might come to visit with his sister before she retired for the night. Maria felt better when he was near, and so did Kate. Stronger somehow. More hopeful.

But this night Maria had gone to bed early, and only Kate was sitting by the fire when he came up the back stairs.

"Your handiwork?" he asked, nodding at the hearth.

"It is, actually," she said. "I'm afraid Sergeant Major Perkins finds my new skill very unsettling."

"He hasn't forbidden you to do it?"

"Well, not yet. And so far I've been able to beat Castine to it enough to keep my hand in."

"Poor Castine," he said, and she smiled. She was looking directly into his eyes, and she shouldn't. She knew that, but she didn't look away.

"I was…surprised," she began, because this was the first opportunity she'd had to speak to him alone.

"About what?"

"About Warrie—that she decided to return to the house."

"I coerced her into doing it."

"How so?"

"She's a good woman—a kind woman—and your brother told me that Maria was having another child."

Kate frowned, and managed to refrain from saying how surprised—shocked—she was that Max would have told him such a personal thing.

"He wanted to make sure I understood what my responsibilities were while he was gone," Robert said as if he had read her thoughts.

"And do you? Understand?"

"I do. And I passed some of them on to Warrie. I told her that Maria needed her—which she does—and that she and I had to find a way not to cause Maria any more worry than she already has."

"It seems to be working."

"So far—if I stay out of her way. She's a long way from forgiving me."

It was Kate's opinion that forgiveness in this situation would be Eleanor's prerogative, but she didn't say so.

"I...take it you've had no answer to your letter," he said without warning, watching her closely as he said it.

Kate shook her head. "I should have heard by now—if John takes what I've said seriously."

"He will."

"You can't know that."

"I know you well enough. And so does he. *I* would take you seriously."

She felt the sudden sting of tears and looked away.

After a long moment she took a deep breath and asked the question she'd been wondering about.

"Did Warrie tell you where Eleanor has gone?"

"No. She thinks I'm not fit to know."

"I'm sorry."

"I think..."

"What?" Kate asked when he didn't continue.

"If Eleanor lets Warrie know where she is, then Warrie will likely tell her I'm here. I just have to...wait and then take it from there."

She gave a quiet sigh. That was exactly what she herself was doing—waiting for something to happen, and then she would take it from there. But the waiting was so *hard,* and most days it was all she could do not to fall back into hiding to solve her problems, hiding so she would have the privacy to weep.

Kate looked at him. "Will you pray with me?" she asked. "For Harrison."

As he had before, he moved his chair to face hers and held out his hands.

"Are you going to tell me what's on your mind or are you going to keep staring at me?" Robert asked, because Maria clearly hadn't insisted on coming to the summer kitchen to join him for breakfast without some—as yet unknown—purpose.

"Nothing is on my mind," she said in a way that would cause any man who had grown up with a sister to realize immediately that such a statement was far and away from the actual truth.

"If you say so," he said, going back to eating the eggs and bacon she had prepared but didn't care to eat herself.

"More coffee?" she asked him after a moment, and when he looked up she was grinning from ear to ear.

"Yes, thank you," he said, ignoring her obvious mirth.

When she'd poured the coffee, she moved the cup back in his direction—and she was smiling again.

"I'm wondering when I got to be so entertaining," he said.

"I'm wondering when you got to be a preacher—despite what you said in church that Sunday."

"I'm not a preacher—yet."

"But you intend to be."

He looked at her. "I… Yes."

"And you're pining over Eleanor."

"No, Maria. I am not pining over her, though I freely admit that I would like to know that she's all right. I will always care about her. She and I were engaged to be married."

"Feeling guilty, then?"

"For what specifically?"

"For 'dying,' of course."

"I'll always feel guilty about that. I hurt the people I loved. But Eleanor wouldn't deliberately ruin her own reputation because she thought I died. Eleanor would come to my memorial service in a red dress."

"I did think it was something like that at first—that whatever scandalous thing she did or didn't do was because she was angry with you—for dying and leaving her."

"But you changed your mind."

"Well, I still think it has something to do with you. I just don't know what it is."

"And neither do I, until I can ask her."

"Aha!" she said, as if she'd uncovered some dark secret he'd been carrying.

"Now what does that mean?"

"You actually don't know, do you?" she said, leaning toward him, smiling still.

"I wouldn't ask if I did."

"What do you think of Kate?"

"What do I think of her?" he said, startled because she had veered off in a completely different direction.

"Don't ask what I ask. Answer."

"I like her," he said easily—because it was true.

"She likes you, too."

"Does she?" he said, surprised by the remark.

"Well, so she said."

"When did she say that?"

"Weeks ago—before she got to know you."

Robert glanced at her. She was teasing him now.

"Right after you came back and disrupted all our lives," she said to qualify her remark. "And you can frown all you like. It doesn't change a thing."

"Maria, you do know I haven't the slightest idea what we're talking about here—"

"Then, dear brother, I will tell you," Maria said, getting up from her chair.

"I wish you would," he said. "And soon."

"You want to be a preacher."

"I do," he said agreeably.

"And you like Kate."

"Yes."

"And she's been…helpful to you when you have your prayer meetings."

"And Mrs. Justice, as well—" he began.

"It's perfectly clear then," Maria said, interrupting.

"What is?"

"Preachers need wives, Robert, and you—my dear, *dear* brother—are grooming her to become one. Yours."

"No, I'm not," he said as soon as he'd recovered enough from Maria's assertion to respond. "'Grooming,' as you put it, is not the reason I'm—"

"Oh, I know you think that," Maria said, dismissing the idea with a wave of her hand. "Max told me Kate is worried about Harrison, and I can see you're trying to help her by keeping her occupied—which is an excellent idea. But you should realize that that isn't the *only* reason. I've seen the way you look at her—and believe me it's not the way you looked at Eleanor. Kate Woodard is important to you. You would have had a much harder time being home again if she weren't here, now wouldn't you?"

She didn't wait for an answer. She smiled prettily and went out the door.

* * *

Kate stood outside the door for a moment, not wanting to cause Maria to lose her place with her knitting.

"There you are," Maria said when she realized Kate was there. "I've been waiting for you."

"Why?" Kate asked, but Maria was counting stitches and didn't answer. Kate glanced around the sitting room. No Robert. In fact she hadn't seen him all day.

"I should learn to knit," Kate said, more to herself than to Maria.

Warrie was putting the boys to bed in the nursery wing. She could hear her singing the song that was, as far as Warrie was concerned, a lullaby, her voice slightly brittle and off-key:

Go tell Aunt Rosie,
Go tell Aunt Rosie,
Go tell Aunt Rosie
The old gray goose is dead.

"I could teach you sometime," Maria said. "Right now I need some company. Come sit down. Mrs. Justice has gone to Mrs. Kinnard's house."

"On a visit or was she summoned?"

"I'm not sure," Maria said. "Whichever it is, the refreshments will be worth it."

Kate sat down in the nearest rocking chair, clutching the book she'd brought with her, the one she had no intention of reading, the one that always held Harrison's photograph. She was so restless. The more time that passed since she'd written that letter to John, the less she was able to sleep. The truth of the matter was that she couldn't remember quite what she'd said. Had she sounded legitimately concerned or completely overwrought?

"Has the mail pouch arrived?" Maria asked, looking up from her knitting.

"Not yet," Kate said. "There must not be any personal mail today."

"No," Maria said. She was clearly disappointed that she wouldn't have a letter from Max to read when she retired. And it wasn't only letters he sent. Kate was more than a little surprised by the romantic gestures her brother made via military postal delivery. Just last week he'd sent Maria some violets he'd dug up from a riverbank along the Neuse and potted in a tin can with a garish yellow Pie Meat label. The can had been wrapped in several layers of wet muslin and placed in a small wooden box before it left New Bern on the train. Incredibly the violets had arrived still fresh and beautiful.

"Is Robert not coming to visit this evening?" Kate suddenly asked, not caring how it sounded. She wanted to know, and if Maria thought the inquiry inappropriately forward, then so be it.

"I'm glad of your friendship with my brother," Maria said instead of answering Kate's bold question.

Kate made no comment, mostly because she didn't know what to think of the remark.

"Did you…know Max had spoken to him?" Maria said next.

"Yes," Kate answered.

"You did?"

"Yes. Robert told me."

"Robert *told* you?" Maria said, clearly surprised, if not out-and-out astounded.

"It's natural that Max would be worried about you—" Kate hesitated because of the expression on Maria's face.

"Natural?" Maria asked.

"Max wanted Robert to know about the baby—so he

would understand what his responsibilities were while Max was gone—or that's how Robert put it."

"But that's not what I meant at all."

"What did you mean, then?"

"I meant that Max talked to Robert about a complaint he'd had from one of his officers."

"What officer?"

"I don't know what officer. Max didn't tell me his name. The complaint had to do with you."

Kate looked at her blankly. "I don't understand."

"This officer felt Robert was being much too familiar where you are concerned, and he thought Max should know about it."

"Max never mentioned anything like that to— Oh. I just realized. One of Max's officers cornered me in the downstairs hallway. He'd been drinking. He kept insisting that he would come here to visit me while Max was away. He was sure I needed the company of 'my own kind.' I couldn't get away from him, and Robert intervened. I'm afraid I let the man think that I might mention his behavior to Max. I suppose he wanted to give Max his version of what happened before I did. This is so aggravating," Kate added.

"What is?"

"My brother—and yours. I don't like being in the middle of some…incident, and not know anything about it. And I'm sure Robert didn't like being put in the wrong for something he didn't do. They didn't come to blows or anything, did they?"

"No. Or if they did, Max didn't tell me."

"Didn't Robert say anything to you about it?"

"No, nothing. According to Max, Robert said that your friendship was very important to him and he had the utmost respect for you and would never do anything to jeopardize it—and Max was satisfied."

Very important? Utmost respect?

Kate had no idea what either of those terms actually meant.

"Kate," Maria said, and she looked at her sister-in-law. "I think I should tell you what I think about this… friendship."

"All right," Kate said.

But Maria hesitated. Warrie had stopped singing, and neither Private Castine nor Sergeant Major Perkins seemed to be wandering about on the ground floor. The house was quiet for a change. Too quiet.

"Maria, what is it?"

"I know my brother very well. I think I even understand why he didn't come home until now. But he's— " Maria stopped and began gathering up her knitting and putting it carefully into her yarn basket. "I've already been an overzealous busybody once today. It's not very becoming."

"For heaven's sake, tell me!"

"All right, I will. Kate, what is 'friendship' to one person may not be friendship to another."

"What do you mean? I have no designs on Robert." Because Robert is *safe,* she nearly said—safe for her to have as a friend, just as she was safe for him—because of Eleanor Hansen.

"I don't mean you. I mean him. I think he has deeper feelings than even he realizes. For you," she added.

"He loves Eleanor," Kate said quietly.

"Yes. But that has nothing to do with this."

Kate opened her mouth to say something, then closed it again.

"I just don't want either of you to be hurt," Maria said.

"Men can be so unobservant sometimes. I think you will see where the situation is heading before he will. If you're privy to what I already suspect and it turns out that I'm right, then you'll be…prepared to handle it. As you said, it's aggravating being in the middle of a situation you know nothing about."

Maria stood.

"I truly am glad of your friendship with Robert, Kate, whatever 'friendship' turns out to be. Think about what I've said. Good night. Pleasant dreams."

Think about it? How could she *not* think about it?

Kate stayed in the sitting room, her mind darting from Robert to Harrison and back again, until she couldn't sit still any longer. She got up from the chair and walked to the window. The summer kitchen windows were dark. Either Robert was not there or he was already asleep.

Very important.

Utmost respect.

Friendship.

Friendship was all that she'd wanted.

But even as that thought formed, she knew it wasn't true. Friendship was the only thing she could allow.

She sighed and went downstairs. Perkins had moved Max's campaign table from the sitting room to a corner of the foyer the day Max departed for New Bern. It was where Perkins left the private mail pouch when there was one. Kate glanced in that direction out of habit, expecting nothing to be there this late in the day, and she was not disappointed. The conversation with Maria had left her too agitated to even think of sleeping, so she wandered toward the kitchen. Mrs. Justice was sitting at the work-table, apparently just returned from her visit, because her bonnet was hanging by its ribbons on the back of one chair and her cloak was draped over another.

"Would you like some tea, my dear," Mrs. Justice asked kindly—a little too kindly, Kate thought.

"Yes, please," she said. She sat down in the only remaining chair and rested her elbows on the table, something her mother would have taken great exception to if she'd seen her.

There was already an extra cup and saucer on the table—which made Kate even more suspicious that offering her tea hadn't been accidental. She gave a heavy sigh as Mrs. Justice poured some and handed the cup and saucer to her.

"You mustn't be upset, my dear," Mrs. Justice said. "The effort he's been making—the grooming—is a compliment, really. It shows he has confidence in your potential."

Kate looked at her. "What grooming?"

"Oh," Mrs. Justice said, somewhat taken aback. "The…um…grooming Maria mentioned?" She looked so hopeful that no further questions would be forthcoming that Kate was almost tempted to let the matter drop. Almost.

"Maria didn't say anything about grooming. Have I not been presentable enough for Mrs. Kinnard? Surely that's not what she wanted to see you about. I have all my dresses now—in fact I was thinking of having Mrs. Russell's sister make me one or two more."

"No, no, not your dresses. It's—Robbie."

"You mean the…friendship?" Kate asked, making a wild guess even though she couldn't see any kind of connection at all between "grooming" and "friendship."

"I wasn't talking about a friendship, my dear. I don't know anything about that. I only know that Maria and I agree—about the grooming."

"I must ask you again, Mrs. Justice. What grooming?"

"The grooming Robbie is doing—and having me do. The grooming to make you a suitable preacher's wife."

Kate stared at her. "You—and Robert Markham—are grooming me to be a preacher's wife," she stated carefully to make sure she'd heard right. She tried—and failed—to keep the incredulity out of her voice.

"Yes," Mrs. Justice said happily. "And you're making wonderful progress."

"And who is this preacher I'm being groomed for?" Kate asked.

"Why, Robbie, of course."

"He's looking for a *wife?*"

"Oh, he says not—according to Maria."

"Well, he should know."

Mrs. Justice leaned toward her as if she didn't want anyone to overhear. "We think he hasn't realized it yet."

"Has everybody forgotten he's going to marry Eleanor Hansen?"

"Oh, no. We haven't forgotten. We've decided that isn't going to work out."

"I see," Kate said. "Well—" She took a sip of her tea. "This has certainly been an evening for interesting... conversations."

Chapter Twelve

Kate came downstairs early to see if there would be a mail pouch on the campaign table after all. The table was bare, except for the small polished brass oil lamp Sergeant Major Perkins had added since the last time she'd looked. It, like the table, seemed lost in the all but empty foyer.

She stood for a moment, making a concerted effort to shore up the courage to face another anxious day. She tried not to worry, but she couldn't seem to help herself. Were other mothers—real mothers—able to let go of the apprehension they felt regarding their children's happiness and safety, or was she merely too excitable because she had always been on the fringes of Harrison's life?

She suddenly remembered Mrs. Justice's prayer.

Thy will.

"Thy will," she whispered. "Not mine." And she turned around just in time to see Robert disappearing into the kitchen—backtracking, unless she was very mistaken.

Is he avoiding me?

She had been avoiding him, of course, since all that talk of "grooming" with Mrs. Justice, but it hadn't occurred to her until this moment that he might be doing the same. She waited, trying to determine which way he was going to go, then she hurried out the front door and around the house to the back. When Robert came outside, she was standing on the slate path, planted firmly between him and the summer kitchen.

"Good morning," she said pointedly.

"Good morning," he replied—once he got over his astonishment at finding her there when she'd only just been in the foyer. He seemed not to want to look at her at first, and then he seemed not to want to stop.

She looked back.

"Mrs. Justice said you were grooming me to be a preacher's wife," she said bluntly, and then she waited.

And waited.

He stood there, not exactly surprised by her comment, she thought, but not exactly...*not* surprised, either.

"Did she?" he said finally.

"No," Kate said. "She *said* you were grooming me to be *your* wife."

He took a quiet breath and then another one. Then, after much too long an interval, he nodded. "Good," he said. And he stepped around her and walked away.

Good?

She pursed her lips to say something, but there was no longer anyone around to talk to. He had disappeared into the summer kitchen and closed the door. She wasn't about to follow him, though it was clear that she would have to if she wanted him to elaborate. Follow him. And corner him.

She looked around at the arrival of a horse and rider— a soldier bringing the mail pouch. She went back inside, hurrying through the kitchen and into the hallway. The soldier was already leaving as she reached the foyer; the private mail pouch lay on the campaign table.

Kate opened the pouch, knowing she was usurping Maria's authority. This was her household and it was her duty to see to the mail. Even so, she dumped everything out, searching through a number of envelopes for a letter with a Philadelphia return address. There was none. She gave a sharp sigh of disappointment, then picked up one of the other pieces, a telegram. Her name was on it.

Her pulse pounded in her ears as she tore the envelope open. It was from John.

She read the message quickly, and then again:

H gone when we arrived. Looking for him here. Advise Max he may come south.
John

"Gone?" Kate said aloud. She read the telegram again, more slowly this time. "Who is 'we'?"

Not Mrs. Howe. She had been ill. Her illness was the reason he'd stayed in Philadelphia. It must be Amanda, his wife, she decided. He wouldn't take his mother with him to the school if he could help it, even if she were well now—unless she'd read Kate's letter and insisted. Mrs. Howe was very good at that—insisting.

She abruptly crumpled the telegram in both hands and stood there, eyes closed, trying not to cry. She had believed all along that something was wrong, and what a bitter thing it was to be proved right.

"Did you say something, Miss Kate?" Perkins said behind her.

"No. Nothing," she said in a rush, turning away so he couldn't see her face. She walked quickly down the hallway toward the back of the house, leaving the sergeant major to think whatever he liked.

Her abrupt entry into the kitchen startled one of the

soldier-cooks who hadn't been there on her first pass through, but she made no apology. She was all but running now, and she didn't stop until she was a short distance from the summer kitchen.

I can't do this. I can't go running to Robert.

But even as the thought came into her mind, she knew she was going to do just that.

Robert caught a glimpse of Kate as she rushed head-long from the house. He immediately opened the door for her, but she had stopped dead.

"What's wrong?" he asked, alarmed by the distress he could see on her face. "Kate?"

She came closer but she didn't say anything. She handed him a crumpled telegram. He had to smooth it out to read it.

"Did you tell Perkins about this?" he asked, looking up at her. It was likely that Perkins would read all the incoming telegrams, but if he hadn't, Robert understood enough about the way the occupation worked to know that the sergeant major would need to be informed immediately.

She shook her head.

"Then that's the first thing you have to do—"

"No," she said.

"He already suspects something. Look," Robert said, nodding toward the house. Perkins was standing at the back door. "He's guessed something is wrong. Harrison's brother wanted Max notified, and he's not here. Perkins will have to handle it. Better him than any of the officers I've seen."

Kate looked toward the house again. Sergeant Major Perkins was on the verge of coming down the slate path. "Yes, all right," she said, trying to force herself to think clearly. Of course Perkins would have to be involved; nobody knew that better than she did.

"Mrs. Howe lives in Philadelphia," Kate said.

"Mrs. Howe?"

"Harrison's mother. If he's run away, I don't think he'll go there. She's a very…exacting woman. He'll think he's let her down and he'd be too ashamed. I think he's more likely to come here. To Max."

"And you," Robert said. "Perkins is coming, Give him the telegram." He handed it back to her.

"He may have already read it."

"Even if he has, that's not the face of a man who understands the situation he's found himself in."

"His sack and burn face," Kate said quietly. She took a deep breath and waited for the inevitable.

"Miss Kate," Perkins said as soon as he was close enough. "You know what I told you the night *he* showed up." He nodded in Robert's direction. "My duty is to the Colonel. I need to know what's going on. Now, if you please."

Kate hesitated, then handed him the telegram.

He read it quickly and looked up at her. "Is that Captain Howe's little brother he's talking about?"

"Yes," Kate said, not at all surprised that he had already discerned who "H" might be.

"The telegram doesn't say much. I reckon he's run off from wherever he was."

"Boarding school," Kate said. "He wasn't happy there."

"Well, if he's coming in this direction, how far he gets will depend on how much money he's got and more on whether or not he can hang on to it. There will be all kinds of riffraff wanting to relieve him of whatever he's carrying. If he runs out, he'll be stuck wherever the train stopped. Best thing is to backtrack from here—check with the conductors and with the people who make a living hanging around the whistle-stops." He looked at Robert. "Soldiers looking for him aren't going to find out much from the locals."

"I'll go," Robert said.

"I'm going with you," Kate said.

"No," both men said in unison.

"You'll slow me down, Kate," Robert said, looking into her eyes. "The places I may need to go, I can't take you. It would be better if you stayed here with Maria. There's no point in having her worry about both of us. If he's stuck somewhere along the line, I can find him, and as soon as I do, I'll get word to the sergeant major. Can you send somebody to find the chaplain?" he said to Perkins.

"What, again?"

"If he's sober enough, he can help."

It was clear to Kate that Perkins didn't see how, but he apparently decided to trust Robert's judgment in the matter.

"Castine!" Perkins suddenly yelled over his shoulder, and the well-trained young soldier burst from the back door of the house as if he'd been alert and waiting for just such a summons.

"I need the chaplain here *now*," Perkins told him. "Take two soldiers with you in case he can't walk."

"Yes, Sergeant Major!" Castine said and hurried away.

"Can you get me some paper, Kate?" Robert said. "Drawing paper if you have any or some sheets of stationery. And pencils, or a pen and ink. Or charcoal sticks— and bring Harrison's photograph. The chaplain is an excellent artist—Reverend Lewis showed me some of his work. Maybe he can do some sketches of the photograph, and Perkins can make sure the soldiers who patrol the wagon roads see them."

Kate looked at him doubtfully. Man of the cloth or not, she'd never gotten the impression that the chaplain was an obliging man, drunk or sober.

"I may need to give him with some of Max's whiskey or brandy. I need you to bring the best he's got out here."

Kate's mind was reeling. She felt better that both Robert and Sergeant Major Perkins were so willing to help, but at the same time, it only made the situation seem all too real. And dire.

"Now, Kate," Robert said, putting his hand briefly on her shoulder.

"Yes, all right," she said, and she hurried back to the house. She had drawing paper. There were a number of sheets she'd never used in the writing box Grey had given her. She had to dodge Maria and Mrs. Justice to get upstairs without having to give some kind of explanation for dashing around the house and yard, and once there, she found everything Robert had said he wanted, including a bottle of Max's best cognac. She had no faith whatsoever that the chaplain wouldn't need it, regardless of the state Castine found him in.

When she returned to the summer kitchen, both Robert and Perkins had gone. She waited by the door for a moment, then went inside. She put everything she was carrying on the table and sat down by the fire. She realized that she didn't have the telegram; Perkins must still have it. She supposed that he would be sending the precise wording of the telegram to Max. In fact, that may be where he was now. She couldn't begin to guess where Robert might be.

She looked around the large kitchen. She couldn't tell where Robert slept—a bedroll on the floor perhaps, one that was kept out of sight during the day in case someone who needed to talk to him arrived. There were a few personal touches—books on the mantel, to be precise. The cookstove sat on the stone floor next to the hearth, sharing the chimney via a secondary flue constructed just for that purpose. She hadn't learned to build a fire in a cookstove yet, and looking at it now, the assorted doors and dampers were nothing if not intimidating.

Groomed.

She had never felt less groomed in her life.

The door rattled; Robert had returned, just ahead of Castine and the chaplain, who didn't seem to need any help. Kate supposed that was a good sign—until she saw him. The chaplain was sober, but he was unsteady on his feet. He sat down immediately in a chair at the table. Kate couldn't smell any whiskey on him, but she saw him look at the bottle of cognac. He glanced at her and then at the bottle again. He was about to be bribed, and he knew it, but he made no mention of that or of the bottle of spirits.

"Am I to know why I've been hurried here?" he asked. "Private Castine was less than forthcoming with his explanations…" He glanced in Kate's direction. "Other than his supposition that Colonel Woodard's sister urgently required my presence."

"We do need your help, Chaplain," Robert said, his voice respectful. "Kate, do you have the photograph?"

"Yes," she said, her voice breaking with emotion when she didn't expect it to. She knew her distress was very close to the surface, but she had thought she had it under better control. She took a deep breath and handed the photograph to him.

"It's very important that we find this boy," Robert said. "It would help us if you would make several sketches of him. Reverend Lewis showed me some of your very fine work," he added, causing the chaplain to look at him in surprise.

"A long time ago, I'm afraid," the chaplain said, but he took the photograph, then held it up and looked at it, squinting as he did so. "My eyes—" he began, but his voice was hoarse sounding now. He cleared his throat. "My eyes aren't what they used to be—I need more light."

Robert and Castine slid the table into a patch of sunlight close to the window. The chaplain picked up his chair and placed it in the location he considered the best for what he needed and sat down again. Once again he looked at the photograph, but not without looking at the bottle of cognac first. He licked his lips and took a deep breath.

"Yes," he said after a moment. "You'll only need sketches of the face, and I can do that well enough to give at least some idea of what this young man looks like."

Kate reached for the paper and pencils she'd brought and placed them in front of him.

"No," he said, holding up his hand when she was about to give him the pen and ink, as well. "Is that charcoal? Charcoal will do nicely."

She handed the charcoal sticks to him, and she watched him closely, moving out of his line of sight so as not to distract him. But he seemed a different man now and completely oblivious to her or anything else around him. He concentrated on the photograph of Harrison and began to work, sketching and smudging as he went. It took him no time at all to make several nearly identical drawings of Harrison's face. Kate stared at them. He had caught the boy's wistful sadness with such accuracy that it was all she could do not to weep.

The chaplain rose from his chair. "I take it I'm free to go now?" he said. He glanced at Castine, who did his best—and rightfully so—to look as if none of this had anything whatsoever to do with him.

"Yes," Kate said quickly, because she thought she understood the difficulty the man must be having, being so close to the cognac and its temptation. "I thank you, sir. I won't forget your kindness."

"You are welcome, Miss Woodard," he said. "Robert, I will see you later. I have some things I'd like to discuss. I wish you Godspeed in your search."

Robert picked up the sketches as soon as the chaplain and Castine had gone.

"I'd like to carry the photograph with me," he said. "I'll leave a sketch with Perkins and the rest I'll distribute to the stationmasters along the line. Kate?" he said, apparently because he realized she wasn't listening.

Kate took one more look at Harrison's face, then handed him the photograph.

"Tell me a passage from the Bible that will help me," she said.

"'Cast thy burden upon the Lord, and He shall sustain thee. He shall never suffer the righteous to be moved,'" he said without hesitation.

And if I'm not righteous? What then? she nearly said. She bowed her head.

"Don't waste time worrying, Kate. Pray."

"I'll…try to do that," she said, looking up at him.

"I'll send word when I find him," he said.

"You will find him, won't you?" she asked, her mouth trembling despite all she could do.

He rested his hands on her shoulders. "Kate—"

They both looked around because Perkins was outside, and Kate stepped away. Perkins opened the door and stuck his head in.

"Train'll be here in about thirty minutes," he said. He

tossed Robert a small leather wallet. "Military authorization so you can ride any train, anywhere you need to. There are some signed chits in there, too. You can use them to pay for whatever the boy needs—Colonel Woodard's orders. Miss Kate, Mrs. Colonel Woodard and Mrs. Justice are looking for you."

Kate had no doubt that they were, and likely at his behest. She looked at Robert. "Thank you," she said, her voice barely a whisper.

He nodded.

She took a few steps toward the door, then looked back at him. "God bless you, Robert," she said.

"I'm going to give you some advice, Mr. Markham," she heard Perkins say as she was walking away. She stopped on the pathway to listen.

"Given our violent history, I'm not sure that would be wise," Robert said.

"Maybe not, but you're going to hear it, anyway. Colonel Woodard left his most precious possessions in my care—his family—and that includes Miss Kate. There's not much that goes on in this town that I haven't heard about, and that includes *you*.

"It would be very good sense on your part if you settled things with one lady before you go starting something up with another one—especially if the second lady happens to be my commanding officer's sister. Are you understanding me?"

"I am, Sergeant Major," Robert said. "I've already had this conversation with the colonel."

"Good. We ought not have a problem then. You just do what you said. You find that boy for Miss Kate."

Chapter Thirteen

When, Kate kept thinking after Robert had gone. *When,* not *if.*

Robert meant to find Harrison; she was certain of that. But whether or not he could do it was another matter entirely. She had been spared having to tell Maria and Mrs. Justice what had happened. Sergeant Major Perkins had taken care of that detail, and she was grateful that she would not have to try to manufacture an acceptable degree of distress at having "a young friend of the family" go missing.

Kate sat at the dining room table now, pushing the cake Maria had served around with her fork rather than actually eating it—while Maria, Mrs. Justice, Mrs. Russell *and* Mrs. Kinnard discussed something pertaining to some aspect of an upcoming Lenten service. It was all she could do to stay seated.

"Well, we'll just have to go right now and see how much space there is," Mrs. Kinnard said.

"This doesn't have to be done until the last Lenten Sunday. We have *weeks* yet," Mrs. Russell said.

"There is no point in leaving everything to the last minute," Mrs. Kinnard insisted, and Kate suddenly realized that they were all getting up from the table. Mrs. Kinnard had spoken—but about what precisely, Kate had no idea.

"It will be dark soon," Maria said.

"I have my carriage. It will only take a few minutes to get there—Miss Woodard, I don't believe we will require *your* presence."

Good, Kate nearly said and her thoughts went immediately to Robert.

She said you were grooming me to be your wife.

Good.

Oh, Robert. What did you mean?

"Kate?" Maria said.

"I'm sorry, what did you say?"

"I said we'll be right back. Will you help Warrie with the boys if she needs it?"

"Of course," Kate said, but both of them knew that Warrie wouldn't ask for help, and she most particularly wouldn't ask for Kate's. Kate wondered if she somehow knew about the "grooming."

She was still sitting at the table when one of the soldiers came in to clear away the plates and put the dining room back in order.

"Sorry, miss," he said, turning to go.

"No, it's all right," Kate said. She went out into the hallway, glancing toward the campaign table as she always did before she went upstairs.

Nothing.

She climbed the stairs quickly, but she didn't go to her room. Instead she went out onto the second-story veranda and stood by the banister, breathing in the cool, fresh air.

Spring was coming. She could feel it, and any other time she would be heartened by it. Jonquils and pink thrift were already in full bloom in nearly every yard, and—according to Sergeant Major Perkins—the trees would be budding soon. On the surface, everything was as it should be. Life went on around her, just as it had after Grey was killed.

She looked up at the late afternoon sky. Four days. Robert had been gone four days.

"Harrison, where are you?" she whispered.

Please, please, Lord. Let Robert find him and let me help him. Please. Whatever he's running from—it doesn't matter. If he needs respite, then let him find it here.

She stood for a long time—until she could see Mrs. Kinnard's carriage returning. She went back inside, and she came downstairs despite the smothering presence of the others. She had to be where she could hear the delivery of the mail pouch if one came.

"Did you find enough space for...whatever it was?" Kate asked no one in particular as she reached the foyer.

"Yes," Mrs. Justice and Mrs. Russell said.

"No," Mrs. Kinnard said. "Two benches will have to be moved."

"There will be extra people there, Acacia. They will need a place to sit," Mrs. Russell said. "Church attendance is always higher during Lent."

"Only because they don't bother to show up the rest of the year. When one's presence at church is so lackadaisical, then one must expect consequences."

"I don't know why I don't have a headache," Maria whispered at Kate's elbow.

"You can have mine," Kate said, and Maria had to stifle a laugh.

"I'm so glad you're here," Maria whispered. "I don't think I could manage them without you."

"You'd still have Sergeant Major Perkins."

"Ladies, I think we've spent enough time on this,"

Mrs. Justice said, and the remark apparently had a direct effect on Mrs. Kinnard's eyebrows.

"I would like for us to have a prayer circle," Mrs. Justice said quietly. "In Bud's sitting room. Now." She looked at Perkins, who had come in from the back of the house. "Are the chairs ready, Sergeant Major?"

"They are, ma'am," he said, and she smiled.

"Then we shall go," she said.

For once Mrs. Kinnard didn't have a more urgent and appropriate alternative. She followed Mrs. Justice up the stairs, giving Kate and the rest of the women a look over her shoulder that suggested she was on the verge of finding all of them recalcitrant for just standing there.

Kate followed along quickly. It was what she needed at the moment, one of Mrs. Justice's quiet and comforting prayers.

Seven chairs had been brought into the sitting room.

"I was expecting that Reverend Lewis would join us," Mrs. Justice said, apparently to explain the seating. "Do please sit down, my dears. Do you remember the last time all of us were gathered like this—here—in Bud's house?"

"I remember," Mrs. Russell said, and it was clear that she didn't appreciate having been reminded.

"When was it?" Kate asked. No one seemed to want to answer.

"It was the night we all sat up waiting for General Stoneman and his horse soldiers to raid the town," Maria said finally.

"I'm reminding you of this for a reason," Mrs. Justice said. "We had that dreadful prison here, and we were all of us certain that the town would be burned to the ground like Atlanta and Columbia. But we prayed for God's mercy and for strength and courage no matter what happened. I would like us to do that again tonight, this time for Robbie and for the young man he has gone to find—" She stopped because someone was coming up the back stairs.

Kate looked at the doorway, expecting to see Reverend Lewis, but it was the army chaplain, Bible in hand. It suddenly occurred to her that she didn't know his name, and clearly, everyone was as surprised to see him as she was—except Mrs. Justice.

"Chaplain Gilford, welcome," Mrs. Justice said. "We are very pleased that you are willing to come out tonight—"

"I hardly think—" Mrs. Kinnard began.

"—*in* Reverend Lewis's stead," Mrs. Justice continued firmly. "It's his gout," she added to the group. "Very painful, I understand. Now. Do let me introduce you to the ladies you have not met."

To their credit Mrs. Kinnard and Mrs. Russell participated in the social amenities because—as Mrs. Justice had pointed out on a previous occasion—their mothers' teaching dictated it, especially in someone else's home. But it was clear to Kate that neither of them wanted to— and for very different reasons, she thought. For Mrs. Russell, the chaplain would be a vivid reminder of how her son had died. For Mrs. Kinnard, he would represent a situation where she had unwillingly experienced a certain loss of control.

But Chaplain Gilford handled both women with courtesy and skillful authority, perhaps the kind he hadn't exhibited in a long time. He clearly wasn't drinking, and he seemed confident and…peaceful. He acknowledged Maria and Kate and then took his seat.

Mrs. Justice kept looking at the doorway, likely for a reason.

Chaplain Gilford looked at each of them and then recited from memory. "'For where two or three are gathered together in my name, there am I in the midst of them.' And so we are here this evening—gathered in *His* name, seeking His help and His comfort. For the boy Robert Markham has gone to find, for Robert and for all of us here who want only to help them both, but have not yet found a way…" He stopped.

Warrie Hansen stood in the doorway.

"Warrie, come in," Maria said. "There's a chair for you."

Warrie stood awkwardly for a moment, then came into the room. "The boys is all asleep," she said. "I reckoned I'd come up here to the prayer circle." She sat down in the empty chair, and Kate wondered if she knew that the prayers tonight would be for Robert.

The chaplain waited until she was situated, then looked at Mrs. Kinnard before he began again. "We are grateful, Lord, that we have this opportunity to offer up our prayers to You. We have come with our troubled hearts and our worry, believing that we may lay our burdens before You. Your word tells us to ask and it shall be given us. Seek, and we will find. Knock and it will be opened unto us. I sought the Lord, and He heard me, and delivered me from all my fears—"

"Excuse me, Chaplain," Perkins said from the doorway. "Miss Kate, you need to come downstairs."

Kate got up immediately and followed him down the wide hallway.

"What is it?" she asked, but he didn't answer her until they had reached the foyer. The mail pouch had come; a stack of letters lay on the campaign table. He picked up one of them.

"Telegram," he said. "For you. It's from Robert Markham."

Kate took it from him, her fingers trembling.

"You've already read it?" she asked as she opened the envelope.

"I have. I thought it couldn't wait."

She struggled to get the telegram free and then began to read:

H found. Come as soon as possible. Perkins has details. Robert

"What's happened? What details?" Kate cried.

"The boy is sick, Miss Kate, and it's bad. He's in some little whistle-stop in Virginia. Markham says he needs some medical supplies. I'm working on getting him what he wants. You need to go pack a trunk. The night train will be here before long, and I've got some more things to figure out."

"What kind of things?"

"Go pack, Miss Kate. Let me do what I need to do."

She stood for a moment, then nodded and hurried up the stairs. She could hear the chaplain praying when she reached the second floor. She went into her room and opened her smallest trunk, her mind in complete turmoil. She had to force herself to *think,* to concentrate on what she might need to take with her.

The boy is sick...

She suddenly realized that she had a good idea of what might be needed—thanks to her constant clashes with Mrs. Kinnard. She wouldn't fill the trunk with her belongings. She would take only the barest minimum for herself and reserve the rest of the space for things that might be necessary to care for someone who was ill.

She hurried downstairs to the kitchen and went into the pantry. The flannel Mrs. Kinnard had asked for— demanded—the night Robert had come home she knew was on the top shelf, and she climbed up on a box to get it. They could be used for heated brick or as washcloths.

She found a bar of soap, some candles and an unopened pack of matches to light them with, and some lumps of sugar wrapped in brown paper. As an afterthought she took down a bag of coffee and some apples, dumping all of it into an empty basket. She took the basket with her through the kitchen to the airing room to get several sheets and two blankets and two pillowcases from the linen cupboard. She put everything that was in the basket into one of them. A stack of clean aprons had been left on one of the ironing tables, and she took one of those, as well. When she came back through the house, Mrs. Kinnard was leaving by the front door.

Kate didn't see Perkins anywhere, and she didn't waste time looking for him. She went upstairs again and changed into her traveling dress with the open side pocket that allowed her to reach the underskirt, which had a pocket where she could hide most of the money she had set aside for traveling. The coins she left in her reticule. She packed the cotton calico dress, along with some clean undergarments, into the trunk. Thanks to recent events she had no qualms about having only two dresses, and with some rearranging, she managed to get everything into the trunk and the lid closed and locked.

When she came out into the hallway, she could no longer hear the chaplain. No doubt Perkins had advised everyone about Robert's telegram by now and had likely given every person in the house some kind of assignment.

Robert.

He had said he would find Harrison. When she had first met him, she had wondered if he were not the Southern version of a knight in shining armor. She didn't have to wonder any longer.

She hurried toward the stairs, not knowing how long it would be before the train came, and then she suddenly stopped.

"Thank you, Lord," she whispered. She had asked for the opportunity to help her son, and she realized suddenly that this was it. The realization brought with it a kind of calmness she hadn't anticipated.

"Help me to do this the best I can," she said. She took a deep breath, and continued down the stairs.

This time Perkins was in the foyer.

"You know you can't go on the train alone—" he began.

"I'm going!" Kate said, alarmed. He was *not* going to stop her. She didn't care how it looked, and she most certainly didn't care how her doing so would affect the smooth running of the occupation.

Perkins held up his hand. "Yes," he said. "*With* a chaperone."

"I don't need a chaperone," Kate said.

"Well, you won't get out of this town without one," he assured her. "Mrs. Colonel Woodard can't do it. Mrs. Justice needs to stay here so she won't wear herself out trying to help Mrs. Hansen with those boys."

"What are you telling me?" Kate asked.

"I'm telling you I got you a chaperone."

"Who?" Kate asked.

He didn't answer her, and because he didn't, Kate knew immediately that there was only one possibility.

"Oh, no," Kate said.

"She's the only one who will do, Miss Kate," Perkins said. "And she is happy to have the job."

"Why?"

"Having authority over the Colonel's sister *and* being able to order people around in another state? Nothing could suit that woman better. Besides that, if anybody else goes, all in this world Mrs. Kinnard would have to do is raise an eyebrow, and she'd cast all kinds of suspicion that things weren't proper and that the Colonel had no regard for the women in his family. And you know—"

"All right! I understand. We have to preserve my brother's standing as well as mine."

"Exactly."

"Does he know about this?"

Perkins hesitated. "I sent him a telegram."

"*Everything* about this?" She was asking if he knew Robert Markham's part in it, but she couldn't quite bring herself to say it.

"Most of it." Perkins was looking at her so directly, and it was all she could do not to avoid his gaze.

"I…thought it best not to tell him Markham sent for you," he said. "If he gave me an order contrary to what Markham is asking, I'd have to carry it out."

"And I'd end up in the stockade."

"Well, I don't think we'd have to go that far—Castine!" he suddenly barked. "What are you doing?"

"Helping Mrs. Justice and Mrs. Colonel Woodard pack a basket for Miss Kate to take with her."

"Well, hurry it along."

"I don't think I know how to hurry ladies, Sergeant Major," he called.

"I don't know how to hurry ladies, either," Perkins said, "but we're not going to tell him that."

Kate gave a brief smile. "Thank you, Sergeant Major Perkins," she said quietly. Perkins hadn't missed her intense worry about Harrison, and regardless of his duty to her brother, he was going out of his way to make it possible for her to go to the boy.

"For what?" he asked innocently.

"You know what," she answered, and surprisingly, he actually smiled in return. She was much more accustomed to his "sack and burn" face.

"Castine's going, too," he said.

Kate looked at him. She didn't know whether this was good news or not—for Castine. Ever since he had escorted her and Valentina to army headquarters and she had seen him being so helpful with the boys, she had found his presence…comforting, but he was even more disconcerted by Mrs. Kinnard than she was.

She heard a long, drawn out train whistle in the distance. Castine came hurrying down the hallway carrying the same basket she was to have taken with her on her last train trip.

"I'll carry the basket," Kate said, because he was juggling a haversack, a knapsack and a repeating rifle as well.

"Yes, miss," he said, handing it over.

"Kate!" Maria called, hurrying from the kitchen with Mrs. Justice in tow. When they reached her, they both embraced her, putting the basket in jeopardy of ending up on the parquet floor.

"Keep praying for him," Kate whispered. "Please."

"Don't you worry about that, my dear," Mrs. Justice said. "We will keep a prayer vigil for him, you can rest assured."

"We've put everything Mrs. Justice and I could think of in the basket. Take care of yourself," Maria said. "And send us word as soon as you know something. If he can be moved, you must bring him here to us."

Kate nodded and hugged them both again. She looked around because Castine was coming down the stairs with her trunk.

"Mrs. Kinnard's carriage is here," Perkins said. "You got everything, Miss Kate?"

"Yes," she said, because she was nearly certain that she had.

"All right then," he said, and he opened the front door.

Chapter Fourteen

Kate stood on the platform watching as the train slowed and lurched and finally stopped. Her mind had gone numb as the terrible significance of having to make this trip finally sank in. Harrison was seriously ill, and she had no idea how long this journey would take. All she knew was that she wanted to board the train as soon as possible and that—please, Lord—she didn't arrive too late.

The passenger car filled rapidly, intensifying the smell of dust and sweat and baskets packed with food. And underneath it all the distinct smell of whiskey and tobacco and babies whose diapers needed changing. She half expected Valentina to show up; this would surely meet her criteria for an "adventure."

Kate had to immediately change seats with Mrs. Kinnard, who couldn't abide being next to the aisle and having people she didn't know—and more importantly, who didn't know *her*—brush and jostle past her. Kate wondered if Mrs. Kinnard had even been on a train before. If she hadn't, this would be an eye-opening experience even under the best of circumstances.

Kate sat with the basket firmly in her lap, clutching the handle tightly as if that would help the situation somehow. She didn't dare let it out of her sight with all these people around. The train car grew more and more crowded, much too crowded for Mrs. Kinnard. She kept giving sharp sighs and holding her perfume-laden handkerchief to her nose, which Kate assumed would continue until they reached wherever they were going. There apparently was no name for the whistle-stop where Harrison was supposed to be, but Perkins, ever efficient, had advised the conductor at what point Colonel Woodard's sister and her party would need to detrain.

Castine, who was standing nearby, suddenly cleared his throat, and Kate looked up just as a man stepped into her line of vision.

"Miss Woodard," the man said, bending low enough for Kate to smell the clover-scented pomade on his hair. "Do forgive me, but I've only just heard that Colonel Woodard's sister was on the train. Might I persuade you to join me in my private car? You will travel much more comfortably there—my cook will prepare us a fine dinner. It would be an honor to offer some assistance to you—and your brother."

"I'm afraid I don't know who you are, sir," she said, despite the fact that Mrs. Kinnard perked up immediately at hearing the words, *private* and *car.* Kate caught a glimpse of Castine, who was clearly trying to tell her something with his eyes. Unfortunately she had no idea what.

"Well, that is easily remedied," the man said. "I'm Welles Burnham." He said his name as if that should explain everything.

Castine seemed to be writing something on a piece of paper.

"Excuse me, sir," Castine said, pushing his way forward. "Miss Woodard, I have a—this message for you."

Kate took it, puzzled but intending to read it later, without this strange man hovering over her.

"You need to look at it now, Miss Woodard," Castine said pointedly.

"Yes. Thank you, Private Castine."

"You're welcome, Miss Woodard," he said as she opened the slip of paper.

She didn't open it far; there was only one word written on it: *carpetbagger.*

Castine had apparently realized immediately that this was a situation that might cause his commanding officer some difficulty. Max could not be seen as a military commander who accepted favors from someone who was profiting from the local residents' plight. Sergeant Major Perkins had taught Castine well.

Kate smiled slightly and handed the note to Mrs. Kinnard, who looked at it much longer than was required to read one word.

"Mr. Welles—" Mrs. Kinnard began when she was ready.

"Burnham," the man corrected.

Mrs. Kinnard made no attempt to backtrack and use his correct name. "I'm sure Miss Woodard—*and I*— would be more comfortable in your private car, however, that is quite impossible. There have been no formal introductions from people we both know. I have no notion of how things are done where *you* come from, but *here*—as Colonel Woodard would certainly tell you—it would be most inappropriate to accept such an invitation. As Miss Woodard's chaperone, I must decline your offer. Now. If you would take your leave."

The man stood for a moment as if he didn't believe Mrs. Kinnard could possibly be serious.

"Surely, an exception—"

"No exceptions. Goodbye, Mr. Welles," Mrs. Kinnard added to underline what he was supposed to do next.

"Mrs. Kinnard," Kate said when he had gone. "I do believe you enjoyed that."

For a moment she thought Acacia Kinnard, the one who had stolen cookies on horseback, might actually smile.

But she didn't.

"Private Castine," she said abruptly, startling the young soldier once again. He looked in her direction. "That was…" She stopped, and Kate could see him bracing himself for yet another of her broadsides.

"Quite…adequately done," Mrs. Kinnard decided, making his ears turn as red as Valentina's indirect compliment had. "If you don't do anything too uncouth for the rest of the journey, I shall be certain to advise Mr. Perkins of your handling of the situation."

"Thank you, Mrs. Kinnard," he said quietly. But clearly he knew enough not to presume when a compliment was in as much danger of being withdrawn as that one was. "I was following orders, ma'am," he said. "The sergeant major intends for you and Miss Woodard to have a safe journey."

He glanced at Kate, and she gave him a small nod of approval.

All the seats were taken now, even the makeshift ones on bundles and baskets in the aisle. The train lurched and then began to move forward as the conductor passed through the car, asking for everyone's ticket except Kate's, Mrs. Kinnard's and Castine's, something that didn't go unnoticed among the other passengers.

Kate closed her eyes as the train gained speed and moved away from the station into the dark countryside. An oil lamp had been lit at each end of the car, and when Kate looked across Mrs. Kinnard toward the window, she could only see their reflections in it. There was nothing to occupy her mind now. No overly familiar carpetbagger, no trip preparations, no handling of Mrs. Kinnard. There was only the worry and the longing to see her son again that suddenly threatened to overwhelm her.

Don't worry—pray.

"Cast thy burden upon the Lord, and He shall sustain thee: He shall never suffer the righteous to be moved," she whispered, not caring if Mrs. Kinnard heard her. But even as she said the words, there was still that nagging truth. She was not righteous. She had shamed her family, and she didn't deserve God's favor. She had thought she might when she'd promised to marry Grey, but after he was killed, she had never been able to convince herself that she could dare to be happy again.

John.

She knew how much he loved Harrison and she knew how distressed he must be now.

Help us both, Lord, she thought. *And please—please— help our son.*

She gave herself up to the constant swaying of the car, and she managed to doze at times. So did Mrs. Kinnard. Castine, on the other hand, seemed to be alert and standing nearby whenever some slowing or accelerating of the train caused her to wake. She lost count of how many times the train actually stopped, but it seemed to her at one point that more people were getting off than were boarding. She kept thinking that there was but one comfort in all of this—Robert was with Harrison. She had no doubt that he would do everything he could for the boy, but all the while she knew she would have to guard against relying on him too much, regardless of what he had *almost* said.

Good.

In retrospect, "good" could have meant anything. She had heard him say Eleanor's name. That alone could leave no doubt that Eleanor Hansen had his heart.

She gave a heavy sigh and dozed again.

Robert stood waiting on the station platform. He kept staring down the tracks for some sign that the train was approaching, but he couldn't hear anything or see the billowing plume of smoke from an engine. All he had was the indifferent stationmaster's best guess as to when the northbound train would get here, and there were any number of events that could alter his estimation.

He walked to the end of the platform and back again—several times. The station itself was unlike any he'd ever encountered in his travels or during the war. It was a three-story wooden structure with a huge wraparound front porch. It didn't look like a train station, and yet it wasn't quite house or hotel, either, but something in between that had evolved as some architectural need arose and was subsequently met. It had seen some rough treatment during the war; there were numerous bullet holes in the wood on one side of the building, as if it had stood in the way of a heavy onslaught of musket fire.

He looked up at the increasingly overcast sky. He expected it to rain before sundown.

Weather prognostication.

He wondered at what point he'd learned to do that—read the sky and air around him and presume to know what the weather would be. He didn't remember having acquired the ability at all, but it had to have been before

Gettysburg—he'd been in no shape to learn anything after that. It must have come from being—living— fighting—outdoors for so many months. It occurred to him that he might have come away from the war with a useful skill besides the killing of his fellow man—if he had decided to become a farmer.

His thoughts went to Harrison Howe. He'd hired the stationmaster's wife to keep watch over him while he came down to meet the train. He both dreaded Kate's arrival and longed for it. By the time she got here, she would have been on the train all night and most of the day. She would be upset and exhausted, and what could he tell her except the truth?

He had managed to locate a country doctor and bring him here to see the boy, but the man had offered no diagnosis beyond the obvious, a fever likely brought on by the beating he'd taken at the hands of a person or persons unknown. Whether it had happened at school and that was the reason the boy had run away, or whether it was the result of a robbery attempt when he'd gotten off the train, Robert didn't know. All he knew was that he could have come to the doctor's conclusion about the boy's condition all on his own. And he didn't need anyone to tell him that young Harrison Howe was not likely to survive. Robert had done the only thing he could. He had sent for Kate.

He looked around sharply at the sound of a train whistle in the distance. The waiting area of the train station began to empty out as more and more people began to crowd onto the platform. He stood back to let them pass, and as he did so, he felt the first drops of rain begin to fall. Clearly his weather prediction had been off by a few hours.

From his vantage point he could see all of the passenger cars, but it was some time before he finally saw Castine helping Mrs. Kinnard down the train car steps to the platform.

Mrs. Kinnard.

He couldn't begin to guess how that had come about, and he braced himself to have to deal with her unexpected presence. She spotted him immediately and came marching across the platform in his direction. He still didn't see Kate.

"Robert Markham," Mrs. Kinnard said as soon as she was close enough. "What is happening with this boy everyone is so concerned about?"

"Where is Kate?" he asked, sidestepping her question. Surely she hadn't sent Acacia Kinnard in her stead.

"She is giving away most of the contents of our food basket to a woman with three hungry children," Mrs. Kinnard said. "As she should. Now, about—"

"Excuse me, Mrs. Kinnard," he said, pushing his way through the crowd again to get closer to the train, because he could see someone he thought must be Kate making her way down the aisle toward the train car exit.

He stood waiting on the platform, watching her progress all the way until she finally appeared. She was so… beautiful to him and had been since the first time he saw her in the downstairs hallway of his father's house.

Maria was right. He did want Kate to be a preacher's wife—*his* wife—and he didn't see how their situation could be any more impossible.

Perkins had been right as well—as far as it went. Robert was not bound to Eleanor, and yet he was, and he would continue to be until he saw her, talked with her, understood what had happened between them and knew she was all right. In the meantime, he could do nothing, say nothing to Kate about the way he felt.

I love her, Lord.

He didn't know when it had happened, or how. All he knew was that it was so, that she was in his mind night and day—and now he was only moments away from breaking her heart.

"Robert!" she cried in obvious relief when she saw him. "How is he? Tell me!"

He helped her down before he answered. "He knows you're coming," he said. "But he's sleeping most of the time now."

She looked at him.

"Sleeping," she repeated as if she thought that he didn't mean "sleeping" at all, that he meant something much more ominous.

"This way," Robert said. "Let's get you and Mrs. Kinnard out of the rain."

"Robert—"

"You need to see him for yourself, Kate."

"He's here, then?"

"Yes. Mrs. Kinnard!" he called. "This way!"

Mrs. Kinnard came in her own good time, unmindful of the rain. "What kind of place *is* this?" she asked when she reached them. "I see no one about to offer a traveler any assistance whatsoever. You have lightened the basket, I take it, Miss Woodard?"

"Yes," Kate said. "Where is he, Robert?"

"That way. Go through those double doors," he said, pointing out the station entrance.

They crossed the wide porch, stepping around sleeping men who sprawled everywhere—salesmen, by the looks of them, "drummers" who preyed upon the unsuspecting traveling public with their "snake oil" cure-alls, as well as the ones who sold legitimate merchandise to the small town and the middle-of-nowhere general stores.

Mrs. Kinnard went inside first. It was as chaotic around the ticket window as it was on the platform.

"Show me to the stationmaster's office," Mrs. Kinnard said to the nearest person she took to be some kind of railroad employee. "I must speak to the man about the way this facility is run," she said to Kate.

A baby began to cry loudly.

"Harrison's on the third floor, Kate," Robert said, leaning down so she could hear him. "Let me have the basket." He had to take it from her hands.

"This isn't what I expected."

"I know. You need to see him now, Kate. Then I'll tell you what I know and you can decide what you want to do."

Kate heard the urgency in Robert's voice. She heard it, and she was afraid. The stairs were steep and difficult to climb. She felt light-headed and unsteady by the time they reached the third-floor landing. She stumbled, and Robert took her by the arm to steady her.

"Which way?" she managed to ask.

He led her to the door and opened it. The room was unoccupied.

"They must have moved him," Robert said. He walked down the hallway, trying one door after another until one of them opened.

"In here," he called to Kate and she hurried in that direction. He said something to someone inside the room but she couldn't hear him clearly or the response.

"The stationmaster apparently took it upon himself to move him in here," he said.

Kate glanced at his face then back again. He was clearly angry.

The room was so dark. There was only one small slit

of a window near the ceiling, and the light from it, combined with that of an oil lamp burning on a nearby table, did little to illuminate her surroundings.

She stepped forward and made her way to the bedside, nodding to a woman who stood nearby.

"This is the stationmaster's wife," Robert said. "I'll leave you now. I need to find Castine."

"All right," Kate said, but she was barely listening. *Harrison!*

He appeared to be clean and the sheets on the bed were fresh, but the room was so damp and close and oppressive.

"Thank you for sitting with him," she said to the woman after a moment, her voice quiet so as not to disturb the boy who lay on the bed, his hair wet with perspiration, his eyes closed.

"I'm supposed to get paid for it," the woman said bluntly. She stopped short of holding her hand out for the money, but Kate wouldn't have been surprised if she had.

Kate touched Harrison's arm, then took his hand. It was cold and clammy.

"Harrison," she said softly. "Can you hear me? It's Kate."

She looked at the woman, who was fidgeting with her apron. "How long has he been like this?" she asked, her mouth trembling despite all she could do. She bit down on her lower lip.

"I reckon since sometime last night. Before that, he'd kind of come and go."

"What does the doctor say?"

"I don't know. He didn't talk to me."

Kate leaned forward to see Harrison better. "His face is bruised. Why is his face bruised?" She knew her voice was rising, but she couldn't help it. "What happened to him?"

"We—my old man—found him like this at the back of the station four…no, five days ago," the woman said. "It ain't hard to figure how he got there."

"What do you mean?"

"The boy had money and he didn't have enough sense to hide it. I reckon he got beat up and robbed and he laid out in the rain all night that night. It ain't our fault he got into trouble, if that's what you're thinking. We've been looking after him as best we could. Then Mr. Markham came and showed us the picture. We knowed it was him the minute we seen it. Mr. Markham, he said we'd get paid for—"

"This room won't do," Kate interrupted, because the rain she could hear beating on the roof was beginning to drip from the ceiling. "I want him moved to someplace with more air and light. Someplace *dry.*"

"The roof don't leak unless there's been a couple days of rain," the woman said as if that somehow negated the leaks.

"I said I want him moved," Kate said.

"Well, there ain't no call to be so—"

"Tell the stationmaster I want to see him. *Now!*" Kate said.

They stared at each other, then the woman gave a sharp sigh and left, returning in a few minutes with a short, rotund man wearing spectacles.

"You're the stationmaster?" Kate asked ahead of whatever excuses he was about to make.

"I am—"

"Then you have the authority to appropriate any room on these premises, is that not correct?"

"That's right—"

"Then I want him moved out of here to a bigger room—one with windows and a ceiling that doesn't leak."

"I done told Markham I ain't got no other place to put him in—ain't no ex-Reb telling me how to run my station. Anyway I don't see how what room he's in can matter now," the man made the mistake of saying.

Kate turned to face him. It took everything she had to sound calm. "As you can see, *I* am not an 'ex-Reb,' as you put it. You will show me the rooms in this place— all of them."

He took a moment, apparently to decide who Kate might be and what would be his most profitable response. He glanced at his wife once before he answered. "If I do," he said finally, "how do I know I'll get paid?"

"You don't," Kate said. "But I can promise you this, you won't get any money at all unless you do as I say. I understand you expect this boy's family to reimburse you for his care before Mr. Markham arrived. Any claims you have will not be honored unless *I* approve them. Do we understand each other?"

The stationmaster didn't say whether he did or didn't; he merely threw up his hands and headed for the door. "The big room," he said to his wife on his way out.

"But we might need that room if there's any rich people coming in on the—"

"You heard what I said!" He shoved past Mrs. Kinnard, who walked up just as he was exiting the doorway.

"What's happening?" Mrs. Kinnard asked. "Who is that rude man?"

"Mrs. Kinnard," Kate said. "Will you kindly go with this woman? We're moving Harrison to another room. I need your opinion as to which one will be the most suitable." Kate looked at the stationmaster's wife. "Mrs. Kinnard ran a wayside hospital during the war, so don't suppose for a minute that she won't know what a gravely ill young man will need to aid his recovery. If she is happy with what you show her, then I will be, as well."

Kate turned her attention back to Harrison, not knowing whether either woman would comply, and she took his hand again. He hadn't stirred during the exchange, not once.

"I'll…tell somebody to bring you some fresh water," the stationmaster's wife said after a moment. "He's fevering again. I reckon he needs sponging."

"Yes. Thank you," Kate said, accepting the woman's token change of attitude—for the moment, at least. She took off her hat and jacket and rolled up her sleeves. She needed her trunk, but she wouldn't worry about that now. She pulled the one chair in the room near the bedside and sat down heavily.

The memory of Warrie Hansen singing to Jake and Joe and Robbie suddenly filled her mind.

Go tell Aunt Rosie,
Go tell Aunt Rosie…

Did anyone ever sing to you? she thought. Mrs. Howe? A nanny hired to make sure you were rarely seen or heard?

God relies on mothers. The midwife who had delivered him had told her that.

And how little help she had been thus far.

"Harrison—Harrison," she said softly to him, covering his hand with hers. "Listen to me, now. You're going to be all right. I'm here—and Mrs. Kinnard. You may have met Mrs. Kinnard when you came to visit John last summer. If you did, then you know she'll get things done for you. We're going to find you a better room so you won't have to be here in the dark and—" Her voice broke and she barely smothered a sob.

She looked around at a small noise. She hadn't realized that Robert was in the room. He came to stand on the other side of the bed, and she looked up at him, shaking her head in despair.

"It's good to talk to him," Robert said. "Sometimes I could hear—understand—what people said. I heard you the night I came home—and I heard soldiers and the people who took care of me after Gettysburg. Talk to him, Kate. Give him hope."

She looked at him, still very close to tears, and he nodded his encouragement.

Hope.

And how could she do that when she herself had none? Even someone so inexperienced in these kinds of things as she, could see how very ill Harrison was. She heard Robert leave, and she sat there trying to think of what to say. Any mention of Mrs. Howe would likely take him right back to whatever had happened at school that had caused him to run away.

"You would be very surprised at the change in me," she said finally, leaning close again. "I can bake cornbread now. Can you believe it? Max and John don't know about that yet. Can you imagine what *they* will say? When you're better, I'll make us some—we'll have cornbread and tea with lots of sugar, just the way you like it, and we'll sit on the upstairs veranda at Max's house. We'll have the tea in tin cups—you know how we both break things.

"And I have some new books. I bought them at that little bookshop—you know the one. We found it when we were supposed to be visiting the museum, but we went looking for Charles Dickens instead. Remember that? Mr. Howe's English friend sent you a bundle of old newspapers—he knew how much you liked to read the London papers, only he didn't know what you really enjoyed were the chapters they published of Mr. Dickens's books. You were missing so many chapters from *David Copperfield*—and nothing would do but we find the whole book—" She stopped again, thinking that the stationmaster's wife had come back.

But it was Castine who brought the fresh water and some hemmed pieces of clean flannel. Robert followed him into the room, and he took the ewer from Castine so he could set the basin on the table near the bed.

"Anything else you need me to do, Mr. Markham?"

"No. Thank you, Castine. Just keep an eye on the vermin in this place."

"Yes, sir. My pleasure, sir."

Robert wet a piece of flannel and handed it to Kate. They began to work together, sponging Harrison's feverish body. Robert showed her how to fan the wet flannel in the air to make it feel colder before she used it to wipe the perspiration away. And all the while Harrison didn't open his eyes, didn't move. There was only the sound of the rain and his labored breaths.

In.

Out.

Mrs. Kinnard returned. She had changed clothes and had put her elaborately dressed hair into a snood. At the moment she looked like someone who might work in the Kinnard household rather than its mistress.

"It took some doing, but the room is ready," she said.

Kate stood back as Robert and Castine—and two men she didn't know—lifted Harrison up, mattress and all and carried him out into the hallway. She gathered up her belongings and followed down the dark passageway to a room on the other side of the building. It was a large and airy corner room with whitewashed walls and double two-over-two windows. Rivulets of rain ran down the windowpanes rather than dripping from the ceiling.

The room didn't look as if it had been recently occupied, but more like one that had been held in reserve for a more important traveler than the gravely ill boy who was being carried into it now.

She waited outside until Harrison had been put to bed.

"Your room is there across the hall," Mrs. Kinnard said. "It's small but I expect you won't want to spend much time in it. Private Castine has brought up your trunk. If you have a dress more suitable for attending the sick, it—"

"I do," Kate said, interrupting. "And I brought sheets and some blankets and some other things I thought we might need as well—apples if you're hungry. I'll go get them."

"Excellent," Mrs. Kinnard said. "I've told those mercenary station people to move a cot and two more chairs in here. I believe we will likely need to take turns sleeping."

"Thank you, Mrs. Kinnard," Kate said, but Mrs. Kinnard had no intention of being thanked for what she considered should be obvious.

"I see what needs to be done and I do it, Miss Woodard. I always have, and with God's help, I always will. There is no need to thank me. It is simply the way I am."

Kate left and went to the small room across from Harrison's and closed the door behind her. She stood waiting for the rush of emotion she knew would come, but she was determined not to waste time weeping. She wiped at her eyes and gathered her strength and set to work unpacking the trunk.

Don't worry—pray.

Don't weep—do.

She closed her eyes, her mind a jumble.

Harrison—the Lord bless thee, and keep thee...thank You for letting me see him again...Thy will, not mine.

Thy will. Thy will!

She changed clothes and put on the apron, making sure she had her money tucked into one of the pockets. She didn't trust the stationmaster or his wife not to harvest whatever they could from her belongings.

When she returned with the sheets and a blanket, and the candles and matches, Mrs. Kinnard had taken over the job of sponging Harrison in an effort to bring his fever down. From time to time she moistened his lips as well, and she filled a quill with water from a glass and fed it to him.

"He can still swallow," she said when she realized Kate was there. "That is a good sign."

Kate believed her without question. How strange it was that she could be so glad, so grateful for this vexing woman's presence.

Thank You, Lord. For Mrs. Kinnard. For Robert. Thank You for them both, and for the others, as well. Max and Maria and Mrs. Justice. Perkins and Castine. I'm not alone... I'll try to remember that...

"Now," Mrs. Kinnard said. "I believe this boy should be allowed to rest for a time before we try to bring down his fever again. He's been bothered enough."

Kate nodded, still willing to accept Mrs. Kinnard's opinion. She sat down in one of the chairs.

"It would be more helpful if you went to find Robert," Mrs. Kinnard said. "We should know everything we can about this situation—even if it isn't much. And you, you're looking...pinched. Go get some air. Eat something—"

"I'm fine."

"You are clearly *not* fine, Miss Woodard, and I would prefer not to have two collapsed people on my hands, if you don't mind. I will stay by the boy until you get back."

Kate stood, trying not to look as "pinched," as Mrs. Kinnard seemed to think she did.

"His name is Harrison," Kate said as she walked toward the door.

She couldn't see Robert in the hallway at first, but she could hear his voice, and she continued in that direction. He was in a small alcove off to the side talking to Castine. She stood and waited until he was finished

"What did the doctor tell you?" she asked immediately.

"He thinks Harrison has a 'morbid fever.' He doesn't know if it's the result of the…"

"The stationmaster's wife told me he was robbed and beaten," Kate said when he didn't go on. "She hinted that it was his own fault, because he didn't know to hide the fact that he had money. She said he lay out in the rain all night."

Robert was watching her so closely. Propriety dictated that she should avoid such an intense gaze, but she didn't. She was so glad that he was here with her and it was all she could do not to tell him so.

"The doctor didn't know if the beating has caused the fever or if it's something else," he said finally. "He didn't offer anything in the way of treatment other than purging. I said no to that. I've seen too many men die from the weakness that comes with it. They're always worse afterward. The doctor didn't know of anything else to try. Perkins sent a field medicine chest—quinine for ague and laudanum for pain are about the only useful things in it. I don't think Harrison is in pain, despite the bruising."

"Or is he past feeling it?" Kate asked bluntly.

Robert didn't try to avoid the question. "That may be the case, but I don't know for sure. It's good that Mrs. Kinnard has come. I think she probably has more experience in this kind of thing than the doctor here does."

"We have to take him home, Robert."

"It's a long way to Philadelphia."

"Not Philadelphia—Salisbury."

"He's very weak, Kate."

"I know. Maria told me to bring him there if I could. I'm going to try to do that. I don't see him getting better in this place. But I don't know what it will take to get him space on the train."

"The authorizations Perkins gave me should take care of that."

"Yes," Kate said in relief. "The authorizations. I'd forgotten about those. I thought I'd have to find another carpetbagger."

"Carpetbagger?"

"There was one on the train. He had a private car, and he knew who I was. He tried to use it to get into Max's good graces."

"I don't think we can count on a private car, a carpetbagger's or otherwise. Most likely Harrison will have to travel the way wounded soldiers traveled—a stretcher placed across the aisle—"

"Miss Woodard!" Mrs. Kinnard called loudly, and Kate ran down the hallway to Harrison's room. Incredibly Harrison was sitting up in bed and struggling with Mrs. Kinnard, who was trying to keep him from falling. But then Kate saw the boy's face, his wild, fever-bright eyes. This was not an improvement in his condition; this was something much worse.

Robert stepped around her to help Mrs. Kinnard. "Find the laudanum in the medicine case, Kate."

"Where is it? It was here on the table—"

Kate looked frantically around the room. There was no medicine case.

She stepped out into the hallway. "Castine!"

He came at a run.

"The medicine case is missing. We need laudanum."

He gave her a sharp nod of acknowledgment—as if that was all he needed to know. He whirled around and disappeared down the hall. He wasn't gone long, and when he returned he had one of the drummers by his collar, and he shoved him into the room. The man looked around wildly, then seemed to be satisfied that he had nothing to worry about—except Castine.

"This man rattled when he walked past me a little while ago," Castine said. "I'm wondering why."

Kate didn't hesitate. She stepped up to him and immediately began going through his pockets—while he leered. She found a number of bottles from the medicine case. The laudanum was in the last pocket she searched.

"Do you know what to do with him, Private Castine?" Robert asked over his shoulder.

"I do, sir."

"Then carry on."

"How much laudanum?" Kate asked Mrs. Kinnard.

"Five drops in water," Mrs. Kinnard said without hesitation. "Put some water in a tin cup—not much—just a swallow or two. Carry it over to the window so you can see the laudanum drops fall into it."

Kate got a tin cup and poured the water. She kept looking over her shoulder as Harrison tried to get free of the hands that held him fast. He was in torment, struggling to get away from something only he could see.

She dropped five drops of laudanum into the cup and handed it to Robert, who administered it quickly despite

Harrison's resistance, and with as much skill as she had seen the hospital orderly use when he'd poured brandy into Robert the night he'd collapsed in the hallway. She wondered if it was something men in the war had to learn to keep each other alive.

Harrison continued to try to get free, but with less and less forcefulness, until at last he stopped fighting altogether and Mrs. Kinnard and Robert laid him back on the bed.

He was quiet now, but he wasn't asleep as he had been before. He was still agitated, only he no longer had the physical strength to respond to it. His eyelids fluttered, and he mumbled unintelligible words. His fingertips plucked at the sheet covering him.

Kate took his hand and held it for a moment. He felt much hotter than he had earlier.

Mrs. Kinnard handed Kate a piece of flannel, and together they began wetting him down until his skin was noticeably cooler. They stopped and waited until it grew hot again and then they started all over. They changed the wet sheets. Castine brought more water, and Robert took over for Mrs. Kinnard. Kate lost all track of time. All her attention was focused on Harrison.

She realized at one point that the windows had grown dark and she thought that Mrs. Kinnard was no longer in the room. But Mrs. Kinnard was sleeping heavily on the cot in the corner, and it was all right. Kate was no longer as helpless at the bedside as she had been when Robert had needed water to drink. She had mastered feeding Harrison with a quill. She mixed some of the sugar she'd brought in water and gave it to him repeatedly with the quill—barely a swallow—and then she let him rest. Then another swallow of sugar water, again and again.

Was it helping? Kate didn't know, but at least she was doing something.

"Kate?"

She looked around, wondering why Robert sounded so insistent.

"Come with me," he said, taking the quill out of her hand.

She shook her head. "No. I can't leave him—"

"Mrs. Kinnard is here. You need to come with me."

She wanted to resist, but he had her firmly by her shoulders, and he walked her out of the room and down the hallway to some kind of storage room she hadn't been in before. There was a cot in the far corner, and it occurred to her that this must be where he slept—if he slept at all.

"Sit," he said, making her sit down on one of several tall stools, the kind she'd seen the clerks sitting on when she'd once gone along with her father to his Philadelphia bank, not because he had business he needed to attend to, but more that he wanted to make it known that he had a daughter of marriageable age. The rows of clerks, the reason for her being there—it was all so…Dickensian somehow.

Oh, Harrison!

She sat there on the stool, her head bowed.

"Look up at me," Robert said, and when she did, he placed a cold and wet piece of flannel over her face. "Let it be for a minute. It will make you feel better."

"How do you know?" she asked wearily, feeling both impatient and overwhelmed.

"Because I was a boxer. Just bear with me. You'll see."

He pressed the flannel gently against her cheeks and forehead, her eyes, then flipped it over, fanned it in the air a few times and reapplied it. The renewed cold against her face felt...wonderful.

"I can do it," she said, not knowing whether she could or not.

"I know. Just sit still."

But she took the flannel away and caught his hand. "I have to go back. I can't leave him, Robert. You don't understand—"

"I think I do," he said.

She shook her head. "No—"

"I can see you in him, Kate. And you keep his photograph with you always. If this situation weren't so dire, you would never have handed it over to me."

"No, that's not—" She wanted to deny it, but tears suddenly welled up in her eyes instead. They spilled over, streaming down her face, years and years of unshed tears. She couldn't stop them no matter how hard she tried. Robert knew the truth, and she was glad.

"Drink this," Robert said.

Kate had cried for a long time, and he had stayed with her while she did it, wiping her face from time to time, but not intruding—until now. It was as if he knew she needed to let go at last.

"Drink it," he said, pressing the tin cup into her hands. "I mean it."

She very nearly smiled. She had no doubt that he could make her do it if he wanted to.

"What is it?" she asked, looking into the cup.

"I'm not sure—some kind of soup. It's good, though. Castine made it. I think he's going to turn into another Perkins."

She did smile this time. "Thank you," she said, looking up at him.

He pulled up another stool and sat down in front of her, she thought to make sure she ate the soup. She tasted it, then took a long swallow. Something with onions and potatoes. It was quite good.

She drank a little more, and she felt the effects of finally having some nourishment almost immediately. She had no idea how long it had been since she'd eaten. She concentrated on holding the tin cup, knowing that Robert was waiting for her to look at him. But she kept sipping until she'd finished the last of Castine's soup, then she sat the tin cup on the nearest stool. She took a deep breath, knowing she was going to tell Robert everything.

"I was very…young," she said quietly.

"Kate—"

"He was born in Italy," she said firmly, looking into his eyes. "I was sent to a place there—for rich young women who needed to hide until their babies were born—I've always been good at hiding, you see.

"*Bambina povera.* That's what the midwife kept saying. 'Poor little girl.' I thought she meant the baby I'd just borne, but she meant me. 'Poor little girl…'"

She wiped at her eyes again. "I was his mother for six hours. The midwife gave him to me and told me to hold him as long as I could. So I did—until someone came and took him away. I don't think she was supposed to let me do that, but I was so…" She stopped.

"You don't have to talk about this, Kate," Robert said.

"No, I want to. I told her I wished I had died, and she said no. It was wrong to think that, because I was a mother now and God relied on mothers. Six hours. I always thought it wasn't long enough to count, but it was. It *is*. He is my child, and this is breaking my heart."

"How did…?" Robert began, then stopped.

"Go ahead," she said. "What were you going to say?"

"I don't understand how people so close to your family raised him."

"It was all part of the plan. Not *my* plan. I had no say about anything. The Howes and my parents were close friends. Their son—John—is Harrison's father. He didn't abandon me," she said quickly because of the look on Robert's face. "When he knew about the child, he wanted to marry me, but my father wouldn't agree to it. He thought I was too young and John was too…wild. And John's father—he wasn't about to let a grandchild of his be given over to strangers. So they did the only thing they could do. The Howes took Harrison. Mrs. Howe came to Italy, too—she was young enough to pass my baby off as her own. It wasn't that difficult. He may look like me in some ways, but he looks more like John. He and John were brought up as brothers."

"And you've always been close by."

"As close as I dared. I knew I couldn't get too close to him. If I did that, I wouldn't be allowed to see him at all. It's still hard—for me. Not so hard for John, I think. He has a firm place in Harrison's life," she said. "It's true that John was wild when he was young—so was Max. It's something young men do, apparently."

"Yes," Robert said.

"Some of them, anyway. I don't think Grey was ever like that."

"Grey?"

"Lieutenant Grey Jamison—I was going to marry Grey." She sighed. "But perhaps he was wild, too. He was a horse soldier in Kilpatrick's cavalry. Isn't that what they say about cavalrymen? That they're reckless and wild?"

"It's what the walkers—infantrymen—say about them."

"He was killed at Bentonville."

"I'm sorry," Robert said.

"When I said yes to his marriage proposal, I thought I could live with the lie of Harrison's birth and never need to tell the man I cared about who Harrison really was. *Now* I know I couldn't have done that. Those kinds of secrets only... It's..."

She sighed. "It happened so... John was... I always thought he was very...lonely, despite his fearlessness when it came to breaking the rules and flaunting authority. He was like an orphan in the storm, and I was—I don't know what I was. He'd come to the house to see Max that night—something had happened—something that upset him terribly. But Max wasn't there. No one was except me and the servants, and they'd all gone to bed. He wouldn't say what was wrong and he was in such... despair. I wanted to...comfort him, but I didn't know how—" She paused to look directly into Robert's eyes. "And then I...did know. I can't blame John for what happened. I could have stopped it, but I didn't. It was all— oh, I'm not making any sense."

She suddenly straightened and wiped her eyes. "So you see, I'm not someone who ought to be groomed." She looked at him.

"I love you, Kate," he said when she did.

It was the wrong thing to say and the wrong time to say it. Kate knew that, and so, she thought, did he. It was so simple and honest, and she believed him.

"I'm not bound to Eleanor—not in the way you think—" Robert said.

Kate shook her head sadly. "Bound is bound, Robert. I'm no more free from my past than you are." She took his hand and held it to her cheek. He rested his head against hers.

Just for a moment, she thought. *I love you, Robert!*

"I have to go back," she said. "Whatever happens, I have to be there."

Chapter Fifteen

There was no carpetbagger with an inappropriate invitation this time. If there had been, Kate thought, it was very likely she would have accepted it. She would have sacrificed Max's reputation for Harrison's comfort without a second thought.

As it was, six seats had been designated for transporting Harrison back down the line to Salisbury. A stretcher had been placed across the aisle with either end resting on a seat. The other four were for Kate and Mrs. Kinnard and items necessary to take care of Harrison for the duration of the trip. A straight chair had been placed close to the stretcher, because the lurching of the train made it too difficult to tend to him standing up. Robert and Castine were located two seats away, primarily to keep any curious passengers from trying to see what was happening. All of them took turns, even Castine, sponging away the fever, feeding Harrison water or a very thin broth.

When it grew dark, a lamp was lit. It hung from a hook in the ceiling, and the constant sway of the train made the shadows sweep back and forth across the car. Despite her exhaustion, Kate was aware of Robert's presence all the time, but never once did he intrude. He quietly made sure she had whatever she needed. She was free to concentrate on her son, and she loved him all the more for it.

She loved him. He loved her. And nothing would ever come of it.

Kate was dozing in one of the seats when Robert lightly touched her arm, startling her awake.

"There's been a change," he whispered, and Kate's heart fell.

"What—?"

"Shhh," Mrs. Kinnard said behind them. "I believe his fever has broken," she whispered. "I think he is sleeping naturally."

Kate immediately maneuvered to where she could see. Because of the moving shadows, it took a moment for her to decide. She reached out to touch Harrison's hand, and when she did, he clasped her fingers.

"Oh—"

"Shhh!" Mrs. Kinnard insisted again. "It would be premature to rejoice. Whatever emotion you're feeling, feel it quietly. Natural sleep is the best healer."

Kate nodded. She realized suddenly that she was crying, and she wiped at her eyes.

"I assume you want to sit by him," Mrs. Kinnard said, still whispering.

"Yes."

"Then do so. But do *not* wake him." She moved the chair so that Kate could sit down without letting go of Harrison's hand.

Kate sat there, trying not to rejoice—but it was so hard not to. At last she had a glimmer of hope.

Thank You for that, Lord.

She looked down the aisle to where Robert sat watching, and she managed to give him the barest of smiles.

She dozed off just as the sun was coming up. When she opened her eyes again, Harrison was looking at her.

"I knew…it was you…" he said.

Kate smiled. "Did you? How?"

"You're the…only one who calls…me 'Harrison.' You…and Mother."

"It's not going away," Robert said.

Kate looked up sharply. She had come outdoors to finish a letter to Max—her latest update regarding Harrison's progress. She had seen Robert at a distance. Surprisingly, he had been talking to Warrie earlier, but Kate hadn't realized he was nearby. He came closer.

"I…don't think I know what you mean," she said, avoiding looking at him directly when that was all in this world she wanted to do. Look at him. Sit with him. Talk to him. But it seemed that they had reached some kind of tacit agreement not to call attention to the change in their friendship, the kind Maria had been so worried about. They were still friends, and both of them knew it would have to stay that way.

"I mean Harrison is getting stronger every day," he said.

Kate glanced at the upstairs veranda where Harrison was sitting in an invalid chair, playing checkers with Castine. They were a quieter but no less intense version of Joe and Jake, who at the moment chased each other around and around the backyard—with two hound pups nipping at their heels.

She knew that Robert expected some kind of response to his remark, but she didn't say anything.

"Do you not see God's plan in all this?" he asked after a moment.

"I'm afraid to see God's plan," she said truthfully.

"Maria told me once that you thought you were brought up useless," he said, and she frowned. "Harrison and I both are proof that that is not the case."

She shook her head. "Robert—"

"You've come a long way from the young woman who missed her train," he said.

She looked at him then, and in a way she hadn't in the days since they had brought Harrison back here to recover. She had *missed* him, even though he was never far away. It was still there. All the feelings—the love—she had for him, and when she looked into his eyes...

"Come walk with me," he said, holding out his hand.

"I don't think that's a good idea—"

"Don't worry. We have more things to discuss than my willingness to die for you. Or live for you—whichever you happen to need."

He was teasing her, and she couldn't help but smile.

"I never know what you're going to say," she said.

"Neither do I," Robert assured her. "Are we walking?"

"All right," she said, putting the letter into her writing box and setting it aside. She took his hand. "Which way?" she asked as he pulled her to her feet.

"That way. I need to see Reverend Lewis."

She took his arm and they began walking down the path to the street that would take them to the church and the church parsonage. As they passed the front of the house, she turned and waved to Harrison.

"He's what I wanted to talk to you about," Robert said.

"Why?"

"Are you going to tell him?" he asked instead of answering her question, and Kate knew exactly what he meant. Robert knew everything about her and Harrison. It wouldn't be difficult for him to guess what was troubling her so.

"I want to," Kate said truthfully. "Are you going to try to talk me out of it?"

"No."

"Are you going to tell me what you think?"

"No," he said again.

"But you think something."

"I do."

"Then tell me."

"I think the same thing you do."

"And what is that?"

"You want whatever is best for your boy. And now you've reached the point where you have to decide what that is."

She stopped walking. They were standing in the shade of an apple tree that grew on the other side of a picket fence. The tree was covered in blossoms, and dozens of insects bobbed from flower to flower. "I want to tell him, Robert."

"Yes," he said.

Yes?

But he was merely acknowledging her desire. He was by no means condoning it.

"He's a lot like you," Robert said as they began walking again.

"Is he? In what way?"

"He's very…forthright. I like that boy quite a lot," Robert said. "He has a very practical way of looking at things."

"What do the two of you talk about?"

"The war. Religion. The benefits of a good education. Samuel."

He stopped walking. "I thought maybe you'd like to wait for me here while I go see the Reverend," he said. The church was only a few yards away.

"I don't—"

"Your lamp is lit late into the night, Kate," he said. "I think there's only one way to find the answer to the question that's keeping you awake."

Kate gave a soft sigh. It was true that she hadn't been sleeping. She was so grateful that Harrison was recovering, and she could manage all the prayers necessary to express her gratitude. What she couldn't manage was asking God what she should do now.

"I'm…afraid, Robert."

"All the more reason to talk to Him. He already knows what's in your heart. *Talk* to Him."

She hesitated, then turned and walked toward the church doors, looking up at the thuya tree as she passed. It was as serene and stately as ever.

It's to show, in God's house, everyone is welcome…

She went into the sanctuary and made her way down the aisle to the front and sat in the same place she had when Robert had spoken so eloquently to the congregation. She didn't think he realized how powerful his message had been.

She could hear the sparrows singing outside the windows, a carriage passing, children playing somewhere. She closed her eyes.

"I'm afraid," she whispered. "Too afraid to say what I want so desperately." She took a quiet breath. "Robert says You already know. Will You show me what to do? Please show me. Help me to understand Your will."

She bowed her head, and she sat there quietly for a long time. But she felt nothing. Neither better nor worse. When she came out of the church, Robert was waiting. He didn't ask her anything. He merely offered her his arm.

She didn't look at him until they had reached the house.

"Don't give up," he said when she did. "You *are* strong, Kate. Remember that."

"Kate!" Harrison called from the upstairs veranda. "Come on up!"

"I'll see you later," Robert said, and he left her standing in the yard.

"Kate!" Harrison called again, and she walked swiftly into the house.

"How is he?" she asked Castine as she passed him in the upstairs hallway.

"He's happy today—got a letter from Philadelphia."

Philadelphia.

If he was happy, then it must have been from John, she decided. Mrs. Howe hadn't written to him personally as yet; there were only a few sentences included in the letters John wrote. Kate could only imagine how displeased the woman must be that he ran away from school. Kate still didn't know the reason. She hoped he had written to John about it because he hadn't said anything to her.

"Kate!" he said as soon as he saw her. "I have something to tell you!"

"I have something to tell you, too," she said, because she knew at that very instant what she was going to do. Harrison was her son. *Her* son. He was part of her, and she was going to tell him the truth.

"You first, then," he said, smiling up at her.

"I can wait. Tell me what has you so excited."

"Well," he said, moving his spectacles up on his nose. There are two things actually. I'll tell you the best first— or maybe I should tell you the other one, I don't know."

"The best one," Kate said.

"All right. I got a letter from Mother today—a *long* letter. She isn't angry with me at all. She wants me home— there's a private railroad car coming to get me—if Max's army doctors say I'm well enough. If they do, I'm to send a telegram right away. I can't wait to see her—she'll know what to do about everything. She'll know how I can make amends—"

"Do you...need to make amends?" Kate asked. It was all she could do to keep her voice steady.

"Yes, of course," he said earnestly. "Robert told me a gentleman always makes amends when he's in the wrong—especially with the people he loves. I ran away and worried everybody. I shouldn't have. Mother will help me to do the right thing. She's very wise—she's the wisest person I know. We're going to have a lot to talk about. She says I'm to thank you for sending Robert to find me."

"Does she?" Kate said, fighting back the tears. She'd hid her true feelings for years and years. She could do it again now—for his sake.

He wants to go home!

"Yes, and she says thank you for taking such good care of me. And for keeping me company when I felt so low. That part is from me—she doesn't know you kept me company. Now I need to tell you something."

"All right."

He was looking at her so intently, and she forced a smile.

"Well, it's this. I think Robert is too shy for his own good. He's like...that Pilgrim—Miles Standish. I think he likes you a lot, and since you're not shy at all and you're not getting any younger, maybe you should ask him if he wants to marry you."

"What?" Kate said, startled because she'd only been half listening. Her mind was filled with but one thought. Mrs. Howe was his mother in every way that mattered, not her. Never her. Regardless of how it began, that was the truth of his life and hers.

I can't tell him. Not ever.

If she did, it would be for her happiness, not his. He loved Mrs. Howe, relied on her, *missed* her. Somehow she hadn't taken that into consideration at all.

"Ask Robert if he wants to marry you," Harrison said.

"I…don't think that's the way it's done," Kate said.

"I don't see why not," he said. "You'd get a good answer. I know you would. Then you wouldn't be alone like you are now and he wouldn't, either. Can you just…think about it? It's a good idea."

"Yes," Kate said. "I'll think about it."

"Good. What were you going to tell me?"

"Oh, nothing important—with all this talk of marriage, I think I've forgotten."

"Then I'm ready for my afternoon nap now—you can tell me later. Would you find Castine? Mrs. Kinnard will be coming by soon, and I don't want to have to explain to her why I'm awake. Unless you'd like to do that for me," he added with a mischievous grin.

"I think not," Kate assured him, and his grin broadened. "I'll see you later."

"Don't forget what I said."

"No. I won't."

Kate left the veranda and went blindly down the stairs. Castine was in the foyer, talking—listening—to Perkins.

"He's ready to be wheeled in," she said. "Do you know where Mr. Markham is?"

"He's outside, Miss Kate," Perkins said, and she nodded.

She needed to find him. The question she'd been so afraid to ask had been answered—Harrison himself had answered it—and Robert was the only person who would understand.

"Wait, Miss Kate," Perkins said when she headed down the hallway. "I don't think you ought to go out there right now," he called.

But she kept going. She saw Robert standing in the yard, and she walked quickly in that direction.

"I was wrong," she said as she approached him. "I was *wrong*."

"Kate, what—?" He held out his arms and she walked into them.

"I was going to tell him," she said into his shirtfront. "I was going to do it, but then I couldn't. I didn't realize how much he loves his—mother. Not me. Oh, it hurt so much listening to him talk about her. I can't take her place—ever. If I told him, I would leave him with nothing but people who had lied to him." She leaned back and looked up at him.

"It's going to be all right," Robert said gently.

"Is it?"

"Yes."

She gave a heavy sigh. All these years she'd had some misguided idea of what Harrison's life had been like, but his sincere words about Mrs. Howe—his mother—had changed everything.

I was blind, but now I see...

She pressed her face into his shirt again, even knowing Mrs. Kinnard was due. "I love you, Robert," she whispered.

"I don't think I heard that," he said, and she looked up at him.

"Yes, you did," she said, and he smiled.

"Rob?" someone said behind them, and they both ooked around.

A woman and a man stood at the edge of the yard. They were both smiling.

"I'm sorry to interrupt, but we have to catch the train. This must be Kate," she said, stepping forward.

"Yes," Kate said, looking to Robert for some guidance.

"This is Eleanor," Robert said to her. "And her fiancé, Dan Ingram."

Eleanor?

No wonder Perkins hadn't wanted her to come outside.

"Pleased to meet you, miss," the man said.

"Kate, do you mind if I have a word with Rob?" Eleanor asked.

"No," Kate said. "Of course not."

She stood there completely bewildered as they walked a short distance away. She suddenly turned her attention to Dan Ingram. He didn't seem to find this situation awkward at all.

"You're catching the train?" she said just to have something to say.

"We're heading back to Wyoming. I was afraid I'd be going home by myself, but Eleanor said yes."

"I...didn't know she was here."

"Nobody did except her mother and Mrs. Woodard. And then Rob. He told us about you—well, he told Eleanor, and she told me."

Kate stared back at him. Clearly a lot had been going on while she was lost in her own troubles.

"If you don't mind my saying so, you're looking like you ought to sit down. How about we walk over there to the porch steps?"

"I— Yes," she decided. Her mind was reeling. Sitting down was definitely a good idea.

When they reached the porch, she sat down on the top step and, surprisingly, so did Dan Ingram.

"It must have been a shock for her—finding out Robert was alive," Kate said. She could see Robert and Eleanor from this vantage point, but she couldn't tell anything about their conversation.

"At first. But then she remembered I'd done about the same thing after the war—run off from everything I knew. Only I went to Wyoming. You love him?" he asked bluntly.

"I— Yes."

"Thought so. It'll help him—if you tell him about it, that is, and you don't go trying to do what you think is best for him. 'Best' is having the woman you care about say she'll take a chance on you—however it turns out." He stood. "Here they come."

He offered Kate his hand, and she stood to meet them. Eleanor Hansen had no reticence whatsoever about calling Kate aside, clearly intending to say something she didn't want Dan or Robert to hear. It occurred to Kate, as she and Eleanor stood looking at each other, that both of them were thinking of the same person.

Robert Markham.

"Yes," Eleanor said after a moment.

"Pardon?"

"I thought you might be wondering if the things you'd heard about me were true. The answer is yes." Eleanor smiled a wry smile. "It's in the past, though. I know that now. Dan came all the way from Wyoming to make sure I know it. And Robert—he helped me to understand... some things. I never thought I'd ever hear myself say something like this, but I believe he's going to make a fine minister."

"So do I," Kate said.

They stared at each other for a moment longer, the conversation clearly ended.

"Dan!" Eleanor suddenly called, holding out her hand to the man she was going to marry. As he approached, she gave Kate an abrupt goodbye hug.

"Be good to him," she whispered in Kate's ear. "He's going to need someone like you. And don't waste time worrying about what people will think." Then she was gone, walking away on Dan Ingram's arm to catch a train to a new life.

Kate walked back to the porch and sat down on the top step again as Robert joined her.

"What did you mean—when you said you weren't bound to Eleanor in the way I thought?" she asked after a moment.

Robert looked at her. A slight breeze ruffled his hair. "She broke our engagement—before Gettysburg—but I still needed to find out if she was all right."

"And is she?"

"Yes. Dan Ingram is a good man."

"What about Warrie? Does she know Eleanor broke your engagement?"

"Eleanor told her. She would never have believed it if it had come from me."

"This has been the most—" She stopped because she had no words for the events of this day.

"Are you all right?" he asked, his eyes searching hers.

"I will be—as soon as I take Harrison's advice. And Eleanor's."

"And what would that be?"

She moved closer so their shoulders touched. "It would be this—Robert Brian Markham, will you marry me? If you think I'm groomed enough, that is."

He smiled. "This is their advice?"

"Harrison's. Eleanor told me not to worry about what people thought. And, since I'm not getting any younger—

to quote Harrison—and both things seem reasonable, given our situation, I want to know—"

"Robert Markham! What would your mother say! Sitting out here like this where everyone can see you—"

"Mrs. Kinnard is here," he advised Kate. "I'm…not sure," he said to Mrs. Kinnard.

"And you, Miss Woodard. What do you think you're doing?"

"I'm asking Robert for his hand in marriage—but he hasn't given me his answer yet. Robert Markham, will you marry me or not?"

"I will, Miss Woodard," he said. "The sooner, the better."

"Good," she said, using his own word for the situation.

He suddenly reached out and took Mrs. Kinnard by the arm. "Come sit with us, Mrs. Kinnard."

"Robert Brian Markham—!" she protested, but he was relentless. She sat, and he put an arm around both of them.

"The very idea!" she said, but she stopped trying to get away.

"I know," Robert said. "But you're the only mother I have—you and Mrs. Justice. I'm happy, Mrs. Kinnard. I want you to be happy, too."

"Well, this is *not* the way."

Perkins came out the front door, took one look at the three of them and went back inside again.

"I love Robert with all my heart, Mrs. Kinnard," Kate said. "And you've just heard him say yes to my bold proposal. Now. Would you be so kind as to arrange my wedding?"

Epilogue

At first Kate had been afraid Mrs. Kinnard would plan something with so much pomp and circumstance it would rival a coronation, but she hadn't. An entirely different Mrs. Kinnard had seemed to be in charge this time, one who understood exactly what Kate and Robert wanted— a wedding that was warm and intimate and joyous all at the same time. And practical.

"We will want an evening wedding," Mrs. Kinnard had said. "So you and Robert can slip away sometime during the reception. And if we schedule it a few days before Christmas, the church will already be decorated."

Which had left Kate free to concentrate on her attendants. Having Maria as her matron of honor had been out of the question, because the wedding date would be too soon after the baby's birth for her to assume the duties required of her—nearly two weeks of her lying-in period would still remain, Kate smiled suddenly, thinking of the beautiful little girl who had been welcomed into Max's family—and hers.

Ann Maria Katherine Woodard.

Max and the boys were absolutely captivated by her

mere presence, and what a job she would have later—keeping *all* of them in line.

And that had left the bridesmaid.

There had been only one other possible bridesmaid who met the age requirement that she be younger than the bride, only one who would see the position as both an honor and an "adventure."

"Kate!" Valentina said now. "Hurry! It's almost time!"

Kate took a deep breath. She could hear the swelling of the first chords from the organ.

"How do I look?" she asked Valentina as she smoothed the flounce on the underskirt of her dress.

"Beautiful," Valentina said earnestly. "And wait till you see Robert. Thanks to Sergeant Major Perkins and Private Castine, he's been polished to within an inch of his *life*."

Kate smiled and followed her into the vestibule. She had no doubt that that was true. And how beautiful the church looked, all candlelit and filled with the scent of Christmas greenery and the boxes of oranges that would be given to the children on Christmas Eve and to the poor. And there were so many people—Mrs. Kinnard hadn't quite accomplished the "intimate" part.

"Here I go!" Valentina said as the organist began playing her musical cue.

Kate could hear the creaking of the pews as people turned to see Valentina make her entrance.

"They're playing the charge," Max said mischievously as he offered Kate his arm. She smiled up at him. Clearly Perkins and Castine had done some work on him, as well.

"Max—"

"He's a good man, Kate. Even I can see that, but if—"

"I don't want to change my mind, Max."

"All right then. I'm ready if you are."

She stood on tiptoe and kissed his cheek. "Thank you, Max. For everything."

She could see Robert and his best man standing at the altar now. Harrison was grinning from ear to ear, and he poked Robert with his elbow as the music changed and she came into view.

She walked with Max down the aisle past a sea of faces, some smiling—Mrs. Justice and Robert's former comrades—and some not—Mrs. Russell and her forlorn daughter.

"Dearly Beloved," Chaplain Gilford began, his voice steady and full of authority. He was doing well now— thanks to Robert's help—and she was so glad they had chosen him to perform the ceremony.

Kate barely heard the rest of it because she was looking into Robert's eyes. It was as if all the many tributaries of her life had been flowing from some unknown source, colliding, joining, carrying her along to this very moment. It was so clear to her now. She could see it—in all that had happened to her and to him. She could see it in her finally understanding her place in Harrison's life and in the remarkable way she and Robert had met. She could see it in his pain and sorrow over Samuel's death and his coming home again. She loved Robert Markham with all her heart, and it was there, too. All of it—*all* of it, was God's plan.

For I know the thoughts that I think toward you, saith the Lord, thoughts of peace, and not of evil, to give you an expected end...

When the wedding was over, she would tell Robert. She would tell her husband how new and joyous she felt.

She smiled suddenly, still looking into his eyes, her heart soaring. She said her vows firmly and with love, and she listened to Robert do the same.

My husband.

She would live with him and grow old with him, and they would do their best to remember that no matter what happened, He would always be there.

* * * * *

Dear Reader,

Years ago, when crewel embroidery was so popular, one of my coworkers brought a beautiful example of her handiwork to the office to show us. As she was taking it out of the bag, she said she'd used this particular piece to teach her Sunday school class.

"How?" I asked her, curious.

"Well, I told them that this piece of embroidery was like our lives," she said, holding it up so the wrong side, the side with all the knots and short pieces of dangling crewel yarn, was facing outward. "This is the side we see, the side that's rough, and unfinished-looking and maybe hard to understand."

Then she flipped it around to show the other side, a stunning array of colorful flowers, greenery and butterflies. It was absolutely beautiful. "And this is the side God sees."

What a simple, yet profound, message, I thought then—and still do. It's the message I kept foremost in my mind when I was writing Robert and Kate's story.

I hope you enjoy reading it.

Love and prayers,

Cheryl Reavis

Questions for Discussion

1. By the time the story begins, Kate has experienced two great losses—the son she gave up for adoption and the young man she would have married had he not been killed in the final days of the war. How do you think these losses shaped her life? How do you think they shaped her faith?

2. Why did Kate suddenly decide to miss her train? What do you think might have happened if she hadn't been in the Markham house when Robert Markham returned home after his long exile?

3. What were Kate's first impressions of Robert and what did she ultimately decide about him? How did it affect her interactions with him? What did Robert think of Kate? How did his first impression affect his interactions with her?

4. Have you ever had to deal with anyone like the forceful Mrs. Kinnard? If so, how did you handle the situation? What did you think of the way Kate managed Mrs. Kinnard? What one specific thing do you think Kate's brother, Colonel Woodard, understood about Mrs. Kinnard's personality?

5. In what ways were Kate and Mrs. Kinnard's daughter, Valentina, alike? In what ways were they different? What private hope did Valentina reveal to Kate regarding the kind of man she wanted to marry?

6. How did Mrs. Justice help Kate reach out to God? Do you think she gave Kate good advice? Why or why not? Have you ever had a spiritual mentor like Mrs. Justice in your life? What was that experience like? Have you ever been a spiritual mentor?

7. Why do you think Mrs. Justice, Mrs. Kinnard and the militant Mrs. Russell remained friends for so long? Do you still have friends you've known since your childhood? What do you think keeps that friendship going?

8. Why did Robert Markham let his family and friends believe he was dead and choose not to come home after the war? What caused him to change his mind? How was he finally able to find God? Why do you think his sister, Maria, was so surprised by this change in him?

9. Why did Robert choose to speak to the members of his church at the Sunday service? How did he feel about Kate being present in the congregation when he did so? How did he feel about Mrs. Hansen, the mother of his former fiancée, Eleanor, being there?

10. How did Robert help Kate when she first learned that her son might be in some kind of trouble? How did he help later when the trouble turned out to be real?

11. Why did Robert need his sister, Maria, and Mrs. Justice to help him understand his true feelings regarding Kate? What did Kate do when she found out about the "helpful" thing the two women had done?

12. What do you think of the decision Kate ultimately made regarding her son? Do you think it was the right thing for her to do? Why or why not? In what way did Robert help her reach her decision?

REQUEST YOUR FREE BOOKS!

2 FREE INSPIRATIONAL NOVELS
PLUS 2
FREE
MYSTERY GIFTS

Love Inspired.

HISTORICAL
INSPIRATIONAL HISTORICAL ROMANCE

YES! Please send me 2 FREE Love Inspired® Historical novels and my 2 FREE mystery gifts (gifts are worth about $10). After receiving them, if I don't wish to receive any more books, I can return the shipping statement marked "cancel." If I don't cancel, I will receive 4 brand-new novels every month and be billed just $4.74 per book in the U.S. or $5.24 per book in Canada. That's a saving of at least 21% off the cover price. It's quite a bargain! Shipping and handling is just 50¢ per book in the U.S. and 75¢ per book in Canada.* I understand that accepting the 2 free books and gifts places me under no obligation to buy anything. I can always return a shipment and cancel at any time. Even if I never buy another book, the two free books and gifts are mine to keep forever.

102/302 IDN F5CN

Name	(PLEASE PRINT)

Address	Apt. #

City	State/Prov.	Zip/Postal Code

Signature (if under 18, a parent or guardian must sign)

Mail to the Harlequin® Reader Service:
IN U.S.A.: P.O. Box 1867, Buffalo, NY 14240-1867
IN CANADA: P.O. Box 609, Fort Erie, Ontario L2A 5X3

Want to try two free books from another series?
Call 1-800-873-8635 or visit www.ReaderService.com.

* Terms and prices subject to change without notice. Prices do not include applicable taxes. Sales tax applicable in N.Y. Canadian residents will be charged applicable taxes. Offer not valid in Quebec. This offer is limited to one order per household. Not valid for current subscribers to Love Inspired Historical books. All orders subject to credit approval. Credit or debit balances in a customer's account(s) may be offset by any other outstanding balance owed by or to the customer. Please allow 4 to 6 weeks for delivery. Offer available while quantities last.

Your Privacy—The Harlequin® Reader Service is committed to protecting your privacy. Our Privacy Policy is available online at www.ReaderService.com or upon request from the Harlequin Reader Service.

We make a portion of our mailing list available to reputable third parties that offer products we believe may interest you. If you prefer that we not exchange your name with third parties, or if you wish to clarify or modify your communication preferences, please visit us at www.ReaderService.com/consumerschoice or write to us at Harlequin Reader Service Preference Service, P.O. Box 9062, Buffalo, NY 14269. Include your complete name and address.

LIH13R

SPECIAL EXCERPT FROM

Love Inspired HISTORICAL

*Oscar White has come to town to tame a horse,
but finds love in the most unexpected of places.*

*Read on for a sneak peek at
ROPING THE WRANGLER by Lacy Williams,
available August 2013 from Love Inspired Historical.*

"They say he's magic with the long reins—"

"I saw him ride once in an exhibition down by Cheyenne...."

Sarah clutched her schoolbooks until her knuckles turned white. The men of Lost Hollow were no better than little boys, excited over a wild cowboy! Unfortunately, her boss, the chairman of the school board and the reason Oscar White was here, had insisted that as the schoolteacher, she should come along as part of the welcoming committee. And because they'd known each other in Bear Creek.

But she hadn't known Oscar White well and hadn't liked what she had known.

And now she just wanted to get this "welcome" over with. Her thoughts wandered until the train came to a hissing stop at the platform.

The man who strode off with a confident gait bore a resemblance to the Oscar White she'd known, but *this* man was assuredly different. With his Stetson tilted back rakishly to reveal brown eyes, his face no longer bore the slight roundness of youth. No, those lean, craggy features belonged to a man, without question. Broad shoulders easily parted the small crowd on the platform, and he headed straight for their group.

Sarah turned away, alarmed by the pulse pounding frantically in her temples. Why this reaction now, *to this man?*

Through the rhythmic beating in her ears—too fast!—she heard the men exchange greetings, and then Mr. Allen cleared his throat.

"And I believe you already know our schoolteacher…"

Obediently she turned and their gazes collided—his brown eyes curious until he glimpsed her face.

"…Miss Sarah Hansen."

His eyes instantly cooled. He quickly looked back to the other men. "I've got to get my horses from the stock car. I'll catch up with you gentlemen in a moment. Miss Hansen." He tipped his hat before rushing off down the line of train cars.

Sarah found herself watching him and forced her eyes away. Obviously he remembered her, and perhaps what had passed between them seven years ago.

That was just fine with her. She had no use for reckless cowboys. She was looking for a responsible man for a husband….

Don't miss ROPING THE WRANGLER
by Lacy Williams,
on sale August 2013 wherever
Love Inspired Historical books are sold!